BORDERS®

CLASSICS

WASHINGTON IRVING

The Legend of Sleepy Hollow

and Other Tales

BORDERS.
CLASSICS

Please direct sales or editorial inquiries to:
BordersTradeBookInventoryQuestions@bordersgroupinc.com

This edition is published by
Borders Classics, an imprint of Borders Group, Inc.,
by special arrangement with
Ann Arbor Media Group, LLC
2500 South State Street, Ann Arbor, MI 48104

Dust jacket copy by Kip Keller
Production team: Mae Barnard, Tina Budzinski, Lori Holland,
Denise Kennedy, Steven Moore, Kathie Radenbaugh,
and Rhonda Welton

Printed and bound in the United States of America
by Edwards Brothers, Inc.

ISBN 1-58726-158-8

07   06   05   04   10 9 8 7 6 5 4 3 2 1

CONTENTS

Rip Van Winkle

A Posthumous Writing of Diedrich Knickerbocker

By Woden, God of Saxons,
From whence comes Wensday, that is Wodensday,
Truth is a thing that ever I will keep
Unto thylke day in which I creep into
My sepulchre—

—Cartwright

[The following Tale was found among the papers of the late Diedrich Knickerbocker, an old gentleman of New York, who was very curious in the Dutch History of the province and the manners of the descendants from its primitive settlers. His historical researches, however, did not lie so much among books as among men; for the former are lamentably scanty on his favorite topics; whereas he found the old burghers, and still more, their wives, rich in that legendary lore, so invaluable to true history. Whenever, therefore, he happened upon a genuine Dutch family, snugly shut up in its low-roofed farm-house, under a spreading sycamore, he looked upon it as a little clasped volume of black-letter, and studied it with the zeal of a bookworm.

The result of all these researches was a history of the province, during the reign of the Dutch governors, which he published some years since. There have been various opinions as to the literary character of his work, and, to tell the truth, it is not a whit better than it should be. Its chief merit is its scrupulous accuracy, which indeed was a little questioned on its first appearance, but has since been completely established; and it is now admitted into all historical collections, as a book of unquestionable authority.

The old gentleman died shortly after the publication of his work; and now that he is dead and gone, it cannot do much harm to his memory to say that his time might have been much better employed in weightier labors. He, however, was apt to ride his hobby his own way; and though it did now and then kick up the dust a little in the eyes of his neighbors, and grieve the spirit of some friends, for whom he felt the truest deference and affection, yet his errors and follies are remembered "more in sorrow than in anger," and it begins to be suspected, that he never intended to injure or offend. But however his memory may be appreciated by critics, it is still held dear among many folks, whose good opinion is well worth having; particularly by certain biscuit-bakers, who have gone so far as to imprint his likeness on their new-year cakes, and have thus given him a chance for immortality, almost equal to the being stamped on a Waterloo medal, or a Queen Anne's farthing.]

Whoever has made a voyage up the Hudson must remember the Kaatskill mountains. They are a dismembered branch of the great Appalachian family, and are seen away to the west of the river, swelling up to a noble height, and lording it over the surrounding country. Every change of season, every change of weather, indeed, every hour of the day produces some change in the magical hues and shapes of these mountains; and they are regarded by all the good wives, far and near, as perfect barometers. When the weather is fair and settled, they are clothed in blue and purple, and print their bold outlines on the clear evening sky; but sometimes, when the rest of the landscape is cloudless, they will gather a hood of gray vapors about their summits, which, in the last rays of the setting sun, will glow and light up like a crown of glory.

At the foot of these fairy mountains, the voyager may have descried the light smoke curling up from a Village, whose shingle roofs gleam among the trees, just where the blue tints of the upland melt away into the fresh green of the nearer landscape. It is a little village of great antiquity, having been founded by some of the Dutch colonists, in the early times of the province, just about the beginning of the government of the good Peter Stuyvesant (may he rest in peace!), and there were some of the houses of the original settlers standing within a few years, built of small yellow bricks, brought from Holland, having latticed windows and gable fronts, surmounted with weathercocks.

In that same village, and in one of these very houses (which, to tell the precise truth, was sadly time-worn and weather-beaten), there lived, many years since, while the country was yet a province of Great Britain, a simple, good-natured fellow, of the name of Rip Van Winkle. He was a descendant of the Van Winkles who figured so gallantly in the chivalrous days of Peter Stuyvesant, and accompanied him to the siege of Fort Christina. He inherited, however, but little of the martial character of his ancestors. I have observed that he was a simple, good-natured man; he was, moreover, a kind neighbor, and an obedient henpecked husband. Indeed, to the latter circumstance might be owing that meekness of spirit which gained him such universal popularity; for those men are apt to be obsequious and conciliating abroad, who are under the discipline of shrews at home. Their tempers, doubtless, are rendered pliant and malleable in the fiery furnace of domestic tribulation, and a curtain-lecture is worth all the sermons in the world for teaching the virtues of patience and long-suffering. A termagant wife may, therefore, in some respects, be considered a tolerable blessing, and if so, Rip Van Winkle was thrice blessed.

Certain it is, that he was a great favorite among all the good wives of the village, who, as usual with the amiable sex, took his part in all family squabbles, and never failed, whenever they talked those matters over in their evening gossipings, to lay all the blame on Dame Van Winkle. The children of the village, too, would shout with joy whenever he approached. He assisted at their sports, made their playthings, taught them to fly kites and shoot marbles, and told them long stories of ghosts, witches, and Indians. Whenever he went dodging about the village, he was surrounded by a troop of them hanging on his skirts, clambering on his back, and playing a thousand tricks on him with impunity; and not a dog would bark at him throughout the neighborhood.

The great error in Rip's composition was an insuperable aversion to all kinds of profitable labor. It could not be for want of assiduity or perseverance; for he would sit on a wet rock, with a rod as long and heavy as a Tartar's lance, and fish all day without a murmur, even though he should not be encouraged by a single nibble. He would carry a fowling-piece on his shoulder, for hours together, trudging through woods and swamps, and up hill and down dale, to shoot a few squirrels or wild pigeons. He would never refuse to assist a neighbor even in the roughest toil, and was a foremost man in all country frolics for husking Indian corn, or building stone fences; the women of the village, too, used to employ him to run their errands, and to do such little odd jobs as their less obliging husbands would not do for them. In a word, Rip was ready to attend to anybody's business but his own; but as to doing family duty, and keeping his farm in order, he found it impossible.

In fact, he declared it was of no use to work on his farm; it was the most pestilent little piece of ground in the whole country; everything about it went wrong, in spite of him. His fences were continually falling to pieces; his cow would either go astray, or get among the cabbages; weeds were sure to grow quicker in his fields than anywhere else; the rain always made a point of setting in just as he had some out-door work to do; so that though his patrimonial estate had dwindled away under his management, acre by acre, until there was little more left than a mere patch of Indian corn and potatoes, yet it was the worst-conditioned farm in the neighborhood.

His children, too, were as ragged and wild as if they belonged to nobody. His son Rip, an urchin begotten in his own likeness, prom-ised to inherit the habits, with the old clothes, of his father. He was generally seen trooping like a colt at his mother's heels, equipped in a pair of his father's cast-off galligaskins, which he had much ado to hold up with one hand, as a fine lady does her train in bad weather.

Rip Van Winkle, however, was one of those happy mortals, of fool-ish, well-oiled dispositions, who take the world easy, eat white bread or brown, whichever can be got with least thought or trouble, and would rather starve on a penny than work for a pound. If left to him-self, he would have whistled life away, in perfect contentment; but his wife kept continually dinning in his ears about his idleness, his care-lessness, and the ruin he was bringing on his family. Morning, noon, and night, her tongue was incessantly going, and every thing he said or did was sure to produce a torrent of household eloquence. Rip had but one way of replying to all lectures of the kind, and that, by fre-quent use, had grown into a habit. He shrugged his shoulders, shook his head, cast up his eyes, but said nothing. This, however, always provoked a fresh volley from his wife, so that he was fain to draw off his forces, and take to the outside of the house—the only side which, in truth, belongs to a henpecked husband.

Rip's sole domestic adherent was his dog Wolf, who was as much henpecked as his master; for Dame Van Winkle regarded them as companions in idleness, and even looked upon Wolf with an evil eye, as the cause of his master's going so often astray. True it is, in all points of spirit befitting in honorable dog, he was as courageous an animal as ever scoured the woods—but what courage can withstand the evil-doing and all-besetting terrors of a woman's tongue? The mo-ment Wolf entered the house, his crest fell, his tail drooped to the ground, or curled between his legs, he sneaked about with a gallows air, casting many a sidelong glance at Dame Van Winkle, and at the least flourish of a broomstick or ladle, he would fly to the door with yelping precipitation.

Times grew worse and worse with Rip Van Winkle as years of matrimony rolled on; a tart temper never mellows with age, and a sharp tongue is the only edged tool that grows keener with constant use. For a long while he used to console himself, when driven from home, by frequenting a kind of perpetual club of the sages, philosophers, and other idle personages of the village, which held its sessions on a bench before a small inn, designated by a rubicund portrait of his Majesty George the Third. Here they used to sit in the shade through a long, lazy summer's day, talking listlessly over village gossip, or telling endless, sleepy stories about nothing. But it would have been worth any statesman's money to have heard the profound discussions which sometimes took place, when by chance an old newspaper fell into their hands from some passing traveller. How solemnly they would listen to the contents, as drawled out by Derrick Van Bummel, the school-master, a dapper learned little man, who was not to be daunted by the most gigantic word in the dictionary; and how sagely they would deliberate upon public events some months after they had taken place.

The opinions of this junto were completely controlled by Nicholas Vedder, a patriarch of the village, and landlord of the inn, at the door of which he took his seat from morning till night, just moving sufficiently to avoid the sun, and keep in the shade of a large tree; so that the neighbors could tell the hour by his movements as accurately as by a sun-dial. It is true, he was rarely heard to speak, but smoked his pipe incessantly. His adherents, however (for every great man has his adherents), perfectly understood him, and knew how to gather his opinions. When any thing that was read or related displeased him, he was observed to smoke his pipe vehemently, and to send forth, frequent, and angry puffs; but when pleased, he would inhale the smoke slowly and tranquilly, and emit it in light and placid clouds, and sometimes, taking the pipe from his mouth, and letting the fragrant vapor curl about his nose, would gravely nod his head in token of perfect approbation.

From even this stronghold the unlucky Rip was at length routed by his termagant wife, who would suddenly break in upon the tranquillity of the assemblage, and call the members all to nought; nor was that august personage, Nicholas Vedder himself, sacred from the daring tongue of this terrible virago, who charged him outright with encouraging her husband in habits of idleness.

Poor Rip was at last reduced almost to despair; and his only alternative, to escape from the labor of the farm and the clamor of his wife, was to take gun in hand, and stroll away into the woods. Here he would sometimes seat himself at the foot of a tree, and share the contents of his wallet with Wolf, with whom he sympathized as a fellow-sufferer in persecution. "Poor Wolf," he would say, "thy mistress leads thee a dog's life of it; but never mind, my lad, whilst I live thou shalt never want a friend to stand by thee!" Wolf would wag his tail, look wistfully in his master's face, and if dogs can feel pity, I verily believe he reciprocated the sentiment with all his heart.

In a long ramble of the kind, on a fine autumnal day, Rip had unconsciously scrambled to one of the highest parts of the Kaatskill mountains. He was after his favorite sport of squirrel-shooting, and the still solitudes had echoed and re-echoed with the reports of his gun. Panting and fatigued, he threw himself, late in the afternoon, on a green knoll, covered with mountain herbage, that crowned the brow of a precipice. From an opening between the trees, he could overlook all the lower country for many a mile of rich woodland. He saw at a distance the lordly Hudson, far, far below him, moving on its silent but majestic course, with the reflection of a purple cloud, or the sail of a lagging bark, here and there sleeping on its glassy bosom and at last losing itself in the blue highlands.

On the other side he looked down into a deep mountain glen, wild, lonely, and shagged, the bottom filled with fragments from the impending cliffs, and scarcely lighted by the reflected rays of the setting sun. For some time Rip lay musing on this scene; evening was gradually advancing; the mountains began to throw their long blue shadows over the valleys; he saw that it would be dark long before he could reach the village; and he heaved a heavy sigh when he thought of encountering the terrors of Dame Van Winkle.

As he was about to descend, he heard a voice from a distance hallooing: "Rip Van Winkle! Rip Van Winkle!" He looked around, but could see nothing but a crow winging its solitary flight across the mountain. He thought his fancy must have deceived him, and turned again to descend, when he heard the same cry ring through the still evening air, "Rip Van Winkle! Rip Van Winkle!"—at the same time Wolf bristled up his back, and giving a low growl, skulked to his master's side, looking fearfully down into the glen. Rip now felt a vague apprehension stealing over him; he looked anxiously in the same direction, and perceived a strange figure slowly toiling up the rocks, and bending under the weight of something he carried on his back. He was surprised to see any human being in this lonely and unfrequented place, but supposing it to be some one of the neighborhood in need of his assistance, he hastened down to yield it.

On nearer approach, he was still more surprised at the singularity of the stranger's appearance. He was a short, square-built old fellow, with thick bushy hair, and a grizzled beard. His dress was of the antique Dutch fashion—a cloth jerkin strapped round the waist—several pairs of breeches, the outer one of ample volume, decorated with rows of buttons down the sides, and bunches at the knees. He bore on his shoulders a stout keg, that seemed full of liquor, and made signs for Rip to approach and assist him with the load. Though rather shy and distrustful of this new acquaintance, Rip complied with his usual alacrity; and mutually relieving each other, they clambered up a narrow gully, apparently the dry bed of a mountain torrent. As they ascended, Rip every now and then heard long rolling peals, like distant thunder, that seemed to issue out of a deep ravine, or rather cleft between lofty rocks, toward which their rugged path conducted. He paused for an instant, but supposing it to be the muttering of one of those transient thunder-showers which often take place in the mountain heights, he proceeded. Passing through the ravine, they came to a hollow, like a small amphitheatre, surrounded by perpendicular precipices, over the brinks of which impending trees shot their branches, so that you only caught glimpses of the azure sky, and the bright evening cloud. During the whole time Rip and his companion had labored on in silence; for though the former marvelled greatly what could be the object of carrying a keg of liquor up this wild mountain, yet there was something strange and incomprehensible about the unknown, that inspired awe, and checked familiarity.

On entering the amphitheatre, new objects of wonder presented themselves. On a level spot in the centre was a company of odd-looking personages playing at ninepins. They were dressed in quaint outlandish fashion; some wore short doublets, others jerkins, with long knives in their belts, and most of them had enormous breeches, of similar style with that of the guide's. Their visages, too, were peculiar; one had a large head, broad face, and small piggish eyes; the face of another seemed to consist entirely of nose, and was surmounted by a white sugar-loaf hat, set off with a little red cock's tail. They all had beards, of various shapes and colors. There was one who seemed to be the commander. He was a stout old gentleman, with a weather-beaten countenance; he wore a laced doublet, broad belt and hanger, high-crowned hat and feather, red stockings, and high-heeled shoes, with roses in them. The whole group reminded Rip of the figures in an old Flemish painting, in the parlor of Dominie Van Schaick, the village parson, and which had been brought over from Holland at the time of the settlement.

What seemed particularly odd to Rip was, that though these folks were evidently amusing themselves, yet they maintained the gravest faces, the most mysterious silence, and were, withal, the most melancholy party of pleasure he had ever witnessed. Nothing interrupted the stillness of the scene but the noise of the balls, which, whenever they were rolled, echoed along the mountains like rumbling peals of thunder.

As Rip and his companion approached them, they suddenly desisted from their play, and stared at him with such a fixed statue-like gaze, and such strange uncouth, lack-lustre countenances, that his heart turned within him, and his knees smote together. His companion now emptied the contents of the keg into large flagons, and made signs to him to wait upon the company. He obeyed with fear and trembling; they quaffed the liquor in profound silence, and then returned to their game.

By degrees, Rip's awe and apprehension subsided. He even ventured, when no eye was fixed upon him, to taste the beverage which he found had much of the flavor of excellent Hollands. He was naturally a thirsty soul, and was soon tempted to repeat the draught. One taste provoked another; and he reiterated his visits to the flagon so often, that at length his senses were overpowered, his eyes swam in his head, his head gradually declined, and he fell into a deep sleep.

On waking, he found himself on the green knoll whence he had first seen the old man of the glen. He rubbed his eyes—it was a bright sunny morning. The birds were hopping and twittering among the bushes, and the eagle was wheeling aloft, and breasting the pure mountain breeze. "Surely," thought Rip, "I have not slept here all night." He recalled the occurrences before he fell asleep. The strange man with the keg of liquor—the mountain ravine—the wild retreat among the rocks—the woe-begone party at ninepins—the flagon— "Oh! that flagon! that wicked flagon!" thought Rip— "what excuse shall I make to Dame Van Winkle?"

He looked round for his gun, but in place of the clean well-oiled fowling-piece, he found an old firelock lying by him, the barrel encrusted with rust, the lock falling off, and the stock worm-eaten. He now suspected that the grave roysterers of the mountains had put a trick upon him, and, having dosed him with liquor, had robbed him of his gun. Wolf, too, had disappeared, but he might have strayed away after a squirrel or partridge. He whistled after him and shouted his name, but all in vain; the echoes repeated his whistle and shout, but no dog was to be seen.

He determined to revisit the scene of the last evening's gambol, and if he met with any of the party, to demand his dog and gun. As he rose to walk, he found himself stiff in the joints, and wanting in his usual activity. "These mountain beds do not agree with me," thought Rip, "and if this frolic, should lay me up with a fit of the rheumatism, I shall have a blessed time with Dame Van Winkle." With some difficulty he got down into the glen: he found the gully up which he and his companion had ascended the preceding evening; but to his astonishment a mountain stream was now foaming down it, leaping from rock to rock, and filling the glen with babbling murmurs. He, however, made shift to scramble up its sides, working his toilsome way through thickets of birch, sassafras, and witch-hazel; and sometimes tripped up or entangled by the wild grape vines that twisted their coils and tendrils from tree to tree, and spread a kind of network in his path.

At length he reached to where the ravine had opened through the cliffs to the amphitheatre; but no traces of such opening remained. The rocks presented a high impenetrable wall, over which the torrent came tumbling in a sheet of feathery foam, and fell into a broad deep basin, black from the shadows of the surrounding forest. Here, then, poor Rip was brought to a stand. He again called and whistled after his dog; he was only answered by the cawing of a flock of idle crows, sporting high in the air about a dry tree that overhung a sunny precipice; and who, secure in their elevation, seemed to look down and scoff at the poor man's perplexities. What was to be done? The morning was passing away, and Rip felt famished for want of his breakfast. He grieved to give up his dog and gun; he dreaded to meet his wife; but it would not do to starve among the mountains. He shook his head, shouldered the rusty firelock, and, with a heart full of trouble and anxiety, turned his steps homeward.

As he approached the village, he met a number of people, but none whom he new, which somewhat surprised him, for he had thought himself acquainted with every one in the country round. Their dress, too, was of a different fashion from that to which he was accustomed. They all stared at him with equal marks of surprise, and whenever they cast eyes upon him, invariably stroked their chins. The constant recurrence of this gesture, induced Rip, involuntarily, to do, the same, when, to his astonishment, he found his beard had grown a foot long!

He had now entered the skirts of the village. A troop of strange children ran at his heels, hooting after him, and pointing at his gray beard. The dogs, too, not one of which he recognized for an old acquaintance, barked at him as he passed. The very village was altered: it was larger and more populous. There were rows of houses which he had never seen before, and those which had been his familiar haunts had disappeared. Strange names were over the doors—strange faces at the windows—everything was strange. His mind now misgave him; he began to doubt whether both he and the world around him were not bewitched. Surely this was his native village, which he had left but a day before. There stood the Kaatskill mountains—there ran the silver Hudson at a distance—there was every hill and dale precisely as it had always been—Rip was sorely perplexed— "That flagon last night," thought he, "has addled my poor head sadly!"

It was with some difficulty that he found the way to his own house, which he approached with silent awe, expecting every moment to hear the shrill voice of Dame Van Winkle. He found the house gone to decay—the roof had fallen in, the windows shattered, and the doors off the hinges. A half-starved dog, that looked like Wolf, was skulking about it. Rip called him by name, but the cur snarled, showed his teeth, and passed on. This was an unkind cut indeed.— "My very dog," sighed poor Rip, "has forgotten me!"

He entered the house, which, to tell the truth, Dame Van Winkle had always kept in neat order. It was empty, forlorn, and apparently abandoned. This desolateness overcame all his connubial fears—he called loudly for his wife and children—the lonely chambers rang for a moment with his voice, and then all again was silence.

He now hurried forth, and hastened to his old resort, the village inn—but it too was gone. A large rickety wooden building stood in its place, with great gaping windows, some of them broken, and mended with old hats and petticoats, and over the door was painted, "The Union Hotel, by Jonathan Doolittle." Instead of the great tree that used to shelter the quiet little Dutch inn of yore, there now was reared a tall naked pole, with something on the top that looked like a red nightcap, and from it was fluttering a flag, on which was a singular assemblage of stars and stripes—all this was strange and incomprehensible. He recognized on the sign, however, the ruby face of King George, under which he had smoked so many a peaceful pipe, but even this was singularly metamorphosed. The red coat was changed for one of blue and buff, a sword was held in the hand instead of a sceptre, the head was decorated with a cocked hat, and underneath was painted in large characters, "GENERAL WASHINGTON."

There was, as usual, a crowd of folk about the door, but none that Rip recollected. The very character of the people seemed changed. There was a busy, bustling, disputatious tone about it, instead of the accustomed phlegm and drowsy tranquillity. He looked in vain for the sage Nicholas Vedder, with his broad face, double chin, and fair long pipe, uttering clouds of tobacco-smoke, instead of idle speeches; or Van Bummel, the schoolmaster, doling forth the contents of an ancient newspaper. In place of these, a lean, bilious-looking fellow, with his pockets full of handbills, was haranguing, vehemently about rights of citizens—elections—members of Congress—liberty—Bunker's hill—heroes of seventy-six—and other words, which were a perfect Babylonish jargon to the bewildered Van Winkle.

The appearance of Rip, with his long, grizzled beard, his rusty fowling-piece, his uncouth dress, and the army of women and children at his heels, soon attracted the attention of the tavern politicians. They crowded round him, eying him from head to foot, with great curiosity. The orator bustled up to him, and, drawing him partly aside, inquired, "on which side he voted?" Rip stared in vacant stupidity. Another short but busy little fellow pulled him by the arm, and, rising on tiptoe, inquired in his ear, "whether he was Federal or Democrat." Rip was equally at a loss to comprehend the question; when a knowing, self-important old gentleman, in a sharp cocked hat, made his way through the crowd, putting them to the right and left with his elbows as he passed, and planting himself before Van Winkle, with one arm akimbo, the other resting on his cane, his keen eyes and sharp hat penetrating, as it were, into his very soul, demanded in an austere tone, "What brought him to the election with a gun on his shoulder, and a mob at his heels; and whether he meant to breed a riot in the village?"

"Alas! gentlemen," cried Rip, somewhat dismayed, "I am a poor, quiet man, a native of the place, and a loyal subject of the King, God bless him!"

Here a general shout burst from the bystanders—"a tory! a tory! a spy! a refugee! hustle him! away with him!" It was with great difficulty that the self-important man in the cocked hat restored order; and having assumed a tenfold austerity of brow, demanded again of the unknown culprit, what he came there for, and whom he was seeking. The poor man humbly assured him that he meant no harm, but merely came there in search of some of his neighbors, who used to keep about the tavern.

"Well—who are they?—name them."

Rip bethought himself a moment, and inquired, Where's Nicholas Vedder?

There was a silence for a little while, when an old man replied, in a thin, piping voice, "Nicholas Vedder? why, be is dead and gone these eighteen years! There was a wooden tombstone in the churchyard that used to tell all about him, but that's rotten and gone too."

"Where's Brom Dutcher?"

"Oh, he went off to the army in the beginning of the war; some say he was killed at the storming of Stony-Point—others say he was drowned in a squall at the foot of Antony's Nose. I don't know—he never came back again."

"Where's Van Bummel, the schoolmaster?"

"He went off to the wars, too; was a great militia general, and is now in Congress."

Rip's heart died away, at hearing of these sad changes in his home and friends, and finding himself thus alone in the world. Every answer puzzled him too, by treating of such enormous lapses of time, and of matters which he could not understand: war—Congress—Stony-Point—he had no courage to ask after any more friends, but cried out in despair, "Does nobody here know Rip Van Winkle?"

"Oh, Rip Van Winkle!" exclaimed two or three. "Oh, to be sure! that's Rip Van Winkle yonder, leaning against the tree."

Rip looked, and beheld a precise counterpart of himself as he went up the mountain; apparently as lazy, and certainly as ragged. The poor fellow was now completely confounded. He doubted his own identity, and whether he was himself or another man. In the midst of his bewilderment, the man in the cocked hat demanded who he was, and what was his name?

"God knows!" exclaimed he at his wit's end; "I'm not myself—I'm somebody else—that's me yonder—no—that's somebody else, got into my shoes—I was myself last night, but I fell asleep on the mountain, and they've changed my gun, and everything's changed, and I'm changed, and I can't tell what's my name, or who I am!"

The by-standers began now to look at each other, nod, wink significantly, and tap their fingers against their foreheads. There was a whisper, also, about securing the gun, and keeping the old fellow from doing mischief; at the very suggestion of which, the self-important man with the cocked hat retired with some precipitation. At this critical moment a fresh, comely woman pressed through the throng to get a peep at the gray-bearded man. She had a chubby child in her arms, which, frightened at his looks, began to cry. "Hush, Rip," cried she, "hush, you little fool; the old man won't hurt you." The name of the child, the air of the mother, the tone of her voice, all awakened a train of recollections in his mind.

"What is your name, my good woman?" asked he.

"Judith Cardenier."

"And your father's name?"

"Ah, poor man, Rip Van Winkle was his name, but it's twenty years since he went away from home with his gun, and never has been heard of since—his dog came home without him; but whether he shot himself, or was carried away by the Indians, nobody can tell. I was then but a little girl."

Rip had but one more question to ask; but he put it with a faltering voice:

"Where's your mother?"

Oh, she too had died but a short time since; she broke a blood-vessel in a fit of passion at a New-England pedler.

There was a drop of comfort, at least, in this intelligence. The honest man could contain himself no longer. He caught his daughter and her child in his arms. "I am your father!" cried he—"Young Rip Van Winkle once—old Rip Van Winkle now—Does nobody know poor Rip Van Winkle!"

All stood amazed, until an old woman, tottering out from among the crowd, put her hand to her brow, and peering under it in his face for a moment exclaimed, "sure enough! it is Rip Van Winkle—it is himself. Welcome home again, old neighbor. Why, where have you been these twenty long years?"

Rip's story was soon told, for the whole twenty years had been to him but as one night. The neighbors stared when they heard it; some were seen to wink at each other, and put their tongues in their cheeks; and the self-important man in the cocked hat, who, when the alarm was over, had returned to the field, screwed down the corners of his mouth, and shook his head—upon which there was a general shaking of the head throughout the assemblage.

It was determined, however, to take the opinion of old Peter Vanderdonk, who was seen slowly advancing up the road. He was a descendant of the historian of that name, who wrote one of the earliest accounts of the province. Peter was the most ancient inhabitant of the village, and well versed in all the wonderful events and traditions of the neighborhood. He recollected Rip at once, and corroborated his story in the most satisfactory manner. He assured the company that it was a fact, handed down from his ancestor, the historian, that the Kaatskill mountains had always been haunted by strange beings. That it was affirmed that the great Hendrick Hudson, the first discoverer of the river and country, kept a kind of vigil there every twenty years, with his crew of the *Half-moon*; being permitted in this way to revisit the scenes of his enterprise, and keep a guardian eye upon the river and the great city called by his name. That his father had once seen them in their old Dutch dresses playing at ninepins in the hollow of the mountain; and that he himself had heard, one summer afternoon, the sound of their balls, like distant peals of thunder.

To make a long story short, the company broke up, and returned to the more important concerns of the election. Rip's daughter took him home to live with her; she had a snug, well-furnished house, and a stout cheery farmer for a husband, whom Rip recollected for one of the urchins that used to climb upon his back. As to Rip's son and heir, who was the ditto of himself, seen leaning against the tree, he was employed to work on the farm; but evinced an hereditary disposition to attend to any thing else but his business.

Rip now resumed his old walks and habits; he soon found many of his former cronies, though all rather the worse for the wear and tear of time; and preferred making friends among the rising generation, with whom be soon grew into great favor.

Having nothing to do at home, and being arrived at that happy age when a man can be idle with impunity, he took his place once more on the bench, at the inn door, and was reverenced as one of the patriarchs of the village, and a chronicle of the old times "before the war." It was some time before he could get into the regular track of gossip, or could be made to comprehend the strange events that had taken place during his torpor. How that there had been a revolutionary war—that the country had thrown off the yoke of old England—and that, instead of being a subject to his Majesty George the Third, he was now a free citizen of the United States. Rip, in fact, was no politician; the changes of states and empires made but little impression on him; but there was one species of despotism under which he had long groaned, and that was—petticoat government. Happily, that was at an end; he had got his neck out of the yoke of matrimony, and could go in and out whenever he pleased, without dreading the tyranny of Dame Van Winkle. Whenever her name was mentioned, however, he shook his head, shrugged his shoulders, and cast up his eyes; which might pass either for an expression of resignation to his fate, or joy at his deliverance.

He used to tell his story to every stranger that arrived at Mr. Doolittle's hotel. He was observed, at first, to vary on some points every time he told it, which was, doubtless, owing to his having so recently awaked. It at last settled down precisely to the tale I have related, and not a man, woman, or child in the neighborhood, but knew it by heart. Some always pretended to doubt the reality of it, and insisted that Rip had been out of his head, and that this was one point on which he always remained flighty. The old Dutch inhabitants, however, almost universally gave it full credit. Even to this day, they never hear a thunder-storm of a summer afternoon about the Kaatskill, but they say Hendrick Hudson and his crew are at their game of ninepins; and it is a common wish of all henpecked husbands in the neighborhood, when life hangs heavy on their hands, that they might have a quieting draught out of Rip Van Winkle's flagon.

Note

The foregoing tale, one would suspect, had been suggested to Mr. Knickerbocker by a little German superstition about the Emperor Frederick der Rothbart and the Kypphauser mountain; the subjoined note, however, which had appended to the tale, shows that it is an absolute fact, narrated with his usual fidelity.

"The story of Rip Van Winkle may seem incredible to many, but nevertheless I give it my full belief, for I know the vicinity of our old Dutch settlements to have been very subject to marvellous events and appearances. Indeed, I have heard many stranger stories than this, in the villages along the Hudson; all of which were too well authenticated to admit of a doubt. I have even talked with Rip Van Winkle myself, who, when last I saw him, was a very venerable old man, and so perfectly rational and consistent on every other point, that I think no conscientious person could refuse to take this into the bargain; nay, I have seen a certificate on the subject taken before a country justice, and signed with cross, in the justice's own handwriting. The story, therefore, is beyond the possibility of doubt.–D. K."

Postscript

The following are travelling notes from a memorandum-book of Mr. Knickerbocker:

The Kaatsberg or Catskill mountains have always been a region full of fable. The Indians considered them the abode of spirits, who influenced the weather, spreading sunshine or clouds over the landscape, and sending good or bad hunting seasons. They were ruled by an old squaw spirit, said to be their mother. She dwelt on the highest peak of the Catskills, and had charge of the doors of day and night to open and shut them at the proper hour. She hung up the new moons in the skies, and cut up the old ones into stars. In times of drought, if properly propitiated, she would spin light summer clouds out of cobwebs and morning dew, and send them off from the crest of the mountain, flake after flake, like flakes of carded cotton, to float in the air; until, dissolved by the heat of the sun, they would fall in gentle showers, causing the grass to spring, the fruits to ripen, and the corn to grow an inch an hour. If displeased, however, she would brew up clouds black as ink, sitting in the midst of them like a bottle-bellied spider in the midst of its web; and when these clouds broke, woe betide the valleys!

In old times, say the Indian traditions, there was a kind of Manitou or Spirit, who kept about the wildest recesses of the Catskill mountains, and took a mischievous pleasure in wreaking all kind of evils and vexations upon the red men. Sometimes he would assume the form of a bear, a panther, or a deer, lead the bewildered hunter a weary chase through tangled forests and among ragged rocks, and then spring off with a loud ho! ho! leaving him aghast on the brink of a beetling precipice or raging torrent.

The favorite abode of this Manitou is still shown. It is a rock or cliff on the loneliest port of the mountains, and, from the flowering vines which clamber about it, and the wild flowers which abound in its neighborhood, is known by the name of the Garden Rock. Near the foot of it is a small lake, the haunt of the solitary bittern, with water-snakes basking in the sun on the leaves of the pond-lilies which lie on the surface. This place was held in great awe by the Indians, insomuch that the boldest hunter would not pursue his game within its precincts. Once upon a time, however, a hunter who had lost his way penetrated to the Garden Rock, where he beheld a number of gourds placed in the crotches of trees. One of these he seized and made off with it, but in the hurry of his retreat he let it fall among the rocks, when a great stream gushed forth, which washed him away and swept him down precipices, where he was dished to pieces, and the stream made its way to the Hudson, and continues to flow to the present day, being the identical stream known by the name of the Kaaterskill.

The Legend of Sleepy Hollow

Found Among the Papers of the Late Diedrich Knickerbocker

> A pleasing land of drowsy-head it was,
> Of dreams that wave before the half-shut eye,
> And of gay castles in the clouds that pass,
> For ever flushing round a summer sky.
> —*Castle of Indolence*

In the bosom of one of those spacious coves which indent the eastern shore of the Hudson, at that broad expansion of the river denominated by the ancient Dutch navigators the Tappan Zee, and where they always prudently shortened sail and implored the protection of St. Nicholas when they crossed, there lies a small market-town or rural port which by some is called Greensburg, but which is more generally and properly known by the name of Tarry Town. This name was given, we are told, in former days by the good housewives of the adjacent country from the inveterate propensity of their husbands to linger about the village tavern on market days. Be that as it may, I do not vouch for the fact, but merely advert to it for the sake of being precise and authentic. Not far from this village, perhaps about two miles, there is a little valley, or rather lap of land, among high hills, which is one of the quietest places in the whole world. A small brook glides through it, with just murmur enough to lull one to repose, and the occasional whistle of a quail or tapping of a woodpecker is almost the only sound that ever breaks in upon the uniform tranquillity.

I recollect that when a stripling my first exploit in squirrel-shooting was in a grove of tall walnut trees that shades one side of the valley. I had wandered into it at noontime, when all Nature is peculiarly quiet, and was startled by the roar of my own gun as it broke the Sabbath stillness around and was prolonged and reverberated by the angry echoes. If ever I should wish for a retreat whither I might steal from the world and its distractions and dream quietly away the remnant of a troubled life, I know of none more promising than this little valley.

From the listless repose of the place and the peculiar character of its inhabitants, who are descendants from the original Dutch settlers, this sequestered glen has long been known by the name of *Sleepy Hollow*, and its rustic lads are called the Sleepy Hollow Boys throughout all the neighboring country. A drowsy, dreamy influence seems to hang over the land and to pervade the very atmosphere. Some say that the place was bewitched by a High German doctor during the early days of the settlement; others, that an old Indian chief, the prophet or wizard of his tribe, held his powwows there before the country was discovered by Master Hendrick Hudson. Certain it is, the place still continues under the sway of some witching power that holds a spell over the minds of the good people, causing them to walk in a continual reverie. They are given to all kinds of marvellous beliefs, are subject to trances and visions, and frequently see strange sights and hear music and voices in the air. The whole neighborhood abounds with local tales, haunted spots, and twilight superstitions; stars shoot and meteors glare oftener across the valley than in any other part of the country, and the nightmare, with her whole ninefold, seems to make it the favorite scene of her gambols.

The dominant spirit, however, that haunts this enchanted region, and seems to be commander-in-chief of all the powers of the air, is the apparition of a figure on horseback without a head. It is said by some to be the ghost of a Hessian trooper whose head had been carried away by a cannonball in some nameless battle during the Revolutionary War, and who is ever and anon seen by the country-folk hurrying along in the gloom of night as if on the wings of the wind. His haunts are not confined to the valley, but extend at times to the adjacent roads, and especially to the vicinity of a church at no great distance. Indeed, certain of the most authentic historians of those parts, who have been careful in collecting and collating the floating facts concerning this spectre, allege that the body of the trooper, having been buried in the churchyard, the ghost rides forth to the scene of battle in nightly quest of his head, and that the rushing speed with which he sometimes passes along the Hollow, like a midnight blast, is owing to his being belated and in a hurry to get back to the churchyard before daybreak.

Such is the general purport of this legendary superstition, which has furnished materials for many a wild story in that region of shadows; and the spectre is known at all the country firesides by the name of the Headless Horseman of Sleepy Hollow.

It is remarkable that the visionary propensity I have mentioned is not confined to the native inhabitants of the valley, but is unconsciously imbibed by every one who resides there for a time. However wide awake they may have been before they entered that sleepy region, they are sure in a little time to inhale the witching influence of the air and begin to grow imaginative—to dream dreams and see apparitions.

I mention this peaceful spot with all possible laud, for it is in such little retired Dutch valleys, found here and there embosomed in the great State of New York, that population, manners, and customs remain fixed, while the great torrent of migration and improvement, which is making such incessant changes in other parts of this restless country, sweeps by them unobserved. They are like those little nooks of still water which border a rapid stream where we may see the straw and bubble riding quietly at anchor or slowly revolving in their mimic harbor, undisturbed by the rush of the passing current. Though many years have elapsed since I trod the drowsy shades of Sleepy Hollow, yet I question whether I should not still find the same trees and the same families vegetating in its sheltered bosom.

In this by-place of Nature there abode, in a remote period of American history—that is to say, some thirty years since—a worthy wight of the name of Ichabod Crane, who sojourned, or, as he expressed it, "tarried," in Sleepy Hollow for the purpose of instructing the children of the vicinity. He was a native of Connecticut, a State which supplies the Union with pioneers for the mind as well as for the forest, and sends forth yearly its legions of frontier woodmen and country schoolmasters. The cognomen of Crane was not inapplicable to his person. He was tall, but exceedingly lank, with narrow shoulders, long arms and legs, hands that dangled a mile out of his sleeves, feet that might have served for shovels, and his whole frame most loosely hung together. His head was small, and flat at top, with huge ears, large green glassy eyes, and a long snip nose, so that it looked like a weathercock perched upon his spindle neck to tell which way the wind blew. To see him striding along the profile of a hill on a windy day, with his clothes bagging and fluttering about him, one might have mistaken him for the genius of Famine descending upon the earth or some scarecrow eloped from a cornfield.

His school-house was a low building of one large room, rudely constructed of logs, the windows partly glazed and partly patched with leaves of old copybooks. It was most ingeniously secured at vacant hours by a withe twisted in the handle of the door and stakes set against the window-shutters, so that, though a thief might get in with perfect ease, he would find some embarrassment in getting out—an idea most probably borrowed by the architect, Yost Van Houten, from the mystery of an eel-pot. The school-house stood in a rather lonely but pleasant situation, just at the foot of a woody hill, with a brook running close by and a formidable birch tree growing at one end of it. From hence the low murmur of his pupils' voices, conning over their lessons, might be heard in a drowsy summer's day like the hum of a bee-hive, interrupted now and then by the authoritative voice of the master in the tone of menace or command, or, peradventure, by the appalling sound of the birch as he urged some tardy loiterer along the flowery path of knowledge. Truth to say, he was a conscientious man, and ever bore in mind the golden maxim, "Spare the rod and spoil the child." Ichabod Crane's scholars certainly were not spoiled.

I would not have it imagined, however, that he was one of those cruel potentates of the school who joy in the smart of their subjects; on the contrary, he administered justice with discrimination rather than severity, taking the burden off the backs of the weak and laying it on those of the strong. Your mere puny stripling, that winced at the least flourish of the rod, was passed by with indulgence; but the claims of justice were satisfied by inflicting a double portion on some little tough, wrong-headed, broad-skirted Dutch urchin, who sulked and swelled and grew dogged and sullen beneath the birch. All this he called "doing his duty by their parents;" and he never inflicted a chastisement without following it by the assurance, so consolatory to the smarting urchin, that "he would remember it and thank him for it the longest day he had to live."

When school-hours were over he was even the companion and playmate of the larger boys, and on holiday afternoons would convoy some of the smaller ones home who happened to have pretty sisters or good housewives for mothers noted for the comforts of the cupboard. Indeed it behooved him to keep on good terms with his pupils. The revenue arising from his school was small, and would have been scarcely sufficient to furnish him with daily bread, for he was a huge feeder, and, though lank, had the dilating powers of an anaconda; but to help out his maintenance he was, according to country custom in those parts, boarded and lodged at the houses of the farmers whose children he instructed. With these he lived successively a week at a time, thus going the rounds of the neighborhood with all his worldly effects tied up in a cotton handkerchief.

That all this might not be too onerous on the purses of his rustic patrons, who are apt to consider the costs of schooling a grievous burden and schoolmasters as mere drones, he had various ways of rendering himself both useful and agreeable. He assisted the farmers occasionally in the lighter labors of their farms, helped to make hay, mended the fences, took the horses to water, drove the cows from pasture, and cut wood for the winter fire. He laid aside, too, all the dominant dignity and absolute sway with which he lorded it in his little empire, the school, and became wonderfully gentle and ingratiating. He found favor in the eyes of the mothers by petting the children, particularly the youngest; and like the lion bold, which whilom so magnanimously the lamb did hold, he would sit with a child on one knee and rock a cradle with his foot for whole hours together.

In addition to his other vocations, he was the singing-master of the neighborhood and picked up many bright shillings by instructing the young folks in psalmody. It was a matter of no little vanity to him on Sundays to take his station in front of the church-gallery with a band of chosen singers, where, in his own mind, he completely carried away the palm from the parson. Certain it is, his voice resounded far above all the rest of the congregation, and there are peculiar quavers still to be heard in that church, and which may even be heard half a mile off, quite to the opposite side of the mill-pond on a still Sunday morning, which are said to be legitimately descended from the nose of Ichabod Crane. Thus, by divers little makeshifts in that ingenious way which is commonly denominated "by hook and by crook," the worthy pedagogue got on tolerably enough, and was thought, by all who understood nothing of the labor of headwork, to have a wonderfully easy life of it.

The schoolmaster is generally a man of some importance in the female circle of a rural neighborhood, being considered a kind of idle, gentleman-like personage of vastly superior taste and accomplishments to the rough country swains, and, indeed, inferior in learning only to the parson. His appearance, therefore, is apt to occasion some little stir at the tea-table of a farmhouse and the addition of a supernumerary dish of cakes or sweetmeats, or, peradventure, the parade of a silver tea-pot. Our man of letters, therefore, was peculiarly happy in the smiles of all the country damsels. How he would figure among them in the churchyard between services on Sundays, gathering grapes for them from the wild vines that overrun the surrounding trees; reciting for their amusement all the epitaphs on the tombstones; or sauntering, with a whole bevy of them, along the banks of the adjacent mill-pond, while the more bashful country bumpkins hung sheepishly back, envying his superior elegance and address.

From his half-itinerant life, also, he was a kind of travelling gazette, carrying the whole budget of local gossip from house to house, so that his appearance was always greeted with satisfaction. He was, moreover, esteemed by the women as a man of great erudition, for he had read several books quite through, and was a perfect master of Cotton Mather's *History of New England Witchcraft*, in which, by the way, he most firmly and potently believed.

He was, in fact, an odd mixture of small shrewdness and simple credulity. His appetite for the marvellous and his powers of digesting it were equally extraordinary, and both had been increased by his residence in this spellbound region. No tale was too gross or monstrous for his capacious swallow. It was often his delight, after his school was dismissed in the afternoon, to stretch himself on the rich bed of clover bordering the little brook that whimpered by his school-house, and there con over old Mather's direful tales until the gathering dusk of the evening made the printed page a mere mist before his eyes. Then, as he wended his way by swamp and stream and awful woodland to the farmhouse where he happened to be quartered, every sound of Nature at that witching hour fluttered his excited imagination—the moan of the whip-poor-will* from the hillside; the boding cry of the tree-toad, that harbinger of storm; the dreary hooting of the screech-owl, or the sudden rustling in the thicket of birds frightened from their roost. The fire-flies, too, which sparkled most vividly in the darkest places, now and then startled him as one of uncommon brightness would stream across his path; and if, by chance, a huge blockhead of a beetle came winging his blundering flight against him, the poor varlet was ready to give up the ghost, with the idea that he was struck with a witch's token. His only resource on such occasions, either to drown thought or drive away evil spirits, was to sing psalm tunes; and the good people of Sleepy Hollow, as they sat by their doors of an evening, were often filled with awe at hearing his nasal melody, "in linked sweetness long drawn out," floating from the distant hill or along the dusky road.

Another of his sources of fearful pleasure was to pass long winter

---

*The whip-poor-will is a bird which is only heard at night. It receives its name from its note, which is thought to resemble those words.

evenings with the old Dutch wives as they sat spinning by the fire, with a row of apples roasting and spluttering along the hearth, and listen to their marvellous tales of ghosts and goblins, and haunted fields, and haunted brooks, and haunted bridges, and haunted houses, and particularly of the headless horseman, or Galloping Hessian of the Hollow, as they sometimes called him. He would delight them equally by his anecdotes of witchcraft and of the direful omens and portentous sights and sounds in the air which prevailed in the earlier times of Connecticut, and would frighten them woefully with speculations upon comets and shooting stars, and with the alarming fact that the world did absolutely turn round and that they were half the time topsy-turvy.

But if there was a pleasure in all this while snugly cuddling in the chimney-corner of a chamber that was all of a ruddy glow from the crackling wood-fire, and where, of course, no spectre dared to show its face, it was dearly purchased by the terrors of his subsequent walk homewards. What fearful shapes and shadows beset his path amidst the dim and ghastly glare of a snowy night! With what wistful look did be eye every trembling ray of light streaming across the waste fields from some distant window! How often was he appalled by some shrub covered with snow, which, like a sheeted spectre, beset his very path! How often did he shrink with curdling awe at the sound of his own steps on the frosty crust beneath his feet, and dread to look over his shoulder, lest he should behold some uncouth being tramping close behind him! And how often was he thrown into complete dismay by some rushing blast howling among the trees, in the idea that it was the Galloping Hessian on one of his nightly scourings!

All these, however, were mere terrors of the night, phantoms of the mind that walk in darkness; and though be had seen many spectres in his time, and been more than once beset by Satan in divers shapes in his lonely perambulations, yet daylight put an end to all these evils; and he would have passed a pleasant life of it, in despite of the devil and all his works, if his path had not been crossed by a being that causes more perplexity to mortal man than ghosts, goblins, and the whole race of witches put together, and that was—a woman.

Among the musical disciples who assembled one evening in each week to receive his instructions in psalmody was Katrina Van Tassel, the daughter and only child of a substantial Dutch farmer. She was a blooming lass of fresh eighteen, plump as a partridge, ripe and melting and rosy-cheeked as one of her father's peaches, and universally famed, not merely for her beauty, but her vast expectations. She was withal a little of a coquette, as might be perceived even in her dress, which was a mixture of ancient and modern fashions, as most suited to set off her charms. She wore the ornaments of pure yellow gold which her great-great-grandmother had brought over from Saardam, the tempting stomacher of the olden time, and withal a provokingly short petticoat to display the prettiest foot and ankle in the country round.

Ichabod Crane had a soft and foolish heart towards the sex, and it is not to be wondered at that so tempting a morsel soon found favor in his eyes, more especially after he had visited her in her paternal mansion. Old Baltus Van Tassel was a perfect picture of a thriving, contented, liberal-hearted farmer. He seldom, it is true, sent either his eyes or his thoughts beyond the boundaries of his own farm, but within those everything was snug, happy, and well-conditioned. He was satisfied with his wealth but not proud of it, and piqued himself upon the hearty abundance, rather than the style, in which he lived. His stronghold was situated on the banks of the Hudson, in one of those green, sheltered, fertile nooks in which the Dutch farmers are so fond of nestling. A great elm tree spread its broad branches over it, at the foot of which bubbled up a spring of the softest and sweetest water in a little well formed of a barrel, and then stole sparkling away through the grass to a neighboring brook that bubbled along among alders and dwarf willows. Hard by the farmhouse was a vast barn, that might have served for a church, every window and crevice of which seemed bursting forth with the treasures of the farm; the flail was busily resounding within it from morning to night; swallows and martins skimmed twittering about the eaves; and rows of pigeons, some with one eye turned up, as if watching the weather, some with their heads under their wings or buried in their bosoms, and others, swelling, and cooing, and bowing about their dames, were enjoying the sunshine on the roof. Sleek, unwieldy porkers were grunting in the repose and abundance of their pens, whence sallied forth, now and then, troops of sucking pigs as if to snuff the air. A stately squadron of snowy geese were riding in an adjoining pond, convoying whole fleets of ducks; regiments of turkeys were gobbling through the farmyard, and guineafowls fretting about it, like ill-tempered housewives, with their peevish, discontented cry. Before the barn-door strutted the gallant cock, that pattern of a husband, a warrior, and a fine gentleman, clapping his burnished wings and crowing in the pride and gladness of his

heart—sometimes tearing up the earth with his feet, and then generously calling his ever-hungry family of wives and children to enjoy the
rich morsel which he had discovered.

The pedagogue's mouth watered as he looked upon this sumptuous promise of luxurious winter fare. In his devouring mind's eye he
pictured to himself every roasting-pig running about with a pudding
in his belly and an apple in his mouth; the pigeons were snugly put to
bed in a comfortable pie and tucked in with a coverlet of crust; the
geese were swimming in their own gravy; and the ducks pairing cosily
in dishes, like snug married couples, with a decent competency of
onion sauce. In the porkers he saw carved out the future sleek side of
bacon and juicy relishing ham; not a turkey but he beheld daintily
trussed up, with its gizzard under its wing, and, peradventure, a necklace of savory sausages; and even bright Chanticleer himself lay sprawling on his back in a side-dish, with uplifted claws, as if craving that
quarter which his chivalrous spirit disdained to ask while living.

As the enraptured Ichabod fancied all this, and as he rolled his
great green eyes over the fat meadow-lands, the rich fields of wheat, of
rye, of buckwheat, and Indian corn, and the orchards burdened with
ruddy fruit, which surrounded the warm tenement of Van Tassel, his
heart yearned after the damsel who was to inherit these domains, and
his imagination expanded with the idea how they might be readily
turned into cash and the money invested in immense tracts of wild
land and shingle palaces in the wilderness. Nay, his busy fancy already
realized his hopes, and presented to him the blooming Katrina, with a
whole family of children, mounted on the top of a wagon loaded with
household trumpery, with pots and kettles dangling beneath, and he
beheld himself bestriding a pacing mare, with a colt at her heels, setting out for Kentucky, Tennessee, or the Lord knows where.

When he entered the house the conquest of his heart was complete. It was one of those spacious farmhouses with high-ridged but
lowly-sloping roofs, built in the style handed down from the first Dutch
settlers, the low projecting eaves forming a piazza along the front capable of being closed up in bad weather. Under this were hung flails,
harness, various utensils of husbandry, and nets for fishing in the
neighboring river. Benches were built along the sides for summer use,
and a great spinning-wheel at one end and a churn at the other showed
the various uses to which this important porch might be devoted.
From this piazza the wondering Ichabod entered the hall, which formed
the centre of the mansion and the place of usual residence. Here rows

of resplendent pewter, ranged on a long dresser, dazzled his eyes. In one corner stood a huge bag of wool ready to be spun; in another a quantity of linsey-woolsey just from the loom; ears of Indian corn and strings of dried apples and peaches hung in gay festoons along the walls, mingled with the gaud of red peppers; and a door left ajar gave him a peep into the best parlor, where the claw-footed chairs and dark mahogany tables shone like mirrors; andirons, with their accompanying shovel and tongs, glistened from their covert of asparagus tops; mock-oranges and conch-shells decorated the mantelpiece; strings of various-colored birds' eggs were suspended above it; a great ostrish egg was hung from the centre of the room, and a corner cupboard, knowingly left open, displayed immense treasures of old silver and well-mended china.

From the moment Ichabod laid his eyes upon these regions of delight the peace of his mind was at an end, and his only study was how to gain the affections of the peerless daughter of Van Tassel. In this enterprise, however, he had more real difficulties than generally fell to the lot of a knight-errant of yore, who seldom had anything but giants, enchanters, fiery dragons, and such-like easily-conquered adversaries to contend with, and had to make his way merely through gates of iron and brass and walls of adamant to the castle keep, where the lady of his heart was confined; all which he achieved as easily as a man would carve his way to the centre of a Christmas pie, and then the lady gave him her hand as a matter of course. Ichabod, on the contrary, had to win his way to the heart of a country coquette beset with a labyrinth of whims and caprices, which were forever presenting new difficulties and impediments, and he had to encounter a host of fearful adversaries of real flesh and blood, the numerous rustic admirers who beset every portal to her heart, keeping a watchful and angry eye upon each other, but ready to fly out in the common cause against any new competitor.

Among these the most formidable was a burly, roaring, roistering blade of the name of Abraham—or, according to the Dutch abbreviation, Brom—Van Brunt, the hero of the country round, which rang with his feats of strength and hardihood. He was broad-shouldered and double-jointed, with short curly black hair and a bluff but not unpleasant countenance, having a mingled air of fun and arrogance. From his Herculean frame and great powers of limb, he had received the nickname of BROM BONES, by which he was universally known. He was famed for great knowledge and skill in horsemanship, being as dexterous on horseback as a Tartar. He was foremost at all races and cockfights, and, with the ascendancy which bodily strength acquires in rustic life, was the umpire in all disputes, setting his hat on one side and giving his decisions with an air and tone admitting of no gainsay or appeal. He was always ready for either a fight or a frolic, but had more mischief than ill-will in his composition; and with all his overbearing roughness there was a strong dash of waggish good-humor at bottom. He had three or four boon companions who regarded him as their model, and at the head of whom he scoured the country, attending every scene of feud or merriment for miles around. In cold weather he was distinguished by a fur cap surmounted with a flaunting fox's tail; and when the folks at a country gathering descried this well-known crest at a distance, whisking about among a squad of hard riders, they always stood by for a squall. Sometimes his crew would be heard dashing along past the farm-houses at midnight with whoop and halloo, like a troop of Don Cossacks, and the old dames, startled out of their sleep, would listen for a moment till the hurry-scurry had clattered by, and then exclaim, "Ay, there goes Brom Bones and his gang!" The neighbors looked upon him with a mixture of awe, admiration, and good-will, and when any madcap prank or rustic brawl occurred in the vicinity always shook their heads and warranted Brom Bones was at the bottom of it.

This rantipole hero had for some time singled out the blooming Katrina for the object of his uncouth gallantries, and, though his amorous toyings were something like the gentle caresses and endearments of a bear, yet it was whispered that she did not altogether discourage his hopes. Certain it is, his advances were signals for rival candidates to retire who felt no inclination to cross a line in his amours; insomuch, that when his horse was scene tied to Van Tassel's paling on a Sunday night, a sure sign that his master was courting—or, as it is termed, "sparking"—within, all other suitors passed by in despair and carried the war into other quarters.

Such was the formidable rival with whom Ichabod Crane had to contend, and, considering all things, a stouter man than he would have shrunk from the competition and a wiser man would have despaired. He had, however, a happy mixture of pliability and perseverance in his nature; he was in form and spirit like a supple jack—yielding, but tough; though he bent, he never broke and though he bowed beneath the slightest pressure, yet the moment it was away, jerk! he was as erect and carried his head as high as ever.

To have taken the field openly against his rival would have been madness for he was not man to be thwarted in his amours, any more than that stormy lover, Achilles. Ichabod, therefore, made his advances in a quiet and gently-insinuating manner. Under cover of his character of singing-master, he made frequent visits at the farm-house; not that he had anything to apprehend from the meddlesome interference of parents, which is so often a stumbling-block in the path of lovers. Balt Van Tassel was an easy, indulgent soul; he loved his daughter better even than his pipe, and, like a reasonable man and an excellent father, let her have her way in everything. His notable little wife, too, had enough to do to attend to her housekeeping and manage her poultry for, as she sagely observed, ducks and geese are foolish things and must be looked after, but girls can take care of themselves. Thus while the busy dame bustled about the house or plied her spinning-wheel at one end of the piazza, honest Balt would sit smoking his evening pipe at the other, watching the achievements of a little wooden warrior who, armed with a sword in each hand, was most valiantly fighting the wind on the pinnacle of the barn. In the meantime, Ichabod would carry on his suit with the daughter by the side of the spring under the great elm, or sauntering along in the twilight, that hour so favorable to the lover's eloquence.

I profess not to know how women's hearts are wooed and won. To me they have always been matters of riddle and admiration. Some seem to have but one vulnerable point, or door of access, while otheres have a thousand avenues and may be captured in a thousand different ways. It is a great triumph of skill to gain the former, but still greater proof of generalship to maintain possession of the latter, for the man must battle for his fortress at every door and window. He who wins a thousand common hearts is therefore entitled to some renown, but he who keeps undisputed sway over the heart of a coquette is indeed a hero. Certain it is, this was not the case with the redoubtable Brom Bones; and from the moment Ichabod Crane made his advances, the interests of the former evidently declined; his horse was no longer seen tied at the palings on Sunday nights, and a deadly feud gradually arose between him and the preceptor of Sleepy Hollow.

Brom, who had a degree of rough chivalry in his nature, would fain have carried matters to open warfare, and have settled their pretensions to the lady according to the mode of those most concise and simple reasoners, the knights-errant of yore—by single combat; but Ichabod was too conscious of the superior might of his adversary to enter the lists against him: he had overheard a boast of Bones, that he would "double the schoolmaster up and lay him on a shelf of his own school-house;" and he was too wary to give him an opportunity. There was something extremely provoking in this obstinately pacific system; it left Brom no alternative but to draw upon the funds of rustic waggery in his disposition and to play off boorish practical jokes upon his rival. Ichabod became the object of whimsical persecution to Bones and his gang of rough riders. They harried his hitherto peaceful domains; smoked out his singing school by stopping up the chimney; broke into the schoolhouse at night in spite of its formidable fastenings of withe and window stakes, and turned everything topsy-turvy; so that the poor schoolmaster began to think all the witches in the country held their meetings there. But, what was still more annoying, Brom took all opportunities of turning him into ridicule in presence of his mistress, and had a scoundrel dog whom he taught to whine in the most ludicrous manner, and introduced as a rival of Ichabod's, to instruct her in psalmody.

In this way, matters went on for some time without producing any material effect on the relative situation of the contending powers. On a fine autumnal afternoon Ichabod, in pensive mood, sat enthroned on the lofty stool whence he usually watched all the concerns of his little literary realm. In his hand he swayed a ferule, that sceptre of despotic power; the birch of justice reposed on three nails behind the throne, a constant terror to evildoers; while on the desk before him might be seen sundry contraband articles and prohibited weapons detected upon the persons of idle urchins, such as half-munched apples, popguns, whirligigs, fly-cages, and whole legions of rampant little paper gamecocks. Apparently there had been some appalling act of justice recently inflicted, for his scholars were all busily intent upon their books or slyly whispering behind them with one eye kept upon the master, and a kind of buzzing stillness reigned throughout the schoolroom. It was suddenly interrupted by the appearance of a negro in tow-cloth jacket and trowsers, a round-crowned fragment of a hat like the cap of Mercury, and mounted on the back of a ragged, wild, half-broken colt, which he managed with a rope by way of halter. He came clattering up to the school door with an invitation to Ichabod to attend a merry-making or "quilting frolic" to be held that evening at Mynheer Van Tassel's; and, having delivered his message with that air of importance and effort at fine language which a negro is apt to display on petty embassies of the kind, he dashed over the brook, and was seen scampering away up the hollow, full of the importance and hurry of his mission.

All was now bustle and hubbub in the late quiet school-room. The scholars were hurried through their lessons without stopping at trifles; those who were nimble skipped over half with impunity, and those who were tardy had a smart application now and then in the rear to quicken their speed or help them over a tall word. Books were flung aside without being put away on the shelves, inkstands were overturned, benches thrown down, and the whole school was turned loose an hour before the usual time, bursting forth like a legion of young imps, yelping and racketing about the green in joy at their early emancipation.

The gallant Ichabod now spent at least an extra half hour at his toilet, brushing and furbishing up his best, and indeed only, suit of rusty black, and arranging his locks by a bit of broken looking-glass that hung up in the school-house. That he might make his appearance before his mistress in the true style of a cavalier, he borrowed a horse from the farmer with whom he was domiciliated, a choleric old Dutchman of the name of Hans Van Ripper, and, thus gallantly mounted, issued forth like a knight-errant in quest of adventures. But it is meet I should, in the true spirit of romantic story, give some account of the looks and equipments of my hero and his steed. The animal he bestrode was a broken-down plough-horse that had outlived almost everything but his viciousness. He was gaunt and shagged, with a ewe neck and a head like a hammer; his rusty mane and tail were tangled and knotted with burrs; one eye had lost its pupil and was glaring and spectral, but the other had the gleam of a genuine devil in it. Still, he must have had fire and mettle in his day, if we may judge from the name he bore of Gunpowder. He had, in fact, been a favorite steed of his master's, the choleric Van Ripper, who was a furious rider, and had infused, very probably, some of his own spirit into the animal; for, old and broken down as he looked, there was more of the lurking devil in him than in any young filly in the country.

Ichabod was a suitable figure for such a steed. He rode with short stirrups, which brought his knees nearly up to the pommel of the saddle; his sharp elbows stuck out like grasshoppers'; he carried his whip perpendicularly in his hand like a sceptre; and as his horse jogged on the motion of his arms was not unlike the flapping of a pair of wings. A small wool hat rested on the top of his nose, for so his scanty strip of forehead might be called, and the skirts of his black coat fluttered out almost to his horse's tail. Such was the appearance of Ichabod and his steed as they shambled out of the gate of Hans Van Ripper, and it was altogether such an apparition as is seldom to be met with in broad daylight.

It was, as I have said, a fine autumnal day, the sky was clear and serene, and Nature wore that rich and golden livery which we always associate with the idea of abundance. The forests had put on their sober brown and yellow, while some trees of the tenderer kind had been nipped by the frosts into brilliant dyes of orange, purple, and scarlet. Streaming files of wild-ducks began to make their appearance high in the air; the bark of the squirrel might be heard from the groves of beech and hickory nuts, and the pensive whistle of the quail at intervals from the neighboring stubble-field.

The small birds were taking their farewell banquets. In the fulness of their revelry they fluttered, chirping and frolicking, from bush to bush and tree to tree, capricious from the very profusion and variety around them. There was the honest cock robin, the favorite game of stripling sportsmen, with its loud querulous note; and the twittering blackbirds, flying in sable clouds; and the golden-winged woodpecker, with his crimson crest, his broad black gorget, and splendid plumage; and the cedar-bird, with its red-tipt wings and yellow-tipt tail and its little monteiro cap of feathers; and the blue jay, that noisy coxcomb, in his gay light-blue coat and white under-clothes, screaming and chattering, bobbing and nodding and bowing, and pretending to be on good terms with every songster of the grove.

As Ichabod jogged slowly on his way his eye, ever open to every symptom of culinary abundance, ranged with delight over the treasures of jolly Autumn. On all sides he beheld vast store of apples—some hanging in oppressive opulence on the trees, some gathered into baskets and barrels for the market, others heaped up in rich piles for the cider-press. Farther on he beheld great fields of Indian corn, with its golden ears peeping from their leafy coverts and holding out the promise of cakes and hasty pudding; and the yellow pumpkins lying beneath them, turning up their fair round bellies to the sun, and giving ample prospects of the most luxurious of pies; and anon he passed the fragrant buckwheat-fields, breathing the odor of the beehive, and as he beheld them soft anticipations stole over his mind of dainty slapjacks, well buttered and garnished with honey or treacle by the delicate little dimpled hand of Katrina Van Tassel.

Thus feeding his mind with many sweet thoughts and "sugared suppositions," he journeyed along the sides of a range of hills which look out upon some of the goodliest scenes of the mighty Hudson. The sun gradually wheeled his broad disk down into the west. The wide bosom of the Tappan Zee lay motionless and glassy, excepting that here and there a gentle undulation waved and prolonged the blue shadow of the distant mountain. A few amber clouds floated in the sky, without a breath of air to move them. The horizon was of a fine golden tint, changing gradually into a pure apple green, and from that into the deep blue of the mid-heaven. A slanting ray lingered on the woody crests of the precipices that overhung some parts of the river, giving greater depth to the dark-gray and purple of their rocky sides. A sloop was loitering in the distance, dropping slowly down with the tide, her sail hanging uselessly against the mast, and as the reflection of the sky gleamed along the still water it seemed as if the vessel was suspended in the air.

It was toward evening that Ichabod arrived at the castle of the Heer Van Tassel, which he found thronged with the pride and flower of the adjacent country—old farmers, a spare leathern-faced race, in homespun coats and breeches, blue stockings, huge shoes, and magnificent pewter buckles; their brisk withered little dames, in close crimped caps, long-waisted shortgowns, homespun petticoats, with scissors and pincushions and gay calico pockets hanging on the outside; buxom lasses, almost as antiquated as their mothers, excepting where a straw hat, a fine ribbon, or perhaps a white frock, gave symptoms of city innovation; the sons, in short square-skirted coats with rows of stupendous brass buttons, and their hair generally queued in the fashion of the times, especially if they could procure an eel-skin for the purpose, it being esteemed throughout the country as a potent nourisher and strengthener of the hair.

Brom Bones, however, was the hero of the scene, having come to the gathering on his favorite steed Daredevil—a creature, like himself full of mettle and mischief, and which no one but himself could manage. He was, in fact, noted for preferring vicious animals, given to all kinds of tricks, which kept the rider in constant risk of his neck, for he held a tractable, well-broken horse as unworthy of a lad of spirit.

Fain would I pause to dwell upon the world of charms that burst upon the enraptured gaze of my hero as he entered the state parlor of Van Tassel's mansion. Not those of the bevy of buxom lasses with their luxurious display of red and white, but the ample charms of a genuine Dutch country tea-table in the sumptuous time of autumn. Such heaped-up platters of cakes of various and almost indescribable

kinds, known only to experienced Dutch housewives! There was the
doughty doughnut, the tenderer oily koek, and the crisp and crumbling cruller; sweet cakes and short cakes, ginger cakes and honey cakes,
and the whole family of cakes. And then there were apple pies and
peach pies and pumpkin pies; besides slices of ham and smoked beef;
and moreover delectable dishes of preserved plums and peaches and
pears and quinces; not to mention broiled shad and roasted chickens;
together with bowls of milk and cream—all mingled higgledy-piggledy,
pretty much as I have enumerated them, with the motherly teapot
sending up its clouds of vapor from the midst. Heaven bless the mark!
I want breath and time to discuss this banquet as it deserves, and am
too eager to get on with my story. Happily, Ichabod Crane was not in
so great a hurry as his historian, but did ample justice to every dainty.

He was a kind and thankful creature, whose heart dilated in proportion as his skin was filled with good cheer, and whose spirits rose
with eating as some men's do with drink. He could not help, too,
rolling his large eyes round him as he ate, and chuckling with the
possibility that he might one day be lord of all this scene of almost
unimaginable luxury and splendor. Then, he thought, how soon he'd
turn his back upon the old school-house, snap his fingers in the face
of Hans Van Ripper and every other niggardly patron, and kick any
itinerant pedagogue out of doors that should dare to call him comrade!

Old Baltus Van Tassel moved about among his guests with a face
dilated with content and good-humor, round and jolly as the harvest
moon. His hospitable attentions were brief, but expressive, being confined to a shake of the hand, a slap on the shoulder, a loud laugh, and
a pressing invitation to "fall to and help themselves."

And now the sound of the music from the common room, or hall,
summoned to the dance. The musician was an old gray-headed negro
who had been the itinerant orchestra of the neighborhood for more
than half a century. His instrument was as old and battered as himself. The greater part of the time he scraped on two or three strings,
accompanying every movement of the bow with a motion of the head,
bowing almost to the ground and stamping with his foot whenever a
fresh couple were to start.

Ichabod prided himself upon his dancing as much as upon his
vocal powers. Not a limb, not a fibre about him was idle; and to have
seen his loosely hung frame in full motion and clattering about the
room you would have thought Saint Vitus himself, that blessed pa-

tron of the dance, was figuring before you in person. He was the admiration of all the negroes, who, having gathered, of all ages and sizes, from the farm and the neighborhood, stood forming a pyramid of shining black faces at every door and window, gazing with delight at the scene, rolling their white eyeballs, and showing grinning rows of ivory from ear to ear. How could the flogger of urchins be otherwise than animated and joyous? The lady of his heart was his partner in the dance, and smiling graciously in reply to all his amorous oglings, while Brom Bones, sorely smitten with love and jealousy, sat brooding by himself in one corner.

When the dance was at an end Ichabod was attracted to a knot of the sager folks, who, with old Van Tassel, sat smoking at one end of the piazza gossiping over former times and drawing out long stories about the war.

This neighborhood, at the time of which I am speaking, was one of those highly favored places which abound with chronicle and great men. The British and American line had run near it during the war; it had therefore been the scene of marauding and infested with refugees, cow-boys, and all kinds of border chivalry. Just sufficient time had elapsed to enable each storyteller to dress up his tale with a little becoming fiction, and in the indistinctness of his recollection to make himself the hero of every exploit.

There was the story of Doffue Martling, a large blue-bearded Dutchman, who had nearly taken a British frigate with an old iron nine-pounder from a mud breastwork, only that his gun burst at the sixth discharge. And there was an old gentleman who shall be nameless, being too rich a mynheer to be lightly mentioned, who, in the battle of Whiteplains, being an excellent master of defence, parried a musket-ball with a small sword, insomuch that he absolutely felt it whiz round the blade and glance off at the hilt: in proof of which he was ready at any time to show the sword, with the hilt a little bent. There were several more that had been equally great in the field, not one of whom but was persuaded that he had a considerable hand in bringing the war to a happy termination.

But all these were nothing to the tales of ghosts and apparitions that succeeded. The neighborhood is rich in legendary treasures of the kind. Local tales and superstitions thrive best in these sheltered, long-settled retreats but are trampled under foot by the shifting throng that forms the population of most of our country places. Besides, there is no encouragement for ghosts in most of our villages, for they have scarcely had time to finish their first nap and turn themselves in their graves before their surviving friends have travelled away from the neighborhood; so that when they turn out at night to walk their rounds they have no acquaintance left to call upon. This is perhaps the reason why we so seldom hear of ghosts except in our long-established Dutch communities.

The immediate causes however, of the prevalence of supernatural stories in these parts, was doubtless owing to the vicinity of Sleepy Hollow. There was a contagion in the very air that blew from that haunted region; it breathed forth an atmosphere of dreams and fancies infecting all the land. Several of the Sleepy Hollow people were present at Van Tassel's, and, as usual, were doling out their wild and wonderful legends. Many dismal tales were told about funeral trains and mourning cries and wailings heard and seen about the great tree where the unfortunate Major André was taken, and which stood in the neighborhood. Some mention was made also of the woman in white that haunted the dark glen at Raven Rock, and was often heard to shriek on winter nights before a storm, having perished there in the snow. The chief part of the stories, however, turned upon the favorite spectre of Sleepy Hollow, the headless horseman, who had been heard several times of late patrolling the country, and, it was said, tethered his horse nightly among the graves in the churchyard.

The sequestered situation of this church seems always to have made it a favorite haunt of troubled spirits. It stands on a knoll surrounded by locust trees and lofty elms, from among which its decent whitewashed walls shine modestly forth, like Christian purity beaming through the shades of retirement. A gentle slope descends from it to a silver sheet of water bordered by high trees, between which peeps may be caught at the blue hills of the Hudson. To look upon its grass-grown yard, where the sunbeams seem to sleep so quietly, one would think that there at least the dead might rest in peace. On one side of the church extends a wide woody dell, along, which raves a large brook among broken rocks and trunks of fallen trees. Over a deep black part of the stream, not far from the church, was formerly thrown a wooden bridge; the road that led to it and the bridge itself were thickly shaded by overhanging trees, which cast a gloom about it even in the daytime, but occasioned a fearful darkness at night. Such was one of the favorite haunts of the headless horseman, and the place where he was most frequently encountered. The tale was told of old Brouwer, a most heretical disbeliever in ghosts, how he met the horseman returning from his foray into Sleepy Hollow, and was obliged to get up behind him; how they galloped over bush and brake, over hill and swamp, until they reached the bridge, when the horseman suddenly turned into a skeleton, threw old Brouwer into the brook, and sprang away over the tree-tops with a clap of thunder.

This story was immediately matched by a thrice-marvellous adventure of Brom Bones, who made light of the galloping Hessian as an arrant jockey. He affirmed that on returning one night from the neighboring village of Sing-Sing he had been over taken by this midnight trooper; that he had offered to race with him for a bowl of punch, and should have won it too, for Daredevil beat the goblin horse all hollow, but just as they came to the church bridge the Hessian bolted and vanished in a flash of fire.

All these tales, told in that drowsy undertone with which men talk in the dark, the countenances of the listeners only now and then receiving a casual gleam from the glare of a pipe, sank deep in the mind of Ichabod. He repaid them in kind with large extracts from his invaluable author, Cotton Mather, and added many marvellous events that had taken place in his native state of Connecticut and fearful sights which he had seen in his nightly walks about Sleepy Hollow.

The revel now gradually broke up. The old farmers gathered together their families in their wagons, and were heard for some time rattling along the hollow roads and over the distant hills. Some of the damsels mounted on pillions behind their favorite swains, and their light-hearted laughter, mingling with the clatter of hoofs, echoed along the silent woodlands, sounding fainter and fainter until they gradually died away, and the late scene of noise and frolic was all silent and deserted. Ichabod only lingered behind, according to the custom of country lovers, to have a tête-à-tête with the heiress, fully convinced that he was now on the high road to success. What passed at this interview I will not pretend to say, for in fact I do not know. Something, however, I fear me, must have gone wrong, for he certainly sallied forth, after no very great interval, with an air quite desolate and chop-fallen. Oh these women! these women! Could that girl have been playing off any of her coquettish tricks? Was her encouragement of the poor pedagogue all a mere sham to secure her conquest of his rival? Heaven only knows, not I! Let it suffice to say, Ichabod stole forth with the air of one who had been sacking a hen-roost, rather than a fair lady's heart. Without looking to the right or left to notice the scene of rural wealth on which he had so often gloated, he went

straight to the stable, and with several hearty cuffs and kicks roused
his steed most uncourteously from the comfortable quarters in which
he was soundly sleeping, dreaming of mountains of corn and oats and
whole valleys of timothy and clover.

It was the very witching time of night that Ichabod, heavy-hearted
and crestfallen, pursued his travel homewards along the sides of the
lofty hills which rise above Tarry Town, and which he had traversed so
cheerily in the afternoon. The hour was as dismal as himself. Far below him the Tappan Zee spread its dusky and indistinct waste of waters, with here and there the tall mast of a sloop riding quietly at
anchor under the land. In the dead hush of midnight he could even
hear the barking of the watch-dog from the opposite shore of the
Hudson; but it was so vague and faint as only to give an idea of his
distance from this faithful companion of man. Now and then, too,
the long-drawn crowing of a cock, accidentally awakened, would sound
far, far off, from some farm-house away among the hills; but it was like
a dreaming sound in his ear. No signs of life occurred near him, but
occasionally the melancholy chirp of a cricket, or perhaps the guttural
twang of a bull-frog from a neighboring marsh, as if sleeping uncomfortably and turning suddenly in his bed.

All the stories of ghosts and goblins that he had heard in the afternoon now came crowding upon his recollection. The night grew darker
and darker; the stars seemed to sink deeper in the sky, and driving
clouds occasionally had them from his sight. He had never felt so
lonely and dismal. He was, moreover, approaching the very place where
many of the scenes of the ghost-stories had been laid. In the centre of
the road stood an enormous tulip tree which towered like a giant above
all the other trees of the neighborhood and formed a: kind of land-
mark. Its limbs were gnarled and fantastic, large enough to form trunks
for ordinary trees, twisting down almost to the earth and rising again
into the air. It was connected with the tragical story of the unfortunate André, who had been taken prisoner hard by, and was universally known by the name of Major André's tree. The common people
regarded it with a mixture of respect and superstition, partly out of
sympathy for the fate of its ill-starred namesake, and partly from the
tales of strange sights and doleful lamentations told concerning it.

As Ichabod approached this fearful tree he began to whistle: he
thought his whistle was answered; it was but a blast sweeping sharply
through the dry branches. As he approached a little nearer he thought
he saw something white hanging in the midst of the tree: he paused

and ceased whistling, but on looking more narrowly perceived that it was a place where the tree had been scathed by lightning and the white wood laid bare. Suddenly he heard a groan: his teeth chattered and his knees smote against the saddle; it was but the rubbing of one huge bough upon another as they were swayed about by the breeze. He passed the tree in safety, but new perils lay before him.

About two hundred yards from the tree a small brook crossed the road and ran into a marshy and thickly-wooded glen known by the name of Wiley's Swamp. A few rough logs, laid side by side, served for a bridge over this stream. On that side of the road where the brook entered the wood a group of oaks and chestnuts, matted thick with wild grape-vines, threw a cavernous gloom over it. To pass this bridge was the severest trial. It was at this identical spot that the unfortunate André was captured, and under the covert of those chestnuts and vines were the sturdy yeomen concealed who surprised him. This has ever since been considered a haunted stream, and fearful are the feelings of the schoolboy who has to pass it alone after dark.

As he approached the stream his heart began to thump; he summoned up, however, all his resolution, gave his horse half a score of kicks in the ribs, and attempted to dash briskly across the bridge; but instead of starting forward, the perverse old animal made a lateral movement and ran broadside against the fence. Ichabod, whose fears increased with the delay, jerked the reins on the other side and kicked lustily with the contrary foot: it was all in vain; his steed started, it is true, but it was only to plunge to the opposite side of the road into a thicket of brambles and alder bushes. The schoolmaster now bestowed both whip and heel upon the starveling ribs of old Gunpowder, who dashed forward, snuffing and snorting, but came to a stand just by the bridge with a suddenness that had nearly sent his rider sprawling over his head. Just at this moment a plashy tramp by the side of the bridge caught the sensitive ear of Ichabod. In the dark shadow of the grove on the margin of the brook he beheld something huge, misshapen, black, and towering. It stirred not, but seemed gathered up in the gloom, like some gigantic monster ready to spring upon the traveller.

The hair of the affrighted pedagogue rose upon his head with terror. What was to be done? To turn and fly was now too late; and besides, what chance was there of escaping ghost or goblin, if such it was, which could ride upon the wings of the wind? Summoning up, therefore, a show of courage, he demanded in stammering accents, "Who are you?" He received no reply. He repeated his demand in a still more agitated voice. Still there was no answer. Once more he cudgelled the sides of the inflexible Gunpowder, and, shutting his eyes, broke forth with involuntary fervor into a psalm tune. Just then the shadowy object of alarm put itself in motion, and with a scramble and a bound stood at once in the middle of the road. Though the night was dark and dismal, yet the form of the unknown might now in some degree be ascertained. He appeared to be a horseman of large dimensions and mounted on a black horse of powerful frame. He made no offer of molestation or sociability, but kept aloof on one side of the road, jogging along on the blind side of old Gunpowder, who had now got over his fright and waywardness.

Ichabod, who had no relish for this strange midnight companion, and bethought himself of the adventure of Brom Bones with the Galloping Hessian, now quickened his steed in hopes of leaving him behind. The stranger, however, quickened his horse to an equal pace. Ichabod pulled up, and fell into a walk, thinking to lag behind; the other did the same. His heart began to sink within him; he endeavored to resume his psalm tune, but his parched tongue clove to the roof of his mouth and he could not utter a stave. There was something in the moody and dogged silence of this pertinacious companion that was mysterious and appalling. It was soon fearfully accounted for. On mounting a rising ground, which brought the figure of his fellow-traveller in relief against the sky, gigantic in height and muffled in a cloak, Ichabod was horror-struck on perceiving that he was headless! but his horror was still more increased on observing that the head, which should have rested on his shoulders, was carried before him on the pommel of the saddle. His terror rose to desperation, he rained a shower of kicks and blows upon Gunpowder, hoping by a sudden movement to give his companion the slip; but the spectre started full jump with him. Away, then, they dashed through thick and thin, stones flying and sparks flashing at every bound. Ichabod's flimsy garments fluttered in the air as he stretched his long lank body away over his horse's head in the eagerness of his flight.

They had now reached the road which turns off to Sleepy Hollow; but Gunpowder, who seemed possessed with a demon, instead of keeping up it, made an opposite turn and plunged headlong down hill to the left. This road leads through a sandy hollow shaded by trees for about a quarter of a mile, where it crosses the bridge famous in goblin story, and just beyond swells the green knoll on which stands the whitewashed church.

As yet the panic of the steed bad given his unskillful rider an apparent advantage in the chase; but just as he had got halfway through the hollow the girths of the saddle gave away and he felt it slipping from under him. He seized it by the pommel and endeavored to hold it firm, but in vain, and had just time to save himself by clasping old Gunpowder round the neck, when the saddle fell to the earth, and he heard it trampled under foot by his pursuer. For a moment the terror of Hans Van Ripper's wrath passed across his mind, for it was his Sunday saddle; but this was no time for petty fears; the goblin was hard on his haunches, and (unskilled rider that he was) he had much ado to maintain his seat, sometimes slipping on one side, sometimes on another, and sometimes jolted on the high ridge of his horse's backbone with a violence that he verily feared would cleave him asunder.

An opening in the trees now cheered him with the hopes that the church bridge was at hand. The wavering reflection of a silver star in the bosom of the brook told him that he was not mistaken. He saw the walls of the church dimly glaring under the trees beyond. He recollected the place where Brom Bones' ghostly competitor had disappeared. "If I can but reach that bridge," thought Ichabod, "I am safe." Just then he heard the, black steed panting and blowing close behind him; he even fancied that he felt his hot breath. Another convulsive kick in the ribs, and old Gunpowder sprang upon the bridge; he thundered over the resounding planks; he gained the opposite side; and now Ichabod cast a look behind to see if his pursuer should vanish, according to rule, in a flash of fire and brimstone. Just then he saw the goblin rising in his stirrups, and in the very act of hurling his head at him. Ichabod endeavored to dodge the horrible missile, but too late. It encountered his cranium with a tremendous crash; he was tumbled headlong into the dust, and Gunpowder, the black steed, and the goblin rider passed by like a whirlwind.

The next morning the old horse was found, without his saddle and with he bridle under his feet, soberly cropping the grass at his master's gate. Ichabod did not make his appearance at breakfast; dinner-hour came, but no Ichabod. The boys assembled at the school-house and strolled idly about the banks of the brook but no schoolmaster. Hans Van Ripper now began to feel some uneasiness about the fate of poor Ichabod and his saddle. An inquiry was set on foot, and after diligent investigation they came upon his traces. In one part of the road leading to the church was found the saddle trampled in the dirt; the tracks of horses' hoofs, deeply dented in the road and evidently at furious speed, were traced to the bridge, beyond which, on the bank of a broad part of the brook, where the water ran deep and black, was found the hat of the unfortunate Ichabod, and close beside it a spattered pumpkin.

The brook was searched, but the body of the schoolmaster was not to be discovered. Hans Van Ripper, as executor of his estate, examined the bundle which contained all his worldly effects. They consisted of two shirts and a half, two stocks for the neck, a pair or two of worsted stockings, an old pair of corduroy small-clothes, a rusty razor, a book of psalm tunes full of dog's ears, and a broken pitch-pipe. As to the books and furniture of the school-house, they belonged to the community, excepting Cotton Mather's *History of Witchcraft*, a *New England Almanac*, and a book of dreams and fortune-telling; in which last was a sheet of foolscap much scribbled and blotted in several fruitless attempts to make a copy of verses in honor of the heiress of Van Tassel. These magic books and the poetic scrawl were forthwith consigned to the flames by Hans Van Ripper, who from that time forward determined to send his children no more to school, observing that he never knew any good come of this same reading and writing. Whatever money the schoolmaster possessed—and he had received his quarter's pay but a day or two before—he must have had about his person at the time of his disappearance.

The mysterious event caused much speculation at the church on the following Sunday. Knots of gazers and gossips were collected in the churchyard, at the bridge, and at the spot where the hat and pumpkin had been found. The stories of Brouwer, of Bones, and a whole budget of others were called to mind, and when they had diligently considered them all, and compared them with the symptoms of the present case, they shook their heads and came to the conclusion that Ichabod had been carried off by the galloping Hessian. As he was a bachelor and in nobody's debt, nobody troubled his head any more about him, the school was removed to a different quarter of the hollow and another pedagogue reigned in his stead.

It is true an old farmer, who had been down to New York on a visit several years after, and from whom this account of the ghostly adventure was received, brought home the intelligence that Ichabod Crane was still alive; that he had left the neighborhood, partly through fear of the goblin and Hans Van Ripper, and partly in mortification at having been suddenly dismissed by the heiress; that he had changed his quarters to a distant part of the country, had kept school and studied law at the same time, had been admitted to the bar, turned politician electioneered, written for the newspapers, and finally had been made a justice of the Ten Pound Court. Brom Bones too, who shortly after his rival's disappearance conducted the blooming Katrina in triumph to the altar, was observed to look exceedingly knowing whenever the story of Ichabod was related, and always burst into a hearty laugh at the mention of the pumpkin; which led some to suspect that he knew more about the matter than he chose to tell.

The old country wives, however, who are the best judges of these matters, maintain to this day that Ichabod was spirited away by supernatural means; and it is a favorite story often told about the neighborhood round the interevening fire. The bridge became more than ever an object of superstitious awe, and that may be the reason why the road has been altered of late years, so as to approach the church by the border of the mill-pond. The schoolhouse, being deserted, soon fell to decay, and was reported to be haunted by the ghost of the unfortunate pedagogue; and the plough-boy, loitering homeward of a still summer evening, has often fancied his voice at a distance chanting a melancholy psalm tune among the tranquil solitudes of Sleepy Hollow.

Postscript

Found in the Handwriting of Mr. Knickerbocker

The preceding tale is given almost in the precise words in which I heard it related at a Corporation meeting of the ancient city of Manhattoes, at which were present many of its sagest and most illustrious burghers. The narrator was a pleasant, shabby, gentlemanly old fellow in pepper-and-salt clothes, with a sadly humorous face, and one whom I strongly suspected of being poor, he made such efforts to be entertaining. When his story was concluded there was much laughter and approbation, particularly from two or three deputy aldermen who had been asleep the greater part of the time. There was, however, one tall, dry-looking old gentleman, with beetling eyebrows, who maintained a grave and rather severe face throughout, now and then folding his arms, inclining his head, and looking down upon the floor, as if turning a doubt over in his mind. He was one of your wary men, who never laugh but upon good grounds—when they have reason and the law on their side. When the mirth of the rest of the company had subsided and silence was restored, he leaned one arm on the elbow of his chair, and sticking the other akimbo, demanded, with a slight but exceedingly sage motion of the head and contraction of the brow, what was the moral of the story and what it went to prove.

The story-teller, who was just putting a glass of wine to his lips as a refreshment after his toils, paused for a moment, looked at his inquirer with an air of infinite deference, and, lowering the glass slowly to the table, observed that the story was intended most logically to prove—

"That there is no situation in life but has its advantages and pleasures—provided we will but take a joke as we find it;

"That, therefore, he that runs races with goblin troopers is likely to have rough riding of it.

"Ergo, for a country schoolmaster to be refused the hand of a Dutch heiress is a certain step to high preferment in the state."

The cautious old gentleman knit his brows tenfold closer after this explanation, being sorely puzzled by the ratiocination of the syllogism, while methought the one in pepper-and-salt eyed him with something of a triumphant leer. At length he observed that all this was very well, but still he thought the story a little on the extravagant—there were one or two points on which he had his doubts.

"Faith, sir," replied the story-teller, "as to that matter, I don't believe one-half of it myself."

D. K.

```
************************************
```

BORDERS REWARDS
MEMBERS ONLY

SAVE 20% OFF
List Price of
Any One Book,
CD OR DVD
WHEN YOU SPEND $10 OR MORE

Valid at Borders, 10/19 - 10/22/2006

```
1 5 9 0 1 5 9 9 0 0 0 0 0 0 0 0 0 0
```

POS: This is a programmed coupon.
If the purchase is $10 or more, scan
the barcode.

One coupon per customer per day.
Excludes online & prior purchases, and
non-stock special orders. Cannot be
used with with other coupons, sale
pricing or standard group discounts.
Cash value .01 cent. Not redeemable
for cash. No copies allowed. Other
uses constitute fraud.
```
************************************
```

Apply for a Borders 3.2.1. Visa
GET A $20 FREE
GIFT CARD

after your first purchase with your
Borders 3-2-1 Visa Card
Apply at
www.chase.com/applyborders
or call 1-877-858-5155
STORE: 0378   REG: 03/94   TRAN#: 7940
SALE   10/16/2006   EMP: 00119
```
************************************
```

10 business days.

Merchandise unaccompanied by the original Borders store receipt, or presented for return beyond 30 days from date of purchase, must be carried by Borders at the time of the return. The lowest price offered for the item during the 12-month period prior to the return will be refunded via a gift card.

Opened videos, discs, and cassettes may only be exchanged for replacement copies of the original item.

Periodicals, newspapers, and out-of-print, collectible and pre-owned items may not be returned.

Returned merchandise must be in saleable condition.

Borders is a T-Mobile HotSpot. Enjoy wireless broadband Internet service for your laptop or PDA.

BORDERS. VISA

GET a $20 Gift Card:

Get the card that gives you points toward books, music, and movies every time you use it. Call 800.294.0038 to apply for the Borders and Waldenbooks Visa Card and get a $20 Gift Card after your first purchase with the card. For complete details, please visit www.chase.com/applybordersvisa.

****
BORDERS.

Returns to Borders Stores:

Merchandise presented for return, including sale or marked-down items, must be accompanied by the original Borders store receipt. Returns must be completed within 30 days of purchase. The purchase price will be refunded in the medium of purchase (cash, credit card, or gift card). Items purchased by check may be returned for cash after 10 business days.

Merchandise unaccompanied by the original Borders store receipt, or presented for return beyond 30 days from date of purchase, must be carried by Borders at

BORDERS

BORDERS
BOOKS MUSIC AND CAFE
500 Bushy Hill Rd.
Simsbury, CT 06070
860-651-7305

STORE: 0378   REG: 03/94   TRAN#: 7940
SALE   10/16/2006   EMP: 00119

LEGEND OF SLEEPY HOLLOW & OTHE
        7574871   CL T   7.95

            Subtotal   7.95
            CT 6.0% SALES TA .48
1 Item   Total   8.43
            CASH   20.00
            Cash Change Due 11.57

        10/16/2006 08:59PM

Check our store inventory online
   at www.bordersstores.com

Shop online at www.borders.com

T··Mobile·
HotSpot

Borders is a T-Mobile HotSpot. Enjoy wireless
broadband Internet service for your laptop or PDA.

BORDERS.   **VISA**

GET a $20 Gift Card:

BORDERS.

Returns to Borders Stores:

The Wife

The treasures of the deep are not so precious
As are the concealed comforts of a man
Lock'd up in woman's love. I scent the air
Of blessings, when I came but near the house,
What a delicious breath marriage sends forth—
The violet bed's no sweeter!

—Middleton

I have often had occasion to remark the fortitude with which women sustain the most overwhelming reverses of fortune. Those disasters which break down the spirit of a man, and prostrate him in the dust, seem to call forth all the energies of the softer sex, and give such intrepidity and elevation to their character, that at times it approaches to sublimity. Nothing can be more touching, than to behold a soft and tender female, who had been all weakness and dependence, and alive to every trivial roughness, while threading the prosperous paths of life, suddenly rising in mental force to be the comforter and support of her husband under misfortune, and abiding with unshrinking firmness the bitterest blasts of adversity.

As the vine, which has long twined its graceful foliage about the oak, and been and been lifted by it into sunshine, will, when the hardy plant is rifted by the thunderbolt, cling round it with its caressing tendrils, and bind up its shattered boughs, so is it beautifully ordered by Providence, that woman, who is the mere dependent and ornament of man in his happier hours, should be his stay and solace when smitten with sudden calamity; winding herself into the rugged recesses of his nature, tenderly supporting the drooping head, and binding up the broken heart.

I was once congratulating a friend, who had around him a blooming family, knit together in the strongest affection. "I can wish you no better lot," said he, with enthusiasm, "than to have a wife and children. If you are prosperous, there they are to share your prosperity; if otherwise, there they are to comfort you." And, indeed, I have observed that a married man falling into misfortune, is more apt to retrieve his situation in the world than a single one; partly, because he is more stimulated to exertion by the necessities of the helpless and be-loved beings who depend upon him for subsistence, but chiefly be-cause his spirits are soothed and relieved by domestic endearments, and his self-respect kept alive by finding, that, though all abroad is darkness and humiliation, yet there is still a little world of love at home, of which he is the monarch. Whereas, a single man is apt to run to waste and self-neglect; to fancy himself lonely and abandoned, and his heart to fall to ruin, like some deserted mansion, for want of an inhabitant.

These observations call to mind a little domestic story, of which I was once a witness. My intimate friend, Leslie, had married a beauti-ful and accomplished girl, who had been brought up in the midst of fashionable life. She had, it is true, no fortune, but that of my friend was ample; and he delighted in the anticipation of indulging her in every elegant pursuit, and administering to those delicate tastes and fancies that spread a kind of witchery about the sex.—"Her life," said he, "shall be like a fairy tale."

The very difference in their characters produced a harmonious combination; he was of a romantic, and somewhat serious cast; she was all life and gladness. I have often noticed the mute rapture with which he would gaze upon her in company, of which her sprightly powers made her the delight: and how, in the midst of applause, her eye would still turn to him, as if there alone she sought favor and acceptance. When leaning on his arm, her slender form contrasted finely with his tall, manly person. The fond, confiding air with which she looked up to him seemed to call forth a flush of triumphant pride and cherishing tenderness, as if he doated on his lovely burden from its very helplessness. Never did a couple set forward on the flowery path of early and well-suited marriage with a fairer prospect of felicity.

It was the misfortune of my friend, however, to have embarked his property in large speculations; and he had not been married many months, when, by a succession of sudden disasters, it was swept from him, and he found himself reduced to almost penury. For a time he kept his situation to himself, and went about with a haggard counte-nance, and a breaking heart. His life was but a protracted agony; and what rendered it more insupportable was the necessity of keeping up a smile in the presence of his wife; for he could not bring himself to overwhelm her with the news. She saw, however, with the quick eyes of affection, that all was not well with him. She marked his altered looks and stifled sighs, and was not to be deceived by his sickly and vapid attempts at cheerfulness. She tasked all her sprightly powers and tender blandishments to win him back to happiness; but she only drove the arrow deeper into his soul. The more he saw cause to love her, the more torturing was the thought that he was soon to make her wretched. A little while, thought he, and the smile will vanish from that cheek—the song will die away from those lips—the lustre of those eyes will be quenched with sorrow and the happy heart which now beats lightly in that bosom, will be weighed down, like mine, by the cares and miseries of the world.

At length he came to me one day, and related his whole situation in a tone of the deepest despair. When I had heard him through, I inquired: "Does your wife know all this?"—At the question he burst into an agony of tears. "For God's sake!" cried he, "if you have any pity on me don't mention my wife; it is the thought of her that drives me almost to madness!"

"And why not?" said I. "She must know it sooner or later: you cannot keep it long from her, and the intelligence may break upon her in a more startling manner than if imparted by yourself; for the accents of those we love soften the harshest tidings. Besides, you are depriving yourself of the comforts of her sympathy; and not merely that, but also endangering the only bond that can keep hearts together—an unreserved community of thought and feeling. She will soon perceive that something is secretly preying upon your mind; and true love will not brook reserve; it feels undervalued and outraged, when even the sorrows of those it loves are concealed from it."

"Oh, but my friend! to think what a blow I am to give to all her future prospects—how I am to strike her very soul to the earth, by telling her that her husband is a beggar! that she is to forego all the elegancies of life—all the pleasures of society—to shrink with me into indigence and obscurity! To tell her that I have dragged her down from the sphere in which she might have continued to move in constant brightness—the light of every eye—the admiration of every heart!—How can she bear poverty? She has been brought up in all the refinements of opulence. How can she bear neglect? She has been the idol of society. Oh, it will break her heart—it will break her heart!"

I saw his grief was eloquent, and I let it have its flow; for sorrow relieves itself by words. When his paroxysm had subsided, and he had relapsed into moody silence, I resumed the subject gently, and urged him to break his situation at once to his wife. He shook his head mournfully, but positively.

"But how are you to keep it from her? It is necessary she should know it, that you may take the steps proper to the alteration of your circumstances. You must change your style of living–nay," observing a pang to pass across his countenance, "don't let that afflict you. I am sure you have never placed your happiness in outward show–you have yet friends, warm friends, who will not think the worse of you for being less splendidly lodged: and surely it does not require a palace to be happy with Mary–"

"I could be happy with her," cried he, convulsively, "in a hovel!–I could go down with her into poverty and the dust!–I could–I could–God bless her!–God bless her!" cried he, bursting into a transport of grief and tenderness.

"And believe me, my friend," said I, stepping up, and grasping him warmly by the hand, "believe me, she can be the same with you. Ay, more; it will be a source of pride and triumph to her–it will call forth all the latent energies and fervent sympathies of her nature; for she will rejoice to prove that she loves you for yourself. There is in every true woman's heart a spark of heavenly fire, which lies dormant in the broad daylight of prosperity; but which kindles up, and beams, and blazes in the dark hour of adversity. No man knows what the wife of his bosom is–no man knows what a ministering angel she is–until he has gone with her through the fiery trials of this world."

There was something in the earnestness of my manner, and the figurative style of my language, that caught the excited imagination of Leslie. I knew the auditor I had to deal with; and following up the impression I had made, I finished by persuading him to go home and unburden his sad heart to his wife.

I must confess, notwithstanding all I had said, I felt some little solicitude for the result. Who can calculate on the fortitude of one whose life has been a round of pleasures? Her gay spirits might revolt at the dark, downward path of low humility suddenly pointed out before her, and might cling to the sunny regions in which they had hitherto revelled. Besides, ruin in fashionable life is accompanied by so many galling mortifications, to which, in other ranks, it is a stranger. In short, I could not meet Leslie, the next morning, without trepidation. He had made the disclosure.

"And how did she bear it?"

"Like an angel! It seemed rather to be a relief to her mind, for she threw her arms around my neck, and asked if this was all that had lately made me unhappy.–But, poor girl," added he, "she cannot realize the change we must undergo. She has no idea of poverty but in the abstract; she has only read of it in poetry, where it is allied to love. She feels as yet no privation; she suffers no loss of accustomed conveniences nor elegancies. When we come practically to experience its sordid cares, its paltry wants, its petty humiliations—then will be the real trial."

"But," said I, "now that you have got over the severest task, that of breaking it to her, the sooner you let the world into the secret the better. The disclosure may be mortifying; but then it is a single misery, and soon over: whereas you otherwise suffer it, in anticipation, every hour in the day. It is not poverty, so much as pretence, that harasses a ruined man—the struggle between a proud mind and an empty purse— the keeping up a hollow show that must soon come to an end. Have the courage to appear poor, and you disarm poverty of its sharpest sting." On this point I found Leslie perfectly prepared. He had no false pride himself, and as to his wife, she was only anxious to conform to their altered fortunes.

Some days afterwards, he called upon me in the evening. He had disposed of his dwelling-house, and taken a small cottage in the country, a few miles from town. He had been busied all day in sending out furniture. The new establishment required few articles, and those of the simplest kind. All the splendid furniture of his late residence had been sold, excepting his wife's harp. That, he said, was too closely associated with the idea of herself it belonged to the little story of their loves; for some of the sweetest moments of their courtship were those when he had leaned over that instrument, and listened to the melting tones of her voice.—I could not but smile at this instance of romantic gallantry in a doating husband.

He was now going out to the cottage, where his wife had been all day superintending its arrangement. My feelings had become strongly interested in the progress of his family story, and, as it was a fine evening, I offered to accompany him.

He was wearied with the fatigues of the day, and, as we walked out, fell into a fit of gloomy musing.

"Poor Mary!" at length broke, with a heavy sigh, from his lips.

"And what of her," asked I, "has anything happened to her?"

"What," said he, darting an impatient glance, is it nothing to be reduced to this paltry situation—to be caged in a miserable cottage—to be obliged to toil almost in the menial concerns of her wretched habitation?"

Has she then repined at the change?

"Repined! she has been nothing but sweetness and good-humor. Indeed, she seems in better spirits than I have ever known her; she has been to me all love, and tenderness, and comfort!"

"Admirable girl!" exclaimed I. "You call yourself poor, my friend; you never were so rich—you never knew the boundless treasures of excellence you possessed in that woman."

"Oh! but, my friend, if this first meeting at the cottage were over, I think I could then be comfortable. But this is her first day of real experience; she has been introduced into a humble dwelling—she has been employed all day in arranging its miserable equipments—she has, for the first time, known the fatigues of domestic employment—she has, for the first time, looked around her on a home destitute of every thing elegant—almost of every thing convenient; and may now be sitting down, exhausted and spiritless, brooding over a prospect of future poverty."

There was a degree of probability in this picture that I could not gainsay, so we walked on in silence.

After turning from the main road up a narrow lane, so thickly shaded with forest-trees as to give it a complete air of seclusion, we came in sight of the cottage. It was humble enough in its appearance for the most pastoral poet; and yet it had a pleasing rural look. A wild vine had overrun one end with a profusion of foliage; a few trees threw their branches gracefully over it; and I observed several pots of flowers tastefully disposed about the door, and on the grass-plot in front. A small wicket-gate opened upon a footpath that wound through some shrubbery to the door. Just as we approached, we heard the sound of music—Leslie grasped my arm; we paused and listened. It was Mary's voice singing, in a style of the most touching simplicity, a little air of which her husband was peculiarly fond.

I felt Leslie's hand tremble on my arm. He stepped forward, to hear more distinctly. His step made a noise on the gravel-walk. A bright beautiful face glanced out at the window, and vanished—a light footstep was heard—and Mary came tripping forth to meet us. She was in a pretty rural dress of white; a few wild flowers were twisted in her fine hair; a fresh bloom was on her cheek; her whole countenance beamed with smiles—I had never seen her look so lovely.

"My dear George," cried she, "I am so glad you are come; I have been watching and watching for you; and running down the lane, and looking out for you. I've set out a table under a beautiful tree behind the cottage; and I've been gathering some of the most delicious strawberries, for I know you are fond of them—and we have such excellent cream—and everything is so sweet and still here—Oh!"—said she, putting her arm within his, and looking up brightly in his face, "Oh, we shall be so happy!"

Poor Leslie was overcome.—He caught her to his bosom—he folded his arms round her—he kissed her again and again—he could not speak, but the tears gushed into his eyes; and he has often assured me, that though the world has since gone prosperously with him, and his life has, indeed, been a happy one, yet never has he experienced a moment of more exquisite felicity.

The Broken Heart

> I never heard
> Of any true affection, but 'twas nipt
> With care, that, like the caterpillar, eats
> The leaves of the spring's sweetest book, the rose.
> —Middleton

It is a common practice with those who have outlived the susceptibility of early feeling, or have been brought up in the gay heartlessness of dissipated life, to laugh at all love stories, and to treat the tales of romantic passion as mere fictions of novelists and poets. My observations on human nature have induced me to think otherwise. They have convinced me that, however the surface of the character may be chilled and frozen by the cares of the world, or cultivated into mere smiles by the arts of society, still there are dormant fires lurking in the depths of the coldest bosom, which, when once enkindled, become impetuous, and are sometimes desolating in their effects. Indeed, I am a true believer in the blind deity, and go to the full extent of his doctrines. Shall I confess it?—I believe in broken hearts, and the possibility of dying of disappointed love! I do not, however, consider it a malady often fatal to my own sex; but I firmly believe that it withers down many a lovely woman into an early grave.

Man is the creature of interest and ambition. His nature leads him forth into the struggle and bustle of the world. Love is but the embellishment of his early life, or a song piped in the intervals of the acts. He seeks for fame, for fortune for space in the world's thought, and dominion over his fellow-men. But a woman's whole life is a history of the affections. The heart is her world; it is there her ambition strives for empire—it is there her avarice seeks for hidden treasures. She sends forth her sympathies on adventure; she embarks her whole soul in the traffic of affection; and if shipwrecked, her case is hopeless—for it is a bankruptcy of the heart.

To a man, the disappointment of love may occasion some bitter pangs; it wounds some feelings of tenderness—it blasts some prospects of felicity; but he is an active being—he may dissipate his thoughts in

the whirl of varied occupation, or may plunge into the tide of pleasure; or, if the scene of disappointment be too full of painful associations, he can shift his abode at will, and taking, as it were, the wings of
the morning, can "fly to the uttermost parts of the earth, and be at
rest."

But woman's is comparatively a fixed, a secluded, and meditative
life. She is more the companion of her own thoughts and feelings;
and if they are turned to ministers of sorrow, where shall she look for
consolation? Her lot is to be wooed and won; and if unhappy in her
love, her heart is like some fortress that has been captured, and sacked,
and abandoned, and left desolate.

How many bright eyes grow dim—how many soft cheeks grow pale—
how many lovely forms fade away into the tomb, and none can tell the
cause that blighted their loveliness! As the dove will clasp its wings to
its side, and cover and conceal the arrow that is preying on its vitals—
so is it the nature of woman, to hide from the world the pangs of
wounded affection. The love of a delicate female is always shy and
silent. Even when fortunate, she scarcely breathes it to herself; but
when otherwise, she buries it in the recesses of her bosom, and there
lets it cower and brood among the ruins of her peace. With her, the
desire of her heart has failed—the great charm of existence is at an
end. She neglects all the cheerful exercises which gladden the spirits,
quicken the pulses, and send the tide of life in healthful currents
through the veins. Her rest is broken—the sweet refreshment of sleep
is poisoned by melancholy dreams—"dry sorrow drinks her blood,"
until her enfeebled frame sinks under the slightest external injury.
Look for her, after a little while, and you find friendship weeping over
her untimely grave, and wondering that one, who but lately glowed
with all the radiance of health and beauty, should so speedily be brought
down to "darkness and the worm." You will be told of some wintry
chill, some casual indisposition, that laid her low—but no one knows
of the mental malady which previously sapped her strength, and made
her so easy a prey to the spoiler.

She is like some tender tree, the pride and beauty of the grove;
graceful in its form, bright in its foliage, but with the worm preying at
its heart. We find it suddenly withering, when it should be most fresh
and luxuriant. We see it drooping its branches to the earth, and shed-
ding leaf by leaf, until, wasted and perished away, it falls even in the
stillness of the forest; and as we muse over the beautiful ruin, we strive

in vain to recollect the blast or thunderbolt that could have smitten it with decay.

I have seen many instances of women running to waste and self-neglect, and disappearing gradually from the earth, almost as if they had been exhaled to heaven; and have repeatedly fancied that I could trace their deaths through the various declensions of consumption, cold, debility, languor, melancholy, until I reached the first symptom of disappointed love. But an instance of the kind was lately told to me; the circumstances are well known in the country where they happened, and I shall but give them in the manner in which they were related.

Everyone must recollect the tragical story of young E——, the Irish patriot; it was too touching to be soon forgotten. During the troubles in Ireland, he was tried, condemned, and executed, on a charge of treason. His fate made a deep impression on public sympathy. He was so young—so intelligent—so generous—so brave—so every thing that we are apt to like in a young man. His conduct under trial, too, was so lofty and intrepid. The noble indignation with which he repelled the charge of treason against his country—the eloquent vindication of his name—and his pathetic appeal to posterity, in the hopeless hour of condemnation—all these entered deeply into every generous bosom, and even his enemies lamented the stern policy that dictated his execution.

But there was one heart whose anguish it would be impossible to describe. In happier days and fairer fortunes, he had won the affections of a beautiful and interesting girl, the daughter of a late celebrated Irish barrister. She loved him with the disinterested fervor of a woman's first and early love. When every worldly maxim arrayed itself against him; when blasted in fortune, and disgrace and danger darkened around his name, she loved him the more ardently for his very sufferings. If, then, his fate could awaken the sympathy even of his foes, what must have been the agony of her, whose whole soul was occupied by his image? Let those tell who have had the portals of the tomb suddenly closed between them and the being they most loved on earth—who have sat at its threshold, as one shut out in a cold and lonely world, whence all that was most lovely and loving had departed.

But then the horrors of such a grave!—so frightful, so dishonored! There was nothing for memory to dwell on that could soothe the pang of separation—none of those tender, though melancholy circumstances which endear the parting scene—nothing to melt sorrow into those blessed tears, sent like the dews of heaven, to revive the heart in the parting hour of anguish.

To render her widowed situation more desolate, she had incurred her father's displeasure by her unfortunate attachment, and was an exile from the parental roof. But could the sympathy and kind offices of friends have reached a spirit so shocked and driven in by horror, she would have experienced no want of consolation, for the Irish are a people of quick and generous sensibilities. The most delicate and cherishing attentions were paid her by families of wealth and distinction. She was led into society, and they tried by all kinds of occupation and amusement to dissipate her grief, and wean her from the tragical story of her love. But it was all in vain. There are some strokes of calamity that scathe and scorch the soul—which penetrate to the vital seat of happiness—and blast it, never again to put forth bud or blossom. She never objected to frequent the haunts of pleasure, but was as much alone there as in the depths of solitude; walking about in a sad revery, apparently unconscious of the world around her. She carried with her an inward woe that mocked at all the blandishments of friendship, and "heeded not the song of the charmer, charm he never so wisely."

The person who told me her story had seen her at a masquerade. There can be no exhibition of far-gone wretchedness more striking and painful than to meet it in such a scene. To find it wandering like a spectre, lonely and joyless, where all around is gay—to see it dressed out in the trappings of mirth, and looking so wan and woe-begone, as if it had tried in vain to cheat the poor heart into momentary forgetfulness of sorrow. After strolling through the splendid rooms and giddy crowd with an air of utter abstraction, she sat herself down on the steps of an orchestra, and, looking about for some time with a vacant air, that showed her insensibility to the garish scene, she began, with the capriciousness of a sickly heart, to warble a little plaintive air. She had an exquisite, voice; but on this occasion it was so simple, so touching, it breathed forth such a soul of wretchedness—that she drew a crowd, mute and silent, around her and melted every one into tears.

The story of one so true and tender could not but excite great interest in a country remarkable for enthusiasm. It completely won the heart of a brave officer, who paid his addresses to her, and thought that one so true to the dead, could not but prove affectionate to the living. She declined his attentions, for her thoughts were irrevocably engrossed by the memory of her former lover. He, however, persisted in his suit. He solicited not her tenderness, but her esteem. He was assisted by her conviction of his worth, and her sense of her own destitute and dependent situation, for she was existing on the kindness of friends. In a word, he at length succeeded in gaining her hand, though with the solemn assurance, that her heart was unalterably another's.

He took her with him to Sicily, hoping that a change of scene might wear out the remembrance of early woes. She was an amiable and exemplary wife, and made an effort to be a happy one; but nothing could cure the silent and devouring melancholy that had entered into her very soul. She wasted away in a slow, but hopeless decline, and at length sunk into the grave, the victim of a broken heart.

It was on her that Moore, the distinguished Irish poet, composed the following lines:

> She is far from the land where her young hero sleeps,
>   And lovers around her are sighing:
> But coldly she turns from their gaze, and weeps,
>   For her heart in his grave is lying.
>
> She sings the wild song of her dear native plains,
>   Every note which he loved awaking—
> Ah! little they think, who delight in her strains,
>   How the heart of the minstrel is breaking!
>
> He had lived for his love—for his country he died,
>   They were all that to life had entwined him—
> Nor soon shall the tears of his country be dried,
>   Nor long will his love stay behind him!
>
> Oh! make her a grave where the sunbeams rest,
>   When they promise a glorious morrow;
> They'll shine o'er her sleep, like a smile from the west,
>   From her own loved island of sorrow!

The Art of Bookmaking

If that severe doom of Synesius be true—"It is a greater offence to steal dead men's labor, than their clothes"—what shall become of most writers?

—Burton's *Anatomy of Melancholy*

I have often wondered at the extreme fecundity of the press, and how it comes to pass that so many heads, on which Nature seems to have inflicted the curse of barrenness, should teem with voluminous productions. As a man travels on, however, in the journey of life, his objects of wonder daily diminish, and he is continually finding out some very simple cause for some great matter of marvel. Thus have I chanced, in my peregrinations about this great metropolis, to blunder upon a scene which unfolded to me some of the mysteries of the bookmaking craft, and at once put an end to my astonishment.

I was one summer's day loitering through the great saloons of the British Museum, with that listlessness with which one is apt to saunter about a museum in warm weather; sometimes lolling over the glass cases of minerals, sometimes studying the hieroglyphics on an Egyptian mummy, and some times trying, with nearly equal success, to comprehend the allegorical paintings on the lofty ceilings. Whilst I was gazing about in this idle way, my attention was attracted to a distant door, at the end of a suite of apartments. It was closed, but every now and then it would open, and some strange-favored being, generally clothed in black, would steal forth, and glide through the rooms, without noticing any of the surrounding objects. There was an air of mystery about this that piqued my languid curiosity, and I determined to attempt the passage of that strait, and to explore the unknown regions beyond. The door yielded to my hand, with all that facility with which the portals of enchanted castles yield to the adventurous knight-errant. I found myself in a spacious chamber, surrounded with great cases of venerable books. Above the cases, and just under the cornice, were arranged a great number of black-looking portraits of ancient authors. About the room were placed long tables, with stands for reading and writing, at which sat many pale, studious personages, poring intently over dusty volumes, rummaging among mouldy manuscripts, and taking copious notes of their contents. A hushed stillness reigned through this mysterious apartment, excepting that you might hear the racing of pens over sheets of paper, and occasionally the deep sigh of one of these sages, as he shifted his position to turn over the page of an old folio; doubtless arising from that hollowness and flatulency incident to learned research.

Now and then one of these personages would write something on a small slip of paper, and ring a bell, whereupon a familiar would appear, take the paper in profound silence, glide out of the room, and return shortly loaded with ponderous tomes, upon which the other would fall, tooth and nail, with famished voracity. I had no longer a doubt that I had happened upon a body of magi, deeply engaged in the study of occult sciences. The scene reminded me of an old Arabian tale, of a philosopher shut up in an enchanted library, in the bosom of a mountain, which opened only once a year; where he made the spirits of the place bring him books of all kinds of dark knowledge, so that at the end of the year, when the magic portal once more swung open on its hinges, he issued forth so versed in forbidden lore, as to be able to soar above the heads of the multitude, and to control the powers of Nature.

My curiosity being now fully aroused, I whispered to one of the familiars, as he was about to leave the room, and begged an interpretation of the strange scene before me. A few words were sufficient for the purpose. I found that these mysterious personages, whom I had mistaken for magi, were principally authors, and were in the very act of manufacturing books. I was, in fact, in the reading-room of the great British Library, an immense collection of volumes of all ages and languages, many of which are now forgotten, and most of which are seldom read: one of these sequestered pools of obsolete literature to which modern authors repair, and draw buckets full of classic lore, or "pure English, undefiled," wherewith to swell their own scanty rills of thought.

Being now in possession of the secret, I sat down in a corner, and watched the process of this book manufactory. I noticed one lean, bilious-looking wight, who sought none but the most worm-eaten volumes, printed in black letter. He was evidently constructing some work of profound erudition, that would be purchased by every man who wished to be thought learned, placed upon a conspicuous shelf of his library, or laid open upon his table—but never read. I observed him, now and then, draw a large fragment of biscuit out of his pocket, and gnaw; whether it was his dinner, or whether he was endeavoring to keep off that exhaustion of the stomach, produced by much pondering over dry works, I leave to harder students than myself to determine.

There was one dapper little gentleman in bright-colored clothes, with a chirping gossiping expression of countenance, who had all the appearance of an author on good terms with his bookseller. After considering him attentively, I recognized in him a diligent getter-up of miscellaneous works, which bustled off well with the trade. I was curious to see how he manufactured his wares. He made more stir and show of business than any of the others; dipping into various books, fluttering over the leaves of manuscripts, taking a morsel out of one, a morsel out of another, "line upon line, precept upon precept, here a little and there a little." The contents of his book seemed to be as heterogeneous as those of the witches' cauldron in *Macbeth*. It was here a finger and there a thumb, toe of frog and blind worm's sting, with his own gossip poured in like "baboon's blood," to make the medley "slab and good."

After all, thought I, may not this pilfering disposition be implanted in authors for wise purposes? may it not be the way in which Providence has taken care that the seeds of knowledge and wisdom shall be preserved from age to age, in spite of the inevitable decay of the works in which they were first produced? We see that Nature has wisely, though whimsically provided for the conveyance of seeds from clime to clime, in the maws of certain birds; so that animals, which, in themselves, are little better than carrion, and apparently the lawless plunderers of the orchard and the corn-field, are, in fact, Nature's carriers to disperse and perpetuate her blessings. In like manner, the beauties and fine thoughts of ancient and obsolete authors are caught up by these flights of predatory writers, and cast forth, again to flourish and bear fruit in a remote and distant tract of time. Many of their works, also, undergo a kind of metempsychosis, and spring up under new forms. What was formerly a ponderous history, revives in the shape of a romance—an old legend changes into a modern play—and a sober philosophical treatise furnishes the body for a whole series of bouncing and sparkling essays. Thus it is in the clearing of our American woodlands; where we burn down a forest of stately pines, a progeny of dwarf oaks start up in their place; and we never see the prostrate trunk of a tree mouldering into soil, but it gives birth to a whole tribe of fungi.

Let us not then, lament over the decay and oblivion into which ancient writers descend; they do but submit to the great law of Nature, which declares that all sublunary shapes of matter shall be limited in their duration, but which decrees, also, that their element shall never perish. Generation after generation, both in animal and vegetable life, passes away, but the vital principle is transmitted to posterity, and the species continue to flourish. Thus, also, do authors beget authors, and having produced a numerous progeny, in a good old age they sleep with their fathers, that is to say, with the authors who preceded them—and from whom they had stolen.

Whilst I was indulging in these rambling fancies I had leaned my head against a pile of reverend folios. Whether it was owing to the soporific emanations for these works; or to the profound quiet of the room; or to the lassitude arising from much wandering; or to an unlucky habit of napping at improper times and places, with which I am grievously afflicted, so it was, that I fell into a doze. Still, however, my imagination continued busy, and indeed the same scene continued before my mind's eye, only a little changed in some of the details. I dreamt that the chamber was still decorated with the portraits of ancient authors, but that the number was increased. The long tables had disappeared, and, in place of the sage magi, I beheld a ragged, threadbare throng, such as may be seen plying about the great repository of cast-off clothes, Monmouth Street. Whenever they seized upon a book, by one of those incongruities common to dreams, methought it turned into a garment of foreign or antique fashion, with which they proceeded to equip themselves. I noticed, however, that no one pretended to clothe himself from any particular suit, but took a sleeve from one, a cape from another, a skirt from a third, thus decking himself out piecemeal, while some of his original rags would peep out from among his borrowed finery.

There was a portly, rosy, well-fed parson, whom I observed ogling several mouldy polemical writers through an eyeglass. He soon contrived to slip on the voluminous mantle of one of the old fathers, and having purloined the gray beard of another, endeavored to look exceedingly wise; but the smirking commonplace of his countenance set at naught all the trappings of wisdom. One sickly-looking gentleman was busied embroidering a very flimsy garment with gold thread drawn out of several old court-dresses of the reign of Queen Elizabeth. Another had trimmed himself magnificently from an illuminated manuscript, had stuck a nosegay in his bosom, culled from "The Paradise of Dainty Devices," and having put Sir Philip Sidney's hat on one side of his head, strutted off with an exquisite air of vulgar elegance. A third, who was but of puny dimensions, had bolstered himself out bravely with the spoils from several obscure tracts of philosophy, so that he had a very imposing front, but he was lamentably tattered in rear, and I perceived that he had patched his small-clothes with scraps of parchment from a Latin author.

There were some well-dressed gentlemen, it is true, who only helped themselves to a gem or so, which sparkled among their own ornaments, without eclipsing them. Some, too, seemed to contemplate the costumes of the old writers, merely to imbibe their principles of taste, and to catch their air and spirit; but I grieve to say, that too many were apt to array themselves, from top to toe, in the patchwork manner I have mentioned. I shall not omit to speak of one genius, in drab breeches and gaiters, and an Arcadian hat, who had a violent propensity to the pastoral, but whose rural wanderings had been confined to the classic haunts of Primrose Hill, and the solitudes of the Regent's Park. He had decked himself in wreaths and ribbons from all the old pastoral poets, and, hanging his head on one side, went about with a fantastical, lackadaisical air, "babbling about green field." But the personage that most struck my attention was a pragmatical old gentleman in clerical robes, with a remarkably large and square but bald head. He entered the room wheezing and puffing, elbowed his way through the throng with a look of sturdy self-confidence, and, having laid hands upon a thick Greek quarto, clapped it upon his head, and swept majestically away in a formidable frizzled wig.

In the height of this literary masquerade, a cry suddenly resounded from every side, of "Thieves! thieves!" I looked, and lo! the portraits about the walls became animated! The old authors thrust out, first a head, then a shoulder, from the canvas, looked down curiously for an instant upon the motley throng, and then descended, with fury in their eyes, to claim their rifled property. The scene of scampering and hubbub that ensued baffles all description. The unhappy culprits endeavored in vain to escape with their plunder. On one side might be seen half a dozen old monks, stripping a modern professor; on another, there was sad devastation carried into the ranks of modern dramatic writers. Beaumont and Fletcher, side by side, raged round the field like Castor and Pollux, and sturdy Ben Jonson enacted more wonders than when a volunteer with the army in Flanders. As to the dapper little compiler of farragos mentioned some time since, he had arrayed himself in as many patches and colors as Harlequin, and there was as fierce a contention of claimants about him, as about the dead body of Patroclus. I was grieved to see many men, to whom I had been accustomed to look up with awe and reverence, fain to steal off with scarce a rag to cover their nakedness. Just then my eye was caught by the pragmatical old gentleman in the Greek grizzled wig, who was scrambling away in sore affright with half a score of authors in full cry after him. They were close upon his haunches; in a twinkling off went his wig; at every turn some strip of raiment was peeled away, until in a few moments, from his domineering pomp, he shrunk into a little, pursy, "chopp'd bald shot," and made his exit with only a few tags and rags fluttering at his back.

There was something so ludicrous in the catastrophe of this learned Theban that I burst into an immoderate fit of laughter, which broke the whole illusion. The tumult and the scuffle were at an end. The chamber resumed its usual appearance. The old authors shrunk back into their picture-frames, and hung in shadowy solemnity along the walls. In short, I found myself wide awake in my corner, with the whole assemblage of bookworms gazing at me with astonishment. Nothing of the dream had been real but my burst of laughter, a sound never before heard in that grave sanctuary, and so abhorrent to the ears of wisdom, as to electrify the fraternity.

The librarian now stepped up to me, and demanded whether I had a card of admission. At first I did not comprehend him, but I soon found that the library was a kind of literary "preserve," subject to game-laws, and that no one must presume to hunt there without special license and permission. In a word, I stood convicted of being an arrant poacher, and was glad to make a precipitate retreat, lest I should have a whole pack of authors let loose upon me.

The Widow and Her Son

Pittie olde age, within whose silver haires
Honour and reverence evermore have rain'd.
—Marlowe's *Tamburlaine*

Those who are in the habit of remarking such matters must have noticed the passive quiet of an English landscape on Sunday. The clacking of the mill, the regularly recurring stroke of the flail, the din of the blacksmith's hammer, the whistling of the ploughman, the rattling of the cart, and all other sounds of rural labor are suspended. The very farm-dogs bark less frequently, being less disturbed by passing travellers. At such times I have almost fancied the wind sunk into quiet, and that the sunny landscape, with its fresh green tints melting into blue haze, enjoyed the hallowed calm.

Sweet day, so pure, so calm, so bright,
The bridal of the earth and sky.

Well was it ordained that the day of devotion should be a day of rest. The holy repose which reigns over the face of nature has its moral influence; every restless passion is charmed down, and we feel the natural religion of the soul gently springing up within us. For my part, there are feelings that visit me, in a country church, amid the beautiful serenity of nature, which I experience nowhere else; and if not a more religious, I think I am a better man on Sunday than on any other day of the seven.

During my recent residence in the country, I used frequently to attend at the old village church. Its shadowy aisles, its mouldering monuments, its dark oaken panelling, all reverend with the gloom of departed years, seemed to fit it for the haunt of solemn meditation; but, being in a wealthy, aristocratic neighborhood, the glitter of fashion penetrated even into the sanctuary; and I felt myself continually thrown back upon the world, by the frigidity and pomp of the poor worms around me. The only being in the whole congregation who appeared thoroughly to feel the humble and prostrate piety of a true

Christian was a poor decrepit old woman, bending under the weight of years and infirmities. She bore the traces of something better than abject poverty. The lingerings of decent pride were visible in her appearance. Her dress, though humble in the extreme, was scrupulously clean. Some trivial respect, too, had been awarded her, for she did not take her seat among the village poor, but sat alone on the steps of the altar. She seemed to have survived all love, all friendship, all society, and to have nothing left her but the hopes of heaven. When I saw her feebly rising and bending her aged form in prayer; habitually conning her prayer-book, which her palsied hand and failing eyes could not permit her to read, but which she evidently knew by heart, I felt persuaded that the faltering voice of that poor woman arose to heaven far before the responses of the clerk, the swell of the organ, or the chanting of the choir.

I am fond of loitering about country churches, and this was so delightfully situated, that it frequently attracted me. It stood on a knoll, round which a small stream made a beautiful bend and then wound its way through a long reach of soft meadow scenery. The church was surrounded by yew trees, which seemed almost coeval with itself. Its tall Gothic spire shot up lightly from among them, with rooks and crows generally wheeling about it. I was seated there one still sunny morning watching two laborers who were digging a grave. They had chosen one of the most remote and neglected corners of the churchyard, where, from the number of nameless graves around, it would appear that the indigent and friendless were huddled into the earth. I was told that the new-made grave was for the only son of a poor widow. While I was meditating on the distinctions of worldly rank, which extend thus down into the very dust, the toll of the bell announced the approach of the funeral. They were the obsequies of poverty, with which pride had nothing to do. A coffin of the plainest materials, without pall or other covering, was borne by some of the villagers. The sexton walked before with an air of cold indifference. There were no mock mourners in the trappings of affected woe, but there was one real mourner who feebly tottered after the corpse. It was the aged mother of the deceased, the poor old woman whom I had seen seated on the steps of the altar. She was supported by a humble friend, who was endeavoring to comfort her. A few of the neighboring poor had joined the train, and some children of the village were running hand in hand, now shouting with unthinking mirth, and now pausing to gaze, with childish curiosity on the grief of the mourner.

As the funeral train approached the grave, the parson issued from the church-porch, arrayed in the surplice, with prayer-book in hand, and attended by the clerk. The service, however, was a mere act of charity. The deceased had been destitute, and the survivor was penniless. It was shuffled through, therefore, in form, but coldly and unfeeling. The well-fed priest moved but a few steps from the church door; his voice could scarcely be heard at the grave; and never did I hear the funeral service, that sublime and touching ceremony, turned into such a frigid mummery of words.

I approached the grave. The coffin was placed on the ground. On it were inscribed the name and age of the deceased—"George Somers, aged 26 years." The poor mother had been assisted to kneel down at the head of it. Her withered hands were clasped, as if in prayer; but I could perceive, by a feeble rocking of the body, and a convulsive motion of the lips, that she was gazing on the last relics of her son with the yearnings of a mother's heart.

Preparations were made to deposit the coffin in the earth. There was that bustling stir, which breaks so harshly on the feelings of grief and affection; directions given in the cold tones of business; the striking of spades into sand and gravel; which, at the grave of those we love, is, of all sounds, the most withering. The bustle around seemed to waken the mother from a wretched revery. She raised her glazed eyes, and looked about with a faint wildness. As the men approached with cords to lower the coffin into the grave, she wrung her hands, and broke into an agony of grief. The poor woman who attended her took her by the arm endeavoring to raise her from the earth, and to whisper something like consolation: "Nay, now—nay, now—don't take it so sorely to heart." She could only shake her head, and wring her hands, as one not to be comforted.

As they lowered the body into the earth, the creaking of the cords seemed to agonize her; but when, on some accidental obstruction, there was a jostling of the coffin, all the tenderness of the mother burst forth, as if any harm could come to him who was far beyond the reach of worldly suffering.

I could see no more—my heart swelled into my throat—my eyes filled with tears; I felt as if I were acting a barbarous part in standing by and gazing idly on this scene of maternal anguish. I wandered to another part of the churchyard, where I remained until the funeral train had dispersed.

When I saw the mother slowly and painfully quitting the grave, leaving behind her the remains of all that was dear to her on earth, and returning to silence and destitution, my heart ached for her. What, thought I, are the distresses of the rich? They have friends to soothe—pleasures to beguile—a world to divert and dissipate their griefs. What are the sorrows of the young? Their growing minds soon close above the wound—their elastic spirits soon rise beneath the pressure—their green and ductile affections soon twine round new objects. But the sorrows of the poor, who have no outward appliances to soothe—the sorrows of the aged, with whom life at best is but a wintry day, and who can look for no after-growth of joy—the sorrows of a widow, aged, solitary, destitute, mourning over an only son, the last solace of her years—these are indeed sorrows which make us feel the impotency of consolation.

It was some time before I left the churchyard. On my way homeward, I met with the woman who had acted as comforter: she was just returning from accompanying the mother to her lonely habitation, and I drew from her some particulars connected with the affecting scene I had witnessed.

The parents of the deceased had resided in the village from childhood. They had inhabited one of the neatest cottages, and by various rural occupations, and the assistance of a small garden, had supported themselves creditably and comfortably, and led a happy and a blameless life. They had one son, who had grown up to be the staff and pride of their age. "Oh, sir!" said the good woman, "he was such a comely lad, so sweet-tempered, so kind to every one around him, so dutiful to his parents! It did one's heart good to see him of a Sunday, drest out in his best, so tall, so straight, so cheery, supporting his old mother to church; for she was always fonder of leaning on George's arm than on her good man's; and, poor soul, she might well be proud of him, for a finer lad there was not in the country round."

Unfortunately, the son was tempted, during a year of scarcity and agricultural hardship, to enter into the service of one of the small craft that plied on a neighboring river. He had not been long in this employ, when he was entrapped by a press-gang, and carried off to sea. His parents received tidings of his seizure, but beyond that they could learn nothing. It was the loss of their main prop. The father, who was already infirm, grew heartless and melancholy and sunk into his grave. The widow, left lonely in her age and feebleness, could no longer support herself, and came upon the parish. Still there was a kind feeling towards her throughout the village, and a certain respect as being one of the oldest inhabitants. As no one applied for the cottage in which she had passed so many happy days, she was permitted to remain in it, where she lived solitary and almost helpless. The few wants of nature were chiefly supplied from the scanty productions of her little garden, which the neighbors would now and then cultivate for her. It was but a few days before the time at which these circumstances were told me, that she was gathering some vegetables for her repast, when she heard the cottage-door which faced the garden, suddenly opened. A stranger came out, and seemed to be looking eagerly and wildly around. He was dressed in seamen's clothes, was emaciated and ghastly pale, and bore the air of one broken by sickness and hardships. He saw her and hastened towards her, but his steps were faint and faltering; he sank on his knees before her and sobbed like a child. The poor woman gazed upon him with a vacant and wandering eye. "Oh, my dear, dear mother! don't you know your son? your poor boy, George?" It was, indeed, the wreck of her once noble lad; who shattered by wounds, by sickness and foreign imprisonment, had, at length, dragged his wasted limbs homeward, to repose among the scenes of his childhood.

I will not attempt to detail the particulars of such a meeting, where sorrow and joy were so completely blended: still, he was alive! he was come home! he might yet live to comfort and cherish her old age! Nature, however, was exhausted in him; and if any thing had been wanting to finish the work of fate, the desolation of his native cottage would have been sufficient. He stretched himself on the pallet on which his widowed mother had passed many a sleepless night, and he never rose from it again.

The villagers, when they heard that George Somers had returned, crowded to see him, offering every comfort and assistance that their humble means afforded. He was too weak, however, to talk—he could only look his thanks. His mother was his constant attendant; and he seemed unwilling to be helped by any other hand.

There is something in sickness that breaks down the pride of manhood, that softens the heart, and brings it back to the feelings of infancy. Who that has languished, even in advanced life, in sickness and despondency, who that has pined on a weary bed in the neglect and loneliness of a foreign land, but has thought on the mother "that looked on his childhood," that smoothed his pillow, and administered to his helplessness? Oh, there is an enduring tenderness in the love of a mother to a son, that transcends all other affections of the heart. It is neither to be chilled by selfishness, nor daunted by danger, nor weakened by worthlessness, nor stifled by ingratitude. She will sacrifice every comfort to his convenience; she will surrender every pleasure to his enjoyment; she will glory in his fame and exult in his prosperity; and, if misfortune overtake him, he will be the dearer to her from misfortune; and if disgrace settle upon his name, she will still love and cherish him in spite of his disgrace; and if all the world beside cast him off, she will be all the world to him.

Poor George Somers had known what it was to be in sickness, and none to soothe—lonely and in prison, and none to visit him. He could not endure his mother from his sight; if she moved away, his eye would follow her. She would sit for hours by his bed watching him as he slept. Sometimes he would start from a feverish dream, and look anxiously up until he saw her bending over him; when he would take her hand, lay it on his bosom, and fall asleep with the tranquillity of a child. In this way he died.

My first impulse on hearing this humble tale of affliction was to visit the cottage of the mourner, and administer pecuniary assistance, and, if possible, comfort. I found, however, on inquiry, that the good feelings of the villagers had prompted them to do everything that the case admitted; and as the poor know best how to console each other's sorrows, I did not venture to intrude.

The next Sunday I was at the village church, when, to my surprise, I saw the poor old woman tottering down the aisle to her accustomed seat on the steps of the altar.

She had made an effort to put on something like mourning for her son; and nothing could be more touching than this struggle between pious affection and utter poverty—a black ribbon or so, a faded black handkerchief, and one or two more such humble attempts to express by outward signs that grief which passes show. When I looked round upon the storied monuments, the stately hatchments, the cold marble pomp with which grandeur mourned magnificently over departed pride, and turned to this poor widow, bowed down by age and sorrow at the altar of her God, and offering up the prayers and praises of a pious though a broken heart, I felt that this living monument of real grief was worth them all.

I related her story to some of the wealthy members of the congregation, and they were moved by it. They exerted themselves to render her situation more comfortable, and to lighten her afflictions. It was, however, but smoothing a few steps to the grave. In the course of a

Sunday or two after, she was missed from her usual seat at church, and before I left the neighborhood I heard, with a feeling of satisfaction, that she had quietly breathed her last, and had gone to rejoin those she loved, in that world where sorrow is never known and friends are never parted.

The Mutability of Literature

A Colloquy in Westminster Abbey

> I know that all beneath the moon decays,
> And what by mortals in this world is brought,
> In time's great periods shall return to nought.
> I know that all the muses' heavenly lays,
> With toil of sprite which are so dearly bought,
> As idle sounds, of few or none are sought—
> That there is nothing lighter than mere praise.
> —Drummond of Hawthornden

There are certain half-dreaming moods of mind in which we naturally steal away from noise and glare, and seek some quiet haunt where we may indulge our reveries and build our air castles undisturbed. In such a mood I was loitering about the old gray cloisters of Westminster Abbey, enjoying that luxury of wandering thought which one is apt to dignify with the name of reflection, when suddenly an irruption of madcap boys from Westminster school, playing at football, broke in upon the monastic stillness of the place, making the vaulted passages and mouldering tombs echo with their merriment. I sought to take refuge from their noise by penetrating still deeper into the solitudes of the pile, and applied to one of the vergers for admission to the library. He conducted me through a portal rich with the crumbling sculpture of former ages, which opened upon a gloomy passage leading to the chapter-house and the chamber in which Doomsday Book is deposited. Just within the passage is a small door on the left. To this the verger applied a key; it was double locked, and opened with some difficulty, as if seldom used. We now ascended a dark narrow staircase, and, passing through a second door, entered the library.

I found myself in a lofty antique hall, the roof supported by massive joists of old English oak. It was soberly lighted by a row of Gothic windows at a considerable height from the floor, and which apparently opened upon the roofs of the cloisters. An ancient picture of some reverend dignitary of the Church in his robes hung over the fireplace. Around the hall and in a small gallery were the books, arranged in carved oaken cases. They consisted principally of old polemical writers, and were much more worn by time than use. In the centre of the library was a solitary table with two or three books on it, an inkstand without ink, and a few pens parched by long disuse. The place seemed fitted for quiet study and profound meditation. It was buried deep among the massive walls of the abbey and shut up from the tumult of the world. I could only hear now and then the shouts of the school-boys faintly swelling from the cloisters, and the sound of a bell tolling for prayers echoing soberly along the roofs of the abbey. By degrees the shouts of merriment grew fainter and fainter, and at length died away; the bell ceased to toll, and a profound silence reigned through the dusky hall.

I had taken down a little thick quarto, curiously bound in parchment, with brass clasps, and seated myself at the table in a venerable elbow-chair. Instead of reading, however, I was beguiled by the solemn monastic air and lifeless quiet of the place, into a train of musing. As I looked around upon the old volumes in their mouldering covers, thus ranged on the shelves and apparently never disturbed in their repose, I could not but consider the library a kind of literary catacomb, where authors, like mummies, are piously entombed and left to blacken and moulder in dusty oblivion.

How much, thought I, has each of these volumes, now thrust aside with such indifference, cost some aching head! how many weary days! how many sleepless nights! How have their authors buried themselves in the solitude of cells and cloisters, shut themselves up from the face of man, and the still more blessed face of Nature; and devoted themselves to painful research and intense reflection! And all for what? To occupy an inch of dusty shelf—to have the titles of their works read now and then in a future age by some drowsy churchman or casual straggler like myself, and in another age to be lost even to remembrance. Such is the amount of this boasted immortality. A mere temporary rumor, a local sound; like the tone of that bell which has tolled among these towers, filling the ear for a moment, lingering transiently in echo, and then passing away, like a thing that was not!

While I sat half-murmuring, half-meditating, these unprofitable speculations with my head resting on my hand, I was thrumming with the other hand upon the quarto, until I accidentally loosened the clasps; when, to my utter astonishment, the little book gave two or three yawns, like one awaking from a deep sleep, then a husky hem, and at length began to talk. At first its voice was very hoarse and broken, being much troubled by a cobweb which some studious spider had woven across it, and having probably contracted a cold from long exposure to the chills and damps of the abbey. In a short time, however, it became more distinct, and I soon found it an exceedingly fluent, conversable little tome. Its language, to be sure, was rather quaint and obsolete, and its pronunciation what, in the present day, would be deemed barbarous; but I shall endeavor, as far as I am able, to render it in modern parlance.

It began with railings about the neglect of the world, about merit being suffered to languish in obscurity, and other such commonplace topics of literary repining, and complained bitterly that it had not been opened for more than two centuries—that the dean only looked now and then into the library, sometimes took down a volume or two, trifled with them for a few moments, and then returned them to their shelves. "What a plague do they mean?" said the little quarto, which I began to perceive was somewhat choleric—"what a plague do they mean by keeping several thousand volumes of us shut up here, and watched by a set of old vergers, like so many beauties in a harem, merely to be looked at now and then by the dean? Books were written to give pleasure and to be enjoyed; and I would have a rule passed that the dean should pay each of us a visit at least once a year; or, if he is not equal to the task, let them once in a while turn loose the whole school of Westminster among us, that at any rate we may now and then have an airing."

"Softly, my worthy friend," replied I; "you are not aware how much better you are off than most books of your generation. By being stored away in this ancient library you are like the treasured remains of those saints and monarchs which lie enshrined in the adjoining chapels, while the remains of their contemporary mortals, left to the ordinary course of Nature, have long since returned to dust."

"Sir," said the little tome, ruffling his leaves and looking big, "I was written for all the world, not for the bookworms of an abbey. I was intended to circulate from hand to hand, like other great contemporary works; but here have I been clasped up for more than two centuries, and might have silently fallen a prey to these worms that are playing the very vengeance with my intestines if you had not by chance given me an opportunity of uttering a few last words before I go to pieces."

"My good friend," rejoined I, "had you been left to the circulation of which you speak, you would long ere this have been no more. To judge from your physiognomy, you are now well stricken in years: very few of your contemporaries can be at present in existence, and those few owe their longevity to being immured like yourself in old libraries; which, suffer me to add, instead of likening to harems, you might more properly and gratefully have compared to those infirmaries attached to religious establishments for the benefit of the old and decrepit, and where, by quiet fostering and no employment, they often endure to an amazingly good-for-nothing old age. You talk of your contemporaries as if in circulation. Where do we meet with their works?. What do we hear of Robert Grosteste of Lincoln? No one could have toiled harder than he for immortality. He is said to have written nearly two hundred volumes. He built, as it were, a pyramid of books to perpetuate his name: but, alas! the pyramid has long since fallen, and only a few fragments are scattered in various libraries, where they are scarcely disturbed even by the antiquarian. What do we hear of Giraldus Cambrensis, the historian, antiquary, philosopher, theologian, and poet? He declined two bishoprics that he might shut himself up and write for posterity; but posterity never inquires after his labors. What of Henry of Huntingdon, who, besides a learned history of England, wrote a treatise on the contempt of the world, which the world has revenged by forgetting him? What is quoted of Joseph of Exeter, styled the miracle of his age in classical composition? Of his three great heroic poems, one is lost forever, excepting a mere fragment; the others are known only to a few of the curious in literature; and as to his love verses and epigrams, they have entirely disappeared. What is in current use of John Wallis the Franciscan, who acquired the name of the tree of life? Of William of Malmsbury—of Simeon of Durham—of Benedict of Peterborough—of John Hanvill of St. Albans—of—"

"Prithee, friend," cried the quarto in a testy tone, "how old do you think me? You are talking of authors that lived long before my time, and wrote either in Latin or French, so that they in a manner expatriated themselves, and deserved to be forgotten;* but I, sir, was ushered into the world from the press of the renowned Wynkyn de Worde. I was written in my own native tongue, at a time when the language had

---

*In Latin and French hath many soueraine wittes had great delyte to endite, and have many noble thinges fulfilde, but certes there ben some that speaken their poisye in French, of which speche the Frenchmen have as good a fantasye as we have in hearying of Frenchmen's Englishe."—Chaucer's *Testament of Love.*

become fixed; and indeed I was considered a model of pure and elegant English."

(I should observe that these remarks were couched in such intoler-
ably antiquated terms, that I have had infinite difficulty in rendering
them into modern phraseology.)

"I cry you mercy," said I, "for mistaking your age; but it matters
little; almost all the writers of your time have likewise passed into
forgetfulness, and De Worde's publications are mere literary rarities
among book-collectors. The purity and stability of language, too, on
which you found your claims to perpetuity, have been the fallacious
dependence of authors of every age, even back to the times of the
worthy Robert of Gloucester, who wrote his history in rhymes of mon-
grel Saxon.* Even now many talk of Spenser's 'well of pure English
undefiled,' as if the language ever sprang from a well or fountain-
head, and was not rather a mere confluence of various tongues per-
petually subject to changes and intermixtures. It is this which has made
English literature so extremely mutable, and the reputation built upon
it so fleeting. Unless thought can be committed to something more
permanent and unchangeable than such a medium, even thought must
share the fate of everything else, and fall into decay. This should serve
as a check upon the vanity and exultation of the most popular writer.
He finds the language in which he has embarked his fame gradually
altering and subject to the dilapidations of time and the caprice of
fashion. He looks back and beholds the early authors of his country,
once the favorites of their day, supplanted by modern writers. A few
short ages have covered them with obscurity, and their merits can
only be relished by the quaint taste of the bookworm. And such, he
anticipates, will be the fate of his own work, which, however it may be
admired in its day and held up as a model of purity, will in the course
of years grow antiquated and obsolete, until it shall become almost as
unintelligible in its native land as an Egyptian obelisk or one of those

---

*Holinshed, in his *Chronicle*, observes, "Afterwards, also, by deligent travell
of Geffry Chaucer and John Gowre, in the time of Richard the Second, and
after them of John Scogan and John Lydgate, monke of Berrie, our said
toong was brought to an excellent passe, notwithstanding that it never came
unto the type of perfection until the time of Queen Elizabeth, wherein John
Jewell, Bishop of Sarum, John Fox, and sundrie learned and excellent writers, have fully accomplished the ornature of the same to their great praise
and mortal commendation."

Runic inscriptions said to exist in the deserts of Tartary. "I declare," added I, with some emotion, "when I contemplate a modern library, filled with new works in all the bravery of rich gilding and binding, I feel disposed to sit down and weep, like the good Xerxes, when he surveyed his army, pranked out in all the splendor of military array, and reflected that in one hundred years not one of them would be in existence."

"Ah," said the little quarto, with a heavy sigh, "I see how it is: these modern scribblers have superseded all the good old authors. I suppose nothing is read nowadays but Sir Philip Sidney's *Arcadia*, Sackville's stately plays and *Mirror for Magistrates*, or the fine-spun euphuisms of the 'unparalleled John Lyly.'"

"There you are again mistaken," said I; "the writers whom you suppose in vogue, because they happened to be so when you were last in circulation, have long since had their day. Sir Philip Sidney's *Arcadia*, the immortality of which was so fondly predicted by his admirers,* and which, in truth, was full of noble thoughts, delicate images, and graceful turns of language, is now scarcely ever mentioned. Sackville has strutted into obscurity; and even Lyly, though his writings were once the delight of a court, and apparently perpetuated by a proverb, is now scarcely known even by name. A whole crowd of authors who wrote and wrangled at the time, have likewise gone down with all their writings and their controversies. Wave after wave of succeeding literature has rolled over them, until they are buried so deep, that it is only now and then that some industrious diver after fragments of antiquity brings up a specimen for the gratification of the curious.

"For my part," I continued, "I consider this mutability of language a wise precaution of Providence for the benefit of the world at large, and of authors in particular. To reason from analogy, we daily behold the varied and beautiful tribes of vegetables springing up, flourishing, adorning the fields for a short time, and then fading into dust, to make way for their successors. Were not this the case, the fecundity of

---

*"Live ever sweete booke; the simple image of his gentle witt, and the golden pillar of his noble courage; and ever notify unto the world that thy writer was the secretary of eloquence, the breath of the muses, the honey bee of the daintyest flowers of witt and arte, the pith of morale and intellectual virtues, the arme of Bellona in the field, the tongue of Suada in the chamber, the sprite of Practise in esse, and the paragon of excellence in print."—Harvey's *Pierce's Supererogation*.

nature would be a grievance instead of a blessing. The earth would groan with rank and excessive vegetation, and its surface become a tangled wilderness. In like manner, the works of genius and learning decline and make way for subsequent productions. Language gradually varies, and with it fade away the writings of authors who have flourished their allotted time; otherwise the creative powers of genius would overstock the world, and the mind would be completely bewildered in the endless mazes of literature. Formerly there were some restraints on this excessive multiplication. Works had to be transcribed by hand, which was a slow and laborious operation; they were written either on parchment, which was expensive, so that one work was often erased to make way for another; or on papyrus, which was fragile and extremely perishable. Authorship was a limited and unprofitable craft, pursued chiefly by monks in the leisure and solitude of their cloisters. The accumulation of manuscripts was slow and costly, and confined almost entirely to monasteries. To these circumstances it may, in some measure, be owing that we have not been inundated by the intellect of antiquity—that the fountains of thought have not been broken up, and modern genius drowned in the deluge. But the inventions of paper and the press have put an end to all these restraints. They have made every one a writer, and enabled every mind to pour itself into print, and diffuse itself over the whole intellectual world. The consequences are alarming. The stream of literature has swollen into a torrent—augmented into a river—expanded into a sea. A few centuries since five or six hundred manuscripts constituted a great library; but what would you say to libraries, such as actually exist, containing three or four hundred thousand volumes; legions of authors at the same time busy; and the press going on with fearfully increasing activity, to double and quadruple the number? Unless some unforeseen mortality should break out among the progeny of the Muse, now that she has become so prolific, I tremble for posterity. I fear the mere fluctuation of language will not be sufficient. Criticism may do much; it increases with the increase of literature, and resembles one of those salutary checks on population spoken of by economists. All possible encouragement, therefore, should be given to the growth of critics, good or bad. But I fear all will be in vain; let criticism do what it may, writers will write, printers will print, and the world will inevitably be overstocked with good books. It will soon be the employment of a lifetime merely to learn their names. Many a man of passable information at the present day reads scarcely anything but reviews, and before long a man of erudition will be little better than a mere walking catalogue."

"My very good sir," said the little quarto, yawning most drearily in my face, "excuse my interrupting you, but I perceive you are rather given to prose. I would ask the fate of an author who was making some noise just as I left the world. His reputation, however, was considered quite temporary. The learned shook their heads at him, for he was a poor, half-educated varlet, that knew little of Latin, and nothing of Greek, and had been obliged to run the country for deer-stealing. I think his name was Shakespeare. I presume he soon sunk into oblivion."

"On the contrary," said I, "it is owing to that very man that the literature of his period has experienced a duration beyond the ordinary term of English literature. There rise authors now and then who seem proof against the mutability of language because they have rooted themselves in the unchanging principles of human nature. They are like gigantic trees that we sometimes see on the banks of a stream, which by their vast and deep roots, penetrating through the mere surface and laying hold on the very foundations of the earth, preserve the soil around them from being swept away by the ever-flowing current, and hold up many a neighboring plant, and perhaps worthless weed, to perpetuity. Such is the case with Shakespeare, whom we behold defying the encroachments of time, retaining in modern use the language and literature of his day, and giving duration to many an indifferent author, merely from having flourished in his vicinity. But even he, I grieve to say, is gradually assuming the tint of age, and his whole form is overrun by a profusion of commentators, who, like clambering vines and creepers, almost bury the noble plant that upholds them."

Here the little quarto began to heave his sides and chuckle, until at length he broke out into a plethoric fit of laughter that had wellnigh choked him by reason of his excessive corpulency. "Mighty well!" cried he, as soon as he could recover breath, "mighty well! and so you would persuade me that the literature of an age is to be perpetuated by a vagabond deer-stealer! by a man without learning! by a poet! forsooth—a poet!" And here he wheezed forth another fit of laughter.

I confess that I felt somewhat nettled at this rudeness, which, however, I pardoned on account of his having flourished in a less polished age. I determined, nevertheless, not to give up my point.

"Yes," resumed I positively, "a poet; for of all writers he has the best chance for immortality. Others may write from the head, but he writes from the heart, and the heart will always understand him. He is the faithful portrayer of Nature, whose features are always the same and always interesting. Prose writers are voluminous and unwieldy; their pages crowded with commonplaces, and their thoughts expanded into tediousness. But with the true poet every thing is terse, touching, or brilliant. He gives the choicest thoughts in the choicest language. He illustrates them by everything that he sees most striking in nature and art. He enriches them by pictures of human life, such as it is passing before him. His writings, therefore, contain the spirit, the aroma, if I may use the phrase, of the age in which he lives. They are caskets which inclose within a small compass the wealth of the language—its family jewels, which are thus transmitted in a portable form to posterity. The setting may occasionally be antiquated, and require now and then to be renewed, as in the case of Chaucer; but the brilliancy and intrinsic value of the gems continue unaltered. Cast a look back over the long reach of literary history. What vast valleys of dulness, filled with monkish legends and academical controversies! What bogs of theological speculations! What dreary wastes of metaphysics! Here and there only do we behold the heaven-illumined bards, elevated like beacons on their widely-separated heights, to transmit the pure light of poetical intelligence from age to age."*

I was just about to launch forth into eulogiums upon the poets of the day when the sudden opening of the door caused me to turn my head. It was the verger, who came to inform me that it was time to close the library. I sought to have a parting word with the quarto, but

---

*Thorow earth and waters deepe,
    The pen by skill doth passe:
And featly nyps the worldes abuse,
    And shoes us in a glasse,
The vertu and the vice
    Of every wight alyve;
The honey comb that bee doth make
    Is not so sweet in hyve,
As are the golden leves
    That drops from poet's head!
Which doth surmount our common talke
    As farre as dross doth lead.
                                Churchyard

the worthy little tome was silent; the clasps were closed: and it looked perfectly unconscious of all that had passed. I have been to the library two or three times since, and have endeavored to draw it into further conversation, but in vain; and whether all this rambling colloquy actually took place, or whether it was another of those old day-dreams to which I am subject, I have never, to this moment, been able to discover.

Rural Funerals

Here's a few flowers! but about midnight more:
The herbs that have on them cold dew o' the night
Are strewings fitt'st for graves—
You were as flowers now withered; even so
These herblets shall, which we upon you strow.
—*Cymbeline*

Among the beautiful and simple-hearted customs of rural life which still linger in some parts of England are those of strewing flowers before the funerals and planting them at the graves of departed friends. These, it is said, are the remains of some of the rites of the primitive Church; but they are of still higher antiquity, having been observed among the Greeks and Romans, and frequently mentioned by their writers, and were no doubt the spontaneous tributes of unlettered affection, originating long before art had tasked itself to modulate sorrow into song or story it on the monument. They are now only to be met with in the most distant and retired places of the kingdom, where fashion and innovation have not been able to throng in and trample out all the curious and interesting traces of the olden time.

In Glamorganshire, we are told, the bed whereon the corpse lies is covered with flowers, a custom alluded to in one of the wild and plaintive ditties of Ophelia:

White his shroud as the mountain snow,
Larded all with sweet flowers;
Which be-wept to the grave did go,
With true love showers.

There is also a most delicate and beautiful rite observed in some of the remote villages of the south at the funeral of a female who has died young and unmarried. A chaplet of white flowers is borne before the corpse by a young girl nearest in age, size, and resemblance, and is afterwards hung up in the church over the accustomed seat of the deceased. These chaplets are sometimes made of white paper, in imitation of flowers, and inside of them is generally a pair of white gloves. They are intended as emblems of the purity of the deceased, and the crown of glory which she has received in heaven.

In some parts of the country, also, the dead are carried to the grave with the singing of psalms and hymns—a kind of triumph, "to show," says Bourne, "that they have finished their course with joy, and are become conquerors." This, I am informed, is observed in some of the northern counties, particularly in Northumberland, and it has a pleasing, though melancholy effect to hear of a still evening in some lonely country scene the mournful melody of a funeral dirge swelling from a distance, and to see the train slowly moving along the landscape.

> Thus, thus, and thus, we compass round
> Thy harmless and unhaunted ground,
> And as we sing thy dirge, we will,
> > The daffodil
> And other flowers lay upon
> The altar of our love, thy stone.
>
> > —Herrick

There is also a solemn respect paid by the traveller to the passing funeral in these sequestered places; for such spectacles, occurring among the quiet abodes of Nature, sink deep into the soul. As the mourning train approaches he pauses, uncovered, to let it go by; he then follows silently in the rear; sometimes quite to the grave, at other times for a few hundred yards, and, having paid this tribute of respect to the deceased, turns and resumes his journey.

The rich vein of melancholy which runs through the English character, and gives it some of its most touching and ennobling graces, is finely evidenced in these pathetic customs, and in the solicitude shown by the common people for an honored and a peaceful grave. The humblest peasant, whatever may be his lowly lot while living, is anxious that some little respect may be paid to his remains. Sir Thomas Overbury, describing the "faire and happy milkmaid," observes, "thus lives she, and all her care is, that she may die in the spring-time, to have store of flowers stucke upon her winding-sheet." The poets, too, who always breathe the feeling of a nation, continually advert to this fond solicitude about the grave. In The Maid's Tragedy, by Beaumont and Fletcher, there is a beautiful instance of the kind describing the capricious melancholy of a broken-hearted girl:

> When she sees a bank
> Stuck full of flowers, she, with a sigh, will tell
> Her servants, what a pretty place it were
> To bury lovers in; and made her maids
> Pluck 'em, and strew her over like a corse.

The custom of decorating graves was once universally prevalent: osiers were carefully bent over them to keep the turf uninjured, and about them were planted evergreens and flowers. "We adorn their graves," says Evelyn, in his *Sylva*, "with flowers and redolent plants, just emblems of the life of man, which has been compared in Holy Scriptures to those fading beauties whose roots, being buried in dishonor, rise, again in glory." This usage has now become extremely rare in England; but it may still be met with in the churchyards of retired villages, among the Welsh mountains; and I recollect an instance of it at the small town of Ruthen, which lies at the head of the beautiful vale of Clewyd. I have been told also by a friend, who was present at the funeral of a young girl in Glamorganshire, that the female attendants had their aprons full of flowers, which, as soon as the body was interred, they stuck about the grave.

He noticed several graves which had been decorated in the same manner. As the flowers had been merely stuck in the ground, and not planted, they had soon withered, and might be seen in various states of decay; some drooping, others quite perished. They were afterwards to be supplanted by holly, rosemary, and other evergreens, which on some graves had grown to great luxuriance, and overshadowed the tombstones.

There was formerly a melancholy fancifulness in the arrangement of these rustic offerings, that had something in it truly poetical. The rose was sometimes blended with the lily, to form a general emblem of frail mortality. "This sweet flower," said Evelyn, "borne on a branch set with thorns and accompanied with the lily, are natural hieroglyphics of our fugitive, umbratile, anxious, and transitory life, which, making so fair a show for a time, is not yet without its thorns and crosses." The nature and color of the flowers, and of the ribbons with which they were tied, had often a particular reference to the qualities or story of the deceased, or were expressive of the feelings of the mourner. In an old poem, entitled "Corydon's Doleful Knell," a lover specifies the decorations he intends to use:

A garland shall be framed
By art and nature's skill,
Of sundry-colored flowers,
In token of good-will.

And sundry-colored ribbons
On it I will bestow;
But chiefly blacke and yellowe
With her to grave shall go.

I'll deck her tomb with flowers
The rarest ever seen;
And with my tears as showers
I'll keep them fresh and green.

The white rose, we are told, was planted at the grave of a virgin; her chaplet was tied with white ribbons, in token of her spotless innocence, though sometimes black ribbons were intermingled, to bespeak the grief of the survivors. The red rose was occasionally used, in remembrance of such as had been remarkable for benevolence; but roses in general were appropriated to the graves of lovers. Evelyn tells us that the custom was not altogether extinct in his time, near his dwelling in the county of Surrey, "where the maidens yearly planted and decked the graves of their defunct sweethearts with rose-bushes." And Camden likewise remarks, in his *Britannia*: "Here is also a certain custom, observed time out of mind, of planting rose-trees upon the graves, especially by the young men and maids who have lost their loves; so that this churchyard is now full of them."

When the deceased had been unhappy in their loves, emblems of a more gloomy character were used, such as the yew and cypress, and if flowers were strewn, they were of the most melancholy colors. Thus, in poems by Thomas Stanley, Esq. (published in 1651), is the following stanza:

Yet strew
Upon my dismall grave
Such offerings as you have,
Forsaken cypresse and yewe;
For kinder flowers can take no birth
Or growth from such unhappy earth.

In *The Maid's Tragedy*, a pathetic little air, is introduced, illustrative of this mode of decorating the funerals of females who had been dis-appointed in love:

> Lay a garland on my hearse
> Of the dismall yew,
> Maidens, willow branches wear,
> Say I died true.
>
> My love was false, but I was firm,
> From my hour of birth;
> Upon my buried body lie
> Lightly, gentle earth.

The natural effect of sorrow over the dead is to refine and elevate the mind; and we have a proof of it in the purity of sentiment and the unaffected elegance of thought which pervaded the whole of these funeral observances. Thus it was an especial precaution that none but sweet-scented evergreens and flowers should be employed. The inten-tion seems to have been to soften the horrors of the tomb, to beguile the mind from brooding over the disgraces of perishing mortality, and to associate the memory of the deceased with the most delicate and beautiful objects in nature. There is a dismal process going on in the grave, ere dust can return to its kindred dust, which the imagina-tion shrinks from contemplating; and we seek still to think of the form we have loved, with those refined associations which it awak-ened when blooming before us in youth and beauty. "Lay her i' the earth," says Laertes, of his virgin sister,

> And from her fair and unpolluted flesh
> May violets spring.

Herrick, also, in his "Dirge of Jephtha," pours forth a fragrant flow of poetical thought and image, which in a manner embalms the dead in the recollections of the living.

> Sleep in thy peace, thy bed of spice,
> And make this place all Paradise:
> May sweets grow here! and smoke from hence
>   Fat frankincense.
> Let balme and cassia send their scent

From out thy maiden monument.
*   *   *   *   *

May all shie maids at wonted hours
Come forth to strew thy tombe with flowers!
May virgins, when they come to mourn
                Male incense burn
Upon thine altar! then return
And leave thee sleeping in thy urn.

I might crowd my pages with extracts from the older British poets, who wrote when these rites were more prevalent, and delighted frequently to allude to them; but I have already quoted more than is necessary. I cannot, however, refrain from giving a passage from Shakespeare, even though it should appear trite, which illustrates the emblematical meaning often conveyed in these floral tributes, and at the same time possesses that magic of language and appositeness of imagery for which he stands pre-eminent.

> With fairest flowers,
> Whilst summer lasts, and I live here, Fidele,
> I'll sweeten thy sad grave; thou shalt not lack
> The flower that's like thy face, pale primrose; nor
> The azured harebell like thy veins; no, nor
> The leaf of eglantine; whom not to slander,
> Outsweetened not thy breath.

There is certainly something more affecting in these prompt and spontaneous offerings of Nature than in the most costly monuments of art; the hand strews the flower while the heart is warm, and the tear falls on the grave as affection is binding the osier round the sod; but pathos expires under the slow labor of the chisel, and is chilled among the cold conceits of sculptured marble.

It is greatly to be regretted that a custom so truly elegant and touching has disappeared from general use, and exists only in the most remote and insignificant villages. But it seems as if poetical custom always shuns the walks of cultivated society. In proportion as people grow polite they cease to be poetical. They talk of poetry, but they have learnt to check its free impulses, to distrust its sallying emotions, and to supply its most affecting and picturesque usages by studied form and pompous ceremonial. Few pageants can be more stately and frigid than an English funeral in town. It is made up of show and gloomy parade: mourning carriages, mourning horses, mourning plumes, and hireling mourners, who make a mockery of grief. "There is a grave digged," says Jeremy Taylor, "and a solemn mourning, and a great talk in the neighborhood, and when the daies are finished, they shall be, and they shall be remembered no more." The associate in the gay and crowded city is soon forgotten; the hurrying succession of new intimates and new pleasures effaces him from our minds, and the very scenes and circles in which he moved are incessantly fluctuating. But funerals in the country are solemnly impressive. The stroke of death makes a wider space in the village circle, and is an awful event in the tranquil uniformity of rural life. The passing bell tolls its knell in every ear; it steals with its pervading melancholy over hill and vale, and saddens all the landscape.

The fixed and unchanging features of the country also perpetuate the memory of the friend with whom we once enjoyed them, who was the companion of our most retired walks, and gave animation to every lonely scene. His idea is associated with every charm of Nature; we hear his voice in the echo which he once delighted to awaken; his spirit haunts the grove which he once frequented; we think of him in the wild upland solitude or amidst the pensive beauty of the valley. In the freshness of joyous morning we remember his beaming smiles and bounding gayety; and when sober evening returns with its gathering shadows and subduing quiet, we call to mind many a twilight hour of gentle talk and sweet-souled melancholy.

> Each lonely place shall him restore,
> For him the tear be duly shed;
> Beloved till life can charm no more,
> And mourn'd till pity's self be dead.

Another cause that perpetuates the memory of the deceased in the country is that the grave is more immediately in sight of the survivors. They pass it on their way to prayer; it meets their eyes when their hearts are softened by the exercises of devotion; they linger about it on the Sabbath, when the mind is disengaged from worldly cares and most disposed to turn aside from present pleasures and present loves and to sit down among the solemn mementos of the past. In North Wales the peasantry kneel and pray over the graves of their deceased friends for several Sundays after the interment; and where the tender

rite of strewing and planting flowers is still practised, it is always renewed on Easter, Whitsuntide, and other festivals, when the season
brings the companion of former festivity more vividly to mind. It is
also invariably performed by the nearest relatives and friends; no
menials nor hirelings are employed, and if a neighbor yields assistance,
it would be deemed an insult to offer compensation.

I have dwelt upon this beautiful rural custom, because as it is one
of the last, so is it one of the holiest, offices of love. The grave is the
ordeal of true affection. It is there that the divine passion of the soul
manifests its superiority to the instinctive impulse of mere animal attachment. The latter must be continually refreshed and kept alive by
the presence of its object, but the love that is seated in the soul can
live on long remembrance. The mere inclinations of sense languish
and decline with the charms which excited them, and turn with shuddering disgust from the dismal precincts of the tomb; but it is thence
that truly spiritual affection rises, purified from every sensual desire,
and returns, like a holy flame, to illumine and sanctify the heart of
the survivor.

The sorrow for the dead is the only sorrow from which we refuse to
be divorced. Every other wound we seek to heal, every other affliction
to forget; but this wound we consider it a duty to keep open, this
affliction we cherish and brood over in solitude. Where is the mother
who would willingly forget the infant that perished like a blossom
from her arms though every recollection is a pang? Where is the child
that would willingly forget the most tender of parents, though to remember be but to lament? Who, even in the hour of agony, would
forget the friend over whom he mourns? Who, even when the tomb is
closing upon the remains of her he most loved, when he feels his
heart, as it were, crushed in the closing of its portal, would accept of
consolation that must be bought by forgetfulness? No, the love which
survives the tomb is one of the noblest attributes of the soul. If it has
its woes, it has likewise its delights; and when the overwhelming burst
of grief is calmed into the gentle tear of recollection, when the sudden
anguish and the convulsive agony over the present ruins of all that we
most loved is softened away into pensive meditation on all that it was
in the days of its loveliness, who would root out such a sorrow from
the heart? Though it may sometimes throw a passing cloud over the
bright hour of gayety, or spread a deeper sadness over the hour of
gloom, yet who would exchange it even for the song of pleasure or the
burst of revelry? No, there is a voice from the tomb sweeter than song.

There is a remembrance of the dead to which we turn even from the charms of the living. Oh, the grave! the grave! It buries every error, covers every defect, extinguishes every resentment! From its peaceful bosom spring none but fond regrets and tender recollections. Who can look down upon the grave even of an enemy, and not feel a compunctious throb that he should ever have warred with the poor handful of earth that lies mouldering before him?

But the grave of those we loved—what a place for meditation! There it is that we call up in long review the whole history of virtue and gentleness, and the thousand endearments lavished upon us almost unheeded in the daily intercourse of intimacy; there it is that we dwell upon the tenderness, the solemn, awful tenderness, of the parting scene. The bed of death, with all its stifled griefs—its noiseless attendance—its mute, watchful assiduities. The last testimonies of expiring love! The feeble, fluttering, thrilling—oh, how thrilling!—pressure of the hand! The faint, faltering accents, struggling in death to give one more assurance of affection! The last fond look of the glazing eye, turning upon us even from the threshold of existence!

Ay, go to the grave of buried love and meditate! There settle the account with thy conscience for every past benefit unrequited—every past endearment unregarded, of that departed being who can never—never—never return to be soothed by thy contrition!

If thou art a child, and hast ever added a sorrow to the soul or a furrow to the silvered brow of an affectionate parent; if thou art a husband, and hast ever caused the fond bosom that ventured its whole happiness in thy arms to doubt one moment of thy kindness or thy truth; if thou art a friend, and hast ever wronged, in thought or word or deed, the spirit that generously confided in thee; if thou art a lover, and hast ever given one unmerited pang to that true heart which now lies cold and still beneath thy feet—then be sure that every unkind look, every ungracious word, every ungentle action will come thronging back upon thy memory and knocking dolefully at thy soul: then be sure that thou wilt lie down sorrowing and repentant on the grave, and utter the unheard groan and pour the unavailing tear, more deep, more bitter because unheard and unavailing.

Then weave thy chaplet of flowers and strew the beauties of Nature about the grave; console thy broken spirit, if thou canst, with these tender yet futile tributes of regret; but take warning by the bitterness of this thy contrite affliction over the dead, and henceforth be more faithful and affectionate in the discharge of thy duties to the living.

In writing the preceding article it was not intended to give a full detail of the funeral customs of the English peasantry, but merely to furnish a few hints and quotations illustrative of particular rites, to be appended, by way of note, to another paper, which has been withheld. The article swelled insensibly into its present form, and this is mentioned as an apology for so brief and casual a notice of these usages after they have been amply and learnedly investigated in other works.

I must observe, also, that I am well aware that this custom of adorning graves with flowers prevails in other countries besides England. Indeed, in some it is much more general, and is observed even by the rich and fashionable; but it is then apt to lose its simplicity and to degenerate into affectation. Bright, in his travels in Lower Hungary, tells of monuments of marble and recesses formed for retirement, with seats placed among bowers of greenhouse plants, and that the graves generally are covered with the gayest flowers of the season. He gives a casual picture of filial piety which I cannot but transcribe; for I trust it is as useful as it is delightful to illustrate the amiable virtues of the sex. "When I was at Berlin," says he, "I followed the celebrated Iffland to the grave. Mingled with some pomp you might trace much real feeling. In the midst of the ceremony my attention was attracted by a young woman who stood on a mound of earth newly covered with turf, which she anxiously protected from the feet of the passing crowd. It was the tomb of her parent; and the figure of this affectionate daughter presented a monument more striking than the most costly work of art."

I will barely add an instance of sepulchral decoration that I once met with among the mountains of Switzerland. It was at the village of Gersau, which stands on the borders of the Lake of Lucerne, at the foot of Mount Rigi. It was once the capital of a miniature republic shut up between the Alps and the lake, and accessible on the land side only by footpaths. The whole force of the republic did not exceed six hundred fighting men, and a few miles of circumference, scooped out as it were from the bosom of the mountains, comprised its territory. The village of Gersau seemed separated from the rest of the world, and retained the golden simplicity of a purer age. It had a small church, with a burying-ground adjoining. At the heads of the graves were placed crosses of wood or iron. On some were affixed miniatures, rudely executed, but evidently attempts at likenesses of the deceased. On the crosses were hung chaplets of flowers, some withering others fresh, as if occasionally renewed. I paused with interest at this scene: I felt that

I was at the source of poetical description, for these were the beautiful but unaffected offerings of the heart which poets are fain to record. In a gayer and more populous place I should have suspected them to have been suggested by factitious sentiment derived from books; but the good people of Gersau knew little of books; there was not a novel nor a love-poem in the village, and I question whether any peasant of the place dreamt, while he was twining a fresh chaplet for the grave of his mistress, that he was fulfilling one of the most fanciful rites of poetical devotion, and that he was practically a poet.

The Spectre Bridegroom

A Traveller's Tale*

> He that supper for is dight,
> He lyes full cold, I trow, this night!
> Yestreen to chamber I him led,
> This night Gray-steel has made his bed!
> —Sir Eger, Sir Grahame, and Sir Gray-Steel

On the summit of one of the heights of the Odenwald, a wild and romantic tract of Upper Germany that lies not far from the confluence of the Main and the Rhine, there stood many, many years since the castle of the Baron Von Landshort. It is now quite fallen to decay, and almost buried among beech trees and dark firs; above which, however, its old watch-tower may still be seen struggling, like the former possessor I have mentioned, to carry a high head and look down upon the neighboring country.

The baron was a dry branch of the great family of Katzenellenbogen,† and inherited the relics of the property and all the pride, of his ancestors. Though the warlike disposition of his predecessors had much impaired the family possessions, yet the baron still endeavored to keep up some show of former state. The times were peaceable, and the German nobles in general had abandoned their inconvenient old castles, perched like eagles' nests among the mountains, and had built more convenient residences in the valleys; still, the baron remained proudly drawn up in his little fortress, cherishing with hereditary inveteracy all the old family feuds, so that he was on ill terms with some of his nearest neighbors, on account of disputes that had happened between their great-great-grandfathers.

The baron had but one child, a daughter, but Nature, when she

---

*The erudite reader, well versed in good-for-nothing lore, will perceive that the above Tale must have been suggested to the old Swiss by a little French anecdote, a circumstance said to have taken place in Paris.

† I.e., Cat's Elbow. The name of a family of those parts, and very powerful in former times. The appellation, we are told, was given in compliment to a peerless dame of the family, celebrated for a fine arm.

grants but one child, always compensates by making it a prodigy; and
so it was with the daughter of the baron. All the nurses, gossips, and
country cousins assured her father that she had not her equal for
beauty in all Germany; and who should know better than they? She
had, moreover, been brought up with great care under the superinten-
dence of two maiden aunts, who had spent some years of their early
life at one of the little German courts, and were skilled in all branches
of knowledge necessary to the education of a fine lady. Under their
instructions she became a miracle of accomplishments. By the time
she was eighteen she could embroider to admiration, and had worked
whole histories of the saints in tapestry with such strength of expression in their countenances that they looked like so many souls in
purgatory. She could read without great difficulty, and had spelled
her way through several Church legends and almost all the chivalric
wonders of the Heldenbuch. She had even made considerable profi-
ciency in writing; could sign her own name without missing a letter,
and so legibly that her aunts could read it without spectacles. She
excelled in making little elegant good-for-nothing, lady-like knicknacks
of all kinds, was versed in the most abstruse dancing of the day, played
a number of airs on the harp and guitar, and knew all the tender
ballads of the Minnelieders by heart.

Her aunts, too, having been great flirts and coquettes in their
younger days, were admirably calculated to be vigilant guardians and
strict censors of the conduct of their niece; for there is no duenna so
rigidly prudent and inexorably decorous as a superannuated coquette.
She was rarely suffered out of their sight; never went beyond the domains of the castle unless well attended, or rather well watched; had
continual lectures read to her about strict decorum and implicit obedience; and, as to the men—pah!—she was taught to hold them at such
a distance and in such absolute distrust that, unless properly autho-
rized, she would not have cast a glance upon the handsomest cavalier
in the world—no, not if he were even dying at her feet.

The good effects of this system were wonderfully apparent. The
young lady was a pattern of docility and correctness. While others
were wasting their sweetness in the glare of the world, and liable to be
plucked and thrown aside by every hand, she was coyly blooming into
fresh and lovely womanhood under the protection of those immacu-
late spinsters, like a rosebud blushing forth among guardian thorns.
Her aunts looked upon her with pride and exultation, and vaunted
that, though all the other young ladies in the world might go astray,

yet thank Heaven, nothing of the kind could happen to the heiress of Katzenellenbogen.

But, however scantily the Baron Von Landshort might be provided with children, his household was by no means a small one; for Providence had enriched him with abundance of poor relations. They, one and all, possessed the affectionate disposition common to humble relatives—were wonderfully attached to the baron, and took every possible occasion to come in swarms and enliven the castle. All family festivals were commemorated by these good people at the baron's expense; and when they were filled with good cheer they would declare that there was nothing on earth so delightful as these family meetings, these jubilees of the heart.

The baron, though a small man, had a large soul, and it swelled with satisfaction at the consciousness of being the greatest man in the little world about him. He loved to tell long stories about the stark old warriors whose portraits looked grimly down from the walls around, and he found no listeners equal to those who fed at his expense. He was much given to the marvellous and a firm believer in all those supernatural tales with which every mountain and valley in Germany abounds. The faith of his guests exceeded even his own: they listened to every tale of wonder with open eyes and mouth, and never failed to be astonished, even though repeated for the hundredth time. Thus lived the Baron Von Landshort, the oracle of his table, the absolute monarch of his little territory, and happy, above all things, in the persuasion that he was the wisest man of the age.

At the time of which my story treats there was a great family gathering at the castle on an affair of the utmost importance: it was to receive the destined bridegroom of the baron's daughter. A negotiation had been carried on between the father and an old nobleman of Bavaria to unite the dignity of their houses by the marriage of their children. The preliminaries had been conducted with proper punctilio. The young people were betrothed without seeing each other, and the time was appointed for the marriage ceremony. The young Count Von Altenburg had been recalled from the army for the purpose, and was actually on his way to the baron's to receive his bride. Missives had even been received from him from Wurtzburg, where he was accidentally detained, mentioning the day and hour when he might be expected to arrive.

The castle was in a tumult of preparation to give him a suitable welcome. The fair bride had been decked out with uncommon care.

The two aunts had superintended her toilet, and quarrelled the whole morning about every article of her dress. The young lady had taken advantage of their contest to follow the bent of her own taste; and fortunately it was a good one. She looked as lovely as youthful bridegroom could desire, and the flutter of expectation heightened the lustre of her charms.

The suffusions that mantled her face and neck, the gentle heaving of the bosom, the eye now and then lost in reverie, all betrayed the soft tumult that was going on in her little heart. The aunts were continually hovering around her, for maiden aunts are apt to take great interest in affairs of this nature. They were giving her a world of staid counsel how to deport herself, what to say, and in what manner to receive the expected lover.

The baron was no less busied in preparations. He had, in truth, nothing exactly to do; but he was naturally a fuming, bustling little man, and could not remain passive when all the world was in a hurry. He worried from top to bottom of the castle with an air of infinite anxiety; he continually called the servants from their work to exhort them to be diligent; and buzzed about every hall and chamber, as idly restless and importunate as a blue-bottle fly on a warm summer's day.

In the mean time the fatted calf had been killed; the forests had rung with the clamor of the huntsmen; the kitchen was crowded with good cheer; the cellars had yielded up whole oceans of Rhein-wein and Ferre-wein; and even the great Heidelberg tun had been laid under contribution. Everything was ready to receive the distinguished guest with Saus und Braus in the true spirit of German hospitality; but the guest delayed to make his appearance. Hour rolled after hour. The sun, that had poured his downward rays upon the rich forest of the Odenwald, now just gleamed along the summits of the mountains. The baron mounted the highest tower and strained his eyes in hopes of catching a distant sight of the count and his attendants. Once he thought he beheld them; the sound of horns came floating from the valley, prolonged by the mountain-echoes. A number of horsemen were seen far below slowly advancing along the road; but when they had nearly reached the foot of the mountain they suddenly struck off in a different direction. The last ray of sunshine departed, the bats began to flit by in the twilight, the road grew dimmer and dimmer to the view, and nothing appeared stirring in it but now and then a peasant lagging homeward from his labor.

While the old castle of Landshort was in this state of perplexity a very interesting scene was transacting in a different part of the Odenwald.

The young Count Von Altenburg was tranquilly pursuing his route in that sober jog-trot way in which a man travels toward matrimony when his friends have taken all the trouble and uncertainty of court-ship off his hands and a bride is waiting for him as certainly as a dinner at the end of his journey. He had encountered at Wurtzburg a youthful companion-in-arms with whom he had seen some service on the frontiers—Herman Von Starkenfaust, one of the stoutest hands and worthiest hearts of German chivalry—who was now returning from the army. His father's castle was not far distant from the old fortress of Landshort, although an hereditary feud rendered the families hostile and strangers to each other.

In the warm-hearted moment of recognition the young friends re-lated all their past adventures and fortunes, and the count gave the whole history of his intended nuptials with a young lady whom he had never seen, but of whose charms he had received the most enrap-turing descriptions.

As the route of the friends lay in the same direction, they agreed to perform the rest of their journey together, and that they might do it the more leisurely, set off from Wurtzburg at an early hour, the count having given directions for his retinue to follow and overtake him.

They beguiled their wayfaring with recollections of their military scenes and adventures; but the count was apt to be a little tedious now and then about the reputed charms of his bride and the felicity that awaited him.

In this way they had entered among the mountains of the Oden-wald, and were traversing one of its most lonely and thickly wooded passes. It is well known that the forests of Germany have always been as much infested by robbers as its castles by spectres; and at this time the former were particularly numerous, from the hordes of disbanded soldiers wandering about the country. It will not appear extraordi-nary, therefore, that the cavaliers were attacked by a gang of these stragglers, in the midst of the forest. They defended themselves with bravery, but were nearly overpowered when the count's retinue ar-rived to their assistance. At sight of them the robbers fled, but not until the count had received a mortal wound. He was slowly and care-fully conveyed back to the city of Wurtzburg, and a friar summoned from a neighboring convent who was famous for his skill in administering to both soul and body; but half of his skill was superfluous; the moments of the unfortunate count were numbered.

With his dying breath he entreated his friend to repair instantly to the castle of Landshort and explain the fatal cause of his not keeping his appointment with his bride. Though not the most ardent of lovers, he was one of the most punctilious of men, and appeared earnestly solicitous that his mission should be speedily and courteously executed. "Unless this is done," said he, "I shall not sleep quietly in my grave." He repeated these last words with peculiar solemnity. A request at a moment so impressive admitted no hesitation. Starkenfaust endeavored to soothe him to calmness, promised faithfully to execute his wish, and gave him his hand in solemn pledge. The dying man pressed it in acknowledgment, but soon lapsed into delirium—raved about his bride, his engagements, his plighted word—ordered his horse, that he might ride to the castle of Landshort, and expired in the fancied act of vaulting into the saddle.

Starkenfaust bestowed a sigh and a soldier's tear on the untimely fate of his comrade and then pondered on the awkward mission he had undertaken. His heart was heavy and his head perplexed; for he was to present himself an unbidden guest among hostile people, and to damp their festivity with tidings fatal to their hopes. Still, there were certain whisperings of curiosity in his bosom to see this far-famed beauty of Katzenellenbogen, so cautiously shut up from the world; for he was a passionate admirer of the sex, and there was a dash of eccentricity and enterprise in his character that made him fond of all singular adventure.

Previous to his departure he made all due arrangements with the holy fraternity of the convent for the funeral solemnities of his friend, who was to be buried in the cathedral of Wurtzburg near some of his illustrious relatives, and the mourning retinue of the count took charge of his remains.

It is now high time that we should return to the ancient family of Katzenellenbogen, who were impatient for their guest, and still more for their dinner, and to the worthy little baron, whom we left airing himself on the watch-tower.

Night closed in, but still no guest arrived. The baron descended from the tower in despair. The banquet, which had been delayed from hour to hour, could no longer be postponed. The meats were already overdone, the cook in an agony, and the whole household had the look of a garrison, that had been reduced by famine. The baron was obliged reluctantly to give orders for the feast without the presence of the guest. All were seated at table, and just on the point of commencing, when the sound of a horn from without the gate gave notice of the approach of a stranger. Another long blast filled the old courts of the castle with its echoes, and was answered by the warder from the walls. The baron hastened to receive his future son-in-law.

The drawbridge had been let down, and the stranger was before the gate. He was a tall gallant cavalier, mounted on a black steed. His countenance was pale, but he had a beaming, romantic eye and an air of stately melancholy. The baron was a little mortified that he should have come in this simple, solitary style. His dignity for a moment was ruffled, and he felt disposed to consider it a want of proper respect for the important occasion and the important family with which he was to be connected. He pacified himself, however, with the conclusion that it must have been youthful impatience which had induced him thus to spur on sooner than his attendants.

"I am sorry," said the stranger, "to break in upon you thus unseasonably——"

Here the baron interrupted him with a world of compliments and greetings, for, to tell the truth, he prided himself upon his courtesy and eloquence. The stranger attempted once or twice to stem the torrent of words, but in vain, so he bowed his head and suffered it to flow on. By the time the baron had come to a pause they had reached the inner court of the castle, and the stranger was again about to speak, when he was once more interrupted by the appearance of the female part of the family, leading forth the shrinking and blushing bride. He gazed on her for a moment as one entranced; it seemed as if his whole soul beamed forth in the gaze and rested upon that lovely form. One of the maiden aunts whispered something in her ear; she made an effort to speak; her moist blue eye was timidly raised, gave a shy glance of inquiry on the stranger, and was cast again to the ground. The words died away, but there was a sweet smile playing about her lips, and a soft dimpling of the cheek that showed her glance had not been unsatisfactory. It was impossible for a girl of the fond age of eighteen, highly predisposed for love and matrimony, not to be pleased with so gallant a cavalier.

The late hour at which the guest had arrived left no time for parley. The baron was peremptory, and deferred all particular conversation until the morning, and led the way to the untasted banquet.

It was served up in the great hall of the castle. Around the walls hung the hard-favored portraits of the heroes of the house of Katzenellenbogen, and the trophies which they had gained in the field, and in the chase. Hacked corselets, splintered jousting-spears, and tattered banners were mingled with the spoils of sylvan warfare: the jaws of the wolf and the tusks of the boar grinned horribly among crossbows and battle-axes, and a huge pair of antlers branched immediately over the head of the youthful bridegroom.

The cavalier took but little notice of the company or the entertainment. He scarcely tasted the banquet, but seemed absorbed in admiration of his bride. He conversed in a low tone that could not be overheard, for the language of love is never loud; but where is the female ear so dull that it cannot catch the softest whisper of the lover? There was a mingled tenderness and gravity in his manner that appeared to have a powerful effect upon the young lady. Her color came and went as she listened with deep attention. Now and then she made some blushing reply, and when his eye was turned away she would steal a sidelong glance at his romantic countenance, and heave a gentle sigh of tender happiness. It was evident that the young couple were completely enamored. The aunts, who were deeply versed in the mysteries of the heart, declared that they had fallen in love with each other at first sight.

The feast went on merrily, or at least noisily, for the guests were all blessed with those keen appetites that attend upon light purses and mountain air. The baron told his best and longest stories, and never had he told them so well or with such great effect. If there was anything marvellous, his auditors were lost in astonishment; and if anything facetious, they were sure to laugh exactly in the right place. The baron, it is true, like most great men, was too dignified to utter any joke but a dull one; it was always enforced, however, by a bumper of excellent Hockheimer, and even a dull joke at one's own table, served up with jolly old wine, is irresistible. Many good things were said by poorer and keener wits that would not bear repeating, except on similar occasions; many sly speeches whispered in ladies' ears that almost convulsed them with suppressed laughter; and a song or two roared out by a poor but merry and broad-faced cousin of the baron that absolutely made the maiden aunts hold up their fans.

Amidst all this revelry the stranger guest maintained a most singular and unseasonable gravity. His countenance assumed a deeper cast of dejection as the evening advanced, and, strange as it may appear, even the baron's jokes seemed only to render him the more melan-

choly. At times he was lost in thought, and at times there was a per-
turbed and restless wandering of the eye that bespoke a mind but ill at
ease. His conversations with the bride became more and more earnest
and mysterious. Lowering clouds began to steal over the fair serenity
of her brow, and tremors to run through her tender frame.

All this could not escape the notice of the company. Their gayety
was chilled by the unaccountable gloom of the bridegroom; their spirits were infected; whispers and glances were interchanged, accompanied by shrugs and dubious shakes of the head. The song and the
laugh grew less and less frequent: there were dreary pauses in the conversation, which were at length succeeded by wild tales and supernatural legends. One dismal story produced another still more dismal,
and the baron nearly frightened some of the ladies into hysterics with
the history of the goblin horseman that carried away the fair Leonora—
a dreadful story which has since been put into excellent verse, and is
read and believed by all the world.

The bridegroom listened to this tale with profound attention. He
kept his eyes steadily fixed on the baron, and, as the story drew to a
close, began gradually to rise from his seat, growing taller and taller,
until in the baron's entranced eye he seemed almost to tower into a
giant. The moment the tale was finished he heaved a deep sigh and
took a solemn farewell of the company. They were all amazement. The
baron was perfectly thunderstruck.

"What! going to leave the castle at midnight? Why, everything was
prepared for his reception; a chamber was ready for him if he wished
to retire."

The stranger shook his head mournfully and mysteriously: "I must
lay my head in a different chamber tonight."

There was something in this reply and the tone in which it was
uttered that made the baron's heart misgive him; but he rallied his
forces and repeated his hospitable entreaties.

The stranger shook his head silently, but positively, at every offer,
and, waving his farewell to the company, stalked slowly out of the hall.
The maiden aunts were absolutely petrified; the bride hung her head
and a tear stole to her eye.

The baron followed the stranger to the great court of the castle,
where the black charger stood pawing the earth and snorting with
impatience. When they had reached the portal, whose deep archway
was dimly lighted by a cresset, the stranger paused, and addressed the

baron in a hollow tone of voice, which the vaulted roof rendered still more sepulchral.

"Now that we are a lone," said he, "I will impart to you the reason of my going. I have a solemn, an indispensable engagement—"

"Why," said the baron, "cannot you send some one in your place?"

"It admits of no substitute—I must attend it in person; I must away to Wurtzburg cathedral—"

"Ay," said the baron, plucking up spirit, "but not until tomorrow— tomorrow you shall take your bride there."

"No! no!" replied the stranger, with tenfold solemnity, "my engagement is with no bride—the worms! the worms expect me! I am a dead man—I have been slain by robbers—my body lies at Wurtzburg—at midnight I am to be buried—the grave is waiting for me—I must keep my appointment!"

He sprang on his black charger, dashed over the drawbridge, and the clattering of his horse's hoofs was lost in the whistling of the night blast.

The baron returned to the hall in the utmost consternation, and related what had passed. Two ladies fainted outright, others sickened at the idea of having banqueted with a spectre. It was the opinion of some that this might be the wild huntsman, famous in German legend. Some talked of mountain-sprites, of wood-demons, and of other supernatural beings with which the good people of Germany have been so grievously harassed since time immemorial. One of the poor relations ventured to suggest that it might be some sportive evasion of the young cavalier, and that the very gloominess of the caprice seemed to accord with so melancholy a personage. This, however, drew on him, the indignation of the whole company, and especially of the baron, who looked upon him as little better than an infidel; so that he was fain to abjure his heresy as speedily as possible and come into the faith of the true believers.

But, whatever may have been the doubts entertained, they were completely put to an end by the arrival next day of regular missives confirming the intelligence of the young count's murder and his interment in Wurtzburg cathedral.

The dismay at the castle may well be imagined. The baron shut himself up in his chamber. The guests, who had come to rejoice with him, could not think of abandoning him in his distress. They wandered about the courts or collected in groups in the hall, shaking their heads and shrugging their shoulders at the troubles of so good a man, and sat longer than ever at table, and ate and drank more stoutly than ever, by way of keeping up their spirits. But the situation of the widowed bride was the most pitiable. To have lost a husband before she had even embraced him—and such a husband! If the very spectre could be so gracious and noble, what must have been the living man? She filled the house with lamentations.

On the night of the second day of her widowhood she had retired to her chamber, accompanied by one of her aunts, who insisted on sleeping with her. The aunt, who was one of the best tellers of ghoststories in all Germany, had just been recounting one of her longest, and had fallen asleep in the very midst of it. The chamber was remote and overlooked a small garden. The niece lay pensively gazing at the beams of the rising moon as they trembled on the leaves of an aspen tree before the lattice. The castle clock had just tolled midnight when a soft strain of music stole up from the garden. She rose hastily from her bed and stepped lightly to the window. A tall figure stood among the shadows of the trees. As it raised its head a beam of moonlight fell upon the countenance. Heaven and earth! she beheld the Spectre Bridegroom! A loud shriek at that moment burst upon her ear, and her aunt, who had been awakened by the music and had followed her silently to the window, fell into her arms. When she looked again the spectre had disappeared.

Of the two females, the aunt now required the most soothing, for she was perfectly beside herself with terror. As to the young lady, there was something even in the spectre of her lover that seemed endearing. There was still the semblance of manly beauty, and, though the shadow of a man is but little calculated to satisfy the affections of a lovesick girl, yet where the substance is not to be had even that is consoling. The aunt declared she would never sleep in that chamber again; the niece, for once, was refractory, and declared as strongly that she would sleep in no other in the castle: the consequence was, that she had to sleep in it alone; but she drew a promise from her aunt not to relate the story of the spectre, lest she should be denied the only melancholy pleasure left her on earth—that of inhabiting the chamber over which the guardian shade of her lover kept its nightly vigils.

How long the good old lady would have observed this promise is uncertain, for she dearly loved to talk of the marvellous, and there is a triumph in being the first to tell a frightful story; it is, however, still quoted in the neighborhood as a memorable instance of female secrecy that she kept it to herself for a whole week, when she was suddenly absolved from all further restraint by intelligence brought to the breakfast-table one morning that the young lady was not to be found. Her room was empty—the bed had not been slept in—the window was open and the bird had flown!

The astonishment and concern with which the intelligence was received can only be imagined by those who have witnessed the agitation which the mishaps of a great man cause among his friends. Even the poor relations paused for a moment from the indefatigable labors of the trencher, when the aunt, who had at first been struck speechless, wrung her hands and shrieked out, "The goblin" the goblin! she's carried away by the goblin!"

In a few words she related the fearful scene of the garden, and concluded that the spectre must have carried off his bride. Two of the domestics corroborated the opinion, for they had heard the clattering of a horse's hoofs down the mountain about midnight, and had no doubt that it was the spectre on his black charger bearing her away to the tomb. All present were struck with the direful probability for events of the kind are extremely common in Germany, as many well-authenticated histories bear witness.

What a lamentable situation was that of the poor baron! What a heart-rending dilemma for a fond father and a member of the great family of Katzenellenbogen! His only daughter had either been rapt away to the grave, or he was to have some wood-demon for a son-in-law, and perchance a troop of goblin grandchildren. As usual, he was completely bewildered, and all the castle in an uproar. The men were ordered to take horse and scour every road and path and glen of the Odenwald. The baron himself had just drawn on his jack-boots, girded on his sword, and was about to mount his steed to sally forth on the doubtful quest, when he was brought to a pause by a new apparition. A lady was seen approaching the castle mounted on a palfrey, attended by a cavalier on horseback. She galloped up to the gate, sprang from her horse, and, falling at the baron's feet, embraced his knees. It was his lost daughter, and her companion—the Spectre Bridegroom! The baron was astounded. He looked at his daughter, then at the spectre, and almost doubted the evidence of his senses. The latter, too, was wonderfully improved in his appearance since his visit to the world of spirits. His dress was splendid, and set off a noble figure of manly symmetry. He was no longer pale and melancholy. His fine countenance was flushed with the glow of youth, and joy rioted in his large dark eye.

The mystery was soon cleared up. The cavalier (for, in truth, as you must have known all the while, he was no goblin) announced himself as Sir Herman Von Starkenfaust. He related his adventure with the young count. He told how he had hastened to the castle to deliver the unwelcome tidings, but that the eloquence of the baron had interrupted him in every attempt to tell his tale. How the sight of the bride had completely captivated him and that to pass a few hours near her he had tacitly suffered the mistake to continue. How he had been sorely perplexed in what way to make a decent retreat, until the baron's goblin stories had suggested his eccentric exit. How, fearing the feudal hostility of the family, he had repeated his visits by stealth—had haunted the garden beneath the young lady's window—had wooed—had won— had borne away in triumph—and, in a word, had wedded the fair.

Under any other circumstances the baron would have been inflexible, for he was tenacious of paternal authority and devoutly obstinate in all family feuds; but he loved his daughter; he had lamented her as lost; he rejoiced to find her still alive; and, though her husband was of a hostile house, yet, thank Heaven! he was not a goblin. There was something, it must he acknowledged, that did not exactly accord with his notions of strict veracity in the joke the knight had passed upon him of his being a dead man; but several old friends present, who had served in the wars, assured him that every stratagem was excusable in love, and that the cavalier was entitled to especial privilege, having lately served as a trooper.

Matters, therefore, were happily arranged. The baron pardoned the young couple on the spot. The revels at the castle were resumed. The poor relations overwhelmed this new member of the family with loving-kindness; he was so gallant, so generous—and so rich. The aunts, it is true, were somewhat scandalized that their system of strict seclusion and passive obedience should be so badly exemplified, but attributed it all to their negligence in not having the windows grated. One of them was particularly mortified at having her marvellous story marred, and that the only spectre she had ever seen should turn out a counterfeit; but the niece seemed perfectly happy at having found him substantial flesh and blood. And so the story ends.

Philip of Pokanoket

An Indian Memoir

As monumental bronze unchanged his look:
A soul that pity touch'd, but never shook;
Train'd from his tree-rock'd cradle to his bier,
The fierce extremes of good and ill to brook
Impassive—fearing but the shame of fear—
Astoic of the woods—a man without a tear.

—Campbell

It is to be regretted that those early writers who treated of the discovery and settlement of America have not given us more particular and candid accounts of the remarkable characters that flourished in savage life. The scanty anecdotes which have reached us are full of peculiarity and interest; they furnish us with nearer glimpses of human nature, and show what man is in a comparatively primitive state and what he owes to civilization. There is something of the charm of discovery in lighting upon these wild and unexplored tracts of human nature—in witnessing, as it were, the native growth of moral sentiment, and perceiving those generous and romantic qualities which have been artificially cultivated by society vegetating in spontaneous hardihood and rude magnificence.

In civilized life, where the happiness, and indeed almost the existence, of man depends so much upon the opinion of his fellow-men, he is constantly acting a studied part. The bold and peculiar traits of native character are refined away or softened down by the levelling influence of what is termed good-breeding, and he practises so many petty deceptions and affects so many generous sentiments for the purposes of popularity that it is difficult to distinguish his real from his artificial character. The Indian, on the contrary, free from the restraints and refinements of polished life, and in a great degree a solitary and independent being, obeys the impulses of his inclination or the dictates of his judgment; and thus the attributes of his nature, being freely indulged, grow singly great and striking. Society is like a lawn, where every roughness is smoothed, every bramble eradicated, and where the eye is delighted by the smiling verdure of a velvet surface;

he, however, who would study Nature in its wildness and variety must plunge into the forest, must explore the glen, must stem the torrent, and dare the precipice.

These reflections arose on casually looking through a volume of early colonial history wherein are recorded, with great bitterness, the outrages of the Indians and their wars with the settlers New England. It is painful to perceive, even from these partial narratives, how the footsteps of civilization may be traced in the blood of the aborigines; how easily the colonists were moved to hostility by the lust of conquest; how merciless and exterminating was their warfare. The imagination shrinks at the idea of how many intellectual beings were hunted from the earth, how many brave and noble hearts, of Nature's sterling coinage, were broken down and trampled in the dust.

Such was the fate of Philip of Pokanoket, an Indian warrior whose name was once a terror throughout Massachusetts and Connecticut. He was the most distinguished of a number of contemporary sachems who reigned over the Pequods, the Narragansetts, the Wampanoags, and the other eastern tribes at the time of the first settlement of New England—a band of native untaught heroes who made the most generous struggle of which human nature is capable, fighting to the last gasp in the cause of their country, without a hope of victory or a thought of renown. Worthy of an age of poetry and fit subjects for local story and romantic fiction, they have left scarcely any authentic traces on the page of history, but stalk like gigantic shadows in the dim twilight of tradition.*

When the Pilgrims, as the Plymouth settlers are called by their descendants, first took refuge on the shores of the New World from the religious persecutions of the Old, their situation was to the last degree gloomy and disheartening. Few in number, and that number rapidly perishing away through sickness and hardships, surrounded by a howling wilderness and savage tribes, exposed to the rigors of an almost arctic winter and the vicissitudes of an ever-shifting climate, their minds were filled with doleful forebodings, and nothing preserved them from sinking into despondency but the strong excitement of religious enthusiasm. In this forlorn situation they were visited by Massasoit, chief sagamore of the Wampanoags, a powerful chief

---

*While correcting the proof-sheets of this article the author is informed that a celebrated English poet has nearly finished an heroic poem on the story of Philip of Pokanoket.

who reigned over a great extent of country. Instead of taking advantage of the scanty number of the strangers and expelling them from his territories, into which they had intruded, he seemed at once to conceive for them a generous friendship, and extended towards them the rites of primitive hospitality. He came early in the spring to their settlement of New Plymouth, attended by a mere handful of followers, entered into a solemn league of peace and amity, sold them a portion of the soil, and promised to secure for them the good-will of his savage allies. Whatever may be said of Indian perfidy, it is certain that the integrity and good faith of Massasoit have never been impeached. He continued a firm and magnanimous friend of the white men, suffering them to extend their possessions and to strengthen themselves in the land, and betraying no jealousy of their increasing power and prosperity. Shortly before his death he came once more to New Plymouth with his son Alexander, for the purpose of renewing the covenant of peace and of securing it to his posterity.

At this conference he endeavored to protect the religion of his forefathers from the encroaching zeal of the missionaries, and stipulated that no further attempt should be made to draw off his people from their ancient faith; but, finding the English obstinately opposed to any such condition, he mildly relinquished the demand. Almost the last act of his life was to bring his two sons, Alexander and Philip (as they bad been named by the English), to the residence of a principal settler, recommending mutual kindness and confidence, and entreating that the same love and amity which had existed between the white men and himself might be continued afterwards with his children. The good old sachem died in peace, and was happily gathered to his fathers before sorrow came upon his tribe; his children remained behind to experience the ingratitude of white men.

His eldest son, Alexander, succeeded him. He was of a quick and impetuous temper, and proudly tenacious of his hereditary rights and dignity. The intrusive policy and dictatorial conduct of the strangers excited his indignation, and he beheld with uneasiness their exterminating wars with the neighboring tribes. He was doomed soon to incur their hostility, being accused of plotting with the Narragansetts to rise against the English and drive them from the land. It is impossible to say whether this accusation was warranted by facts or was grounded on mere suspicions. It is evident, however, by the violent and overbearing measures of the settlers that they had by this time begun to feel conscious of the rapid increase of their power, and to grow harsh and inconsiderate in their treatment of the natives. They despatched an armed force to seize upon Alexander and to bring him before their courts. He was traced to his woodland haunts, and surprised at a hunting-house where he was reposing with a band of his followers, unarmed, after the toils of the chase. The suddenness of his arrest and the outrage offered to his sovereign dignity so preyed upon the irascible feelings of this proud savage as to throw him into a raging fever. He was permitted to return home on condition of sending his son as a pledge for his re-appearance; but the blow he had received was fatal, and before he reached his home he fell a victim to the agonies of a wounded spirit.

The successor of Alexander was Metamocet, or King Philip, as he was called by the settlers on account of his lofty spirit and ambitious temper. These, together with his well-known energy and enterprise, had rendered him an object of great jealousy and apprehension, and he was accused of having always cherished a secret and implacable hostility towards the whites. Such may very probably and very naturally have been the case. He considered them as originally but mere intruders into the country, who had presumed upon indulgence and were extending an influence baneful to savage life. He saw the whole race of his countrymen melting before them from the face of the earth, their territories slipping from their hands, and their tribes becoming feeble, scattered, and dependent. It may be said that the soil was originally purchased by the settlers; but who does not know the nature of Indian purchases in the early periods of colonization? The Europeans always made thrifty bargains through their superior adroitness in traffic, and they gained vast accessions of territory by easily-provoked hostilities. An uncultivated savage is never a nice inquirer into the refinements of law by which an injury may be gradually and legally inflicted. Leading facts are all by which he judges; and it was enough for Philip to know that before the intrusion of the Europeans his countrymen were lords of the soil, and that now they were becoming vagabonds in the land of their fathers.

But whatever may have been his feelings of general hostility and his particular indignation at the treatment of his brother, he suppressed them for the present, renewed the contract with the settlers, and resided peaceably for many years at Pokanoket, or as, it was called by the English, Mount Hope,* the ancient seat of dominion of his tribe.

---

*Now Bristol, Rhode Island.

Suspicions, however, which were at first but vague and indefinite, began to acquire form and substance, and he was at length charged with attempting to instigate the various eastern tribes to rise at once, and by a simultaneous effort to throw off the yoke of their oppressors. It is difficult at this distant period to assign the proper credit due to these early accusations against the Indians. There was a proneness to suspicion and an aptness to acts of violence on the part of the whites that gave weight and importance to every idle tale. Informers abounded where tale-bearing met with countenance and reward, and the sword was readily unsheathed when its success was certain and it carved out empire.

The only positive evidence on record against Philip is the accusation of one Sausaman, a renegado Indian, whose natural cunning had been quickened by a partial education which be had received among the settlers. He changed his faith and his allegiance two or three times with a facility that evinced the looseness of his principles. He had acted for some time as Philip's confidential secretary and counsellor, and had enjoyed his bounty and protection. Finding, however, that the clouds of adversity were gathering round his patron, he abandoned his service and went over to the whites, and in order to gain their favor charged his former benefactor with plotting against their safety. A rigorous investigation took place. Philip and several of his subjects submitted to be examined, but nothing was proved against them. The settlers, however, had now gone too far to retract; they had previously determined that Philip was a dangerous neighbor; they had publicly evinced their distrust, and had done enough to insure his hostility; according, therefore, to the usual mode of reasoning in these cases, his destruction had become necessary to their security. Sausaman, the treacherous informer, was shortly afterwards found dead in a pond, having fallen a victim to the vengeance of his tribe. Three Indians, one of whom was a friend and counsellor of Philip, were apprehended and tried, and on the testimony of one very questionable witness were condemned and executed as murderers.

This treatment of his subjects and ignominious punishment of his friend outraged the pride and exasperated the passions of Philip. The bolt which had fallen thus at his very feet awakened him to the gathering storm, and he determined to trust himself no longer in the power of the white men. The fate of his insulted and broken-hearted brother still rankled in his mind; and he had a further warning in the tragical story of Miantonimo, a great Sachem of the Narragansetts, who, after

manfully facing his accusers before a tribunal of the colonists, excul-
pating himself from a charge of conspiracy and receiving assurances
of amity, had been perfidiously despatched at their instigation. Philip
therefore gathered his fighting-men about him, persuaded all strangers that he could to join his cause, sent the women and children to the
Narragansetts for safety, and wherever he appeared was continually
surrounded by armed warriors.

When the two parties were thus in a state of distrust and irritation,
the least spark was sufficient to set them in a flame. The Indians,
having weapons in their hands, grew mischievous and committed various petty depredations. In one of their maraudings a warrior was fired
on and killed by a settler. This was the signal for open hostilities; the
Indians pressed to revenge the death of their comrade, and the alarm
of war resounded through the Plymouth colony.

In the early chronicles of these dark and melancholy times we meet
with many indications of the diseased state of the public mind. The
gloom of religious abstraction and the wildness of their situation among
trackless forests and savage tribes had disposed the colonists to superstitious fancies, and had filled their imaginations with the frightful
chimeras of witchcraft and spectrology. They were much given also to
a belief in omens. The troubles with Philip and his Indians were preceded, we are told, by a variety of those awful warnings which forerun
great and public calamities. The perfect form of an Indian bow appeared in the air at New Plymouth, which was looked upon by the
inhabitants as a "prodigious apparition." At Hadley, Northampton,
and other towns in their neighborhood "was heard the report of a
great piece of ordnance, with a shaking of the earth and a considerable echo."* Others were alarmed on a still sunshiny morning by the
discharge of guns and muskets; bullets seemed to whistle past them,
and the noise of drums resounded in the air, seeming to pass away to
the westward; others fancied that they heard the galloping of horses
over their heads; and certain monstrous births which took place about
the time filled the superstitious in some towns with doleful forebodings. Many of these portentous sights and sounds may be ascribed to
natural phenomena—to the northern lights which occur vividly in those
latitudes, the meteors which explode in the air, the casual rushing of a
blast through the top branches of the forest, the crash of fallen trees

---

*The Rev. Increase Mather's History.

or disrupted rocks, and to those other uncouth sounds and echoes which will sometimes strike the ear so strangely amidst the profound stillness of woodland solitudes. These may have startled some melancholy imaginations, may have been exaggerated by the love for the marvellous, and listened to with that avidity with which we devour whatever is fearful and mysterious. The universal currency of these superstitious fancies and the grave record made of them by one of the learned men of the day are strongly characteristic of the times.

The nature of the contest that ensued was such as too often distinguishes the warfare between civilized men and savages. On the part of the whites it was conducted with superior skill and success, but with a wastefulness of the blood and a disregard of the natural rights of their antagonists: on the part of the Indians it was waged with the desperation of men fearless of death, and who had nothing to expect from peace but humiliation, dependence, and decay.

The events of the war are transmitted to us by a worthy clergyman of the time, who dwells with horror and indignation on every hostile act of the Indians, however justifiable, whilst he mentions with applause the most sanguinary atrocities of the whites. Philip is reviled as a murderer and a traitor, without considering that he was a true-born prince gallantly fighting at the head of his subjects to avenge the wrongs of his family, to retrieve the tottering power of his line, and to deliver his native land from the oppression of usurping strangers.

The project of a wide and simultaneous revolt, if such had really been formed, was worthy of a capacious mind, and had it not been prematurely discovered might have been overwhelming in its consequences. The war that actually broke out was but a war of detail, a mere succession of casual exploits and unconnected enterprises. Still, it sets forth the military genius and daring prowess of Philip, and wherever, in the prejudiced and passionate narrations that have been given of it, we can arrive at simple facts, we find him displaying a vigorous mind, a fertility of expedients, a contempt of suffering and hardship, and an unconquerable resolution that command our sympathy and applause.

Driven from his paternal domains at Mount Hope, he threw himself into the depths of those vast and trackless forests that skirted the settlements and were almost impervious to anything but a wild beast or an Indian. Here he gathered together his forces, like the storm accumulating its stores of mischief in the bosom of the thundercloud, and would suddenly emerge at a time and place least expected, carry-

ing havoc and dismay into the villages. There were now and then indications of these impending ravages that filled the minds of the colonists with awe and apprehension. The report of a distant gun would
perhaps be heard from the solitary woodland, where there was known
to be no white man; the cattle which had been wandering in the woods
would sometimes return home wounded; or an Indian or two would
be seen lurking about the skirts of the forests and suddenly disappearing, as the lightning will sometimes be seen playing silently about the
edge of the cloud that is brewing up the tempest.

Though sometimes pursued and even surrounded by the settlers,
yet Philip as often escaped almost miraculously from their toils, and,
plunging into the wilderness, would be lost to all search or inquiry
until he again emerged at some far distant quarter, laying the country
desolate. Among his strongholds were the great swamps or morasses
which extend in some parts of New England, composed of loose bogs
of deep black mud, perplexed with thickets, brambles, rank weeds,
the shattered and mouldering trunks of fallen trees, overshadowed by
lugubrious hemlocks. The uncertain footing and the tangled mazes of
these shaggy wilds rendered them almost impracticable to the white
man, though the Indian could thread their labyrinths with the agility
of a deer. Into one of these, the great swamp of Pocasset Neck, was
Philip once driven with a band of his followers. The English did not
dare to pursue him, fearing to venture into these dark and frightful
recesses, where they might perish in fens and miry pits or be shot
down by lurking foes. They therefore invested the entrance to the Neck,
and began to build a fort with the thought of starving out the foe; but
Philip and his warriors wafted themselves on a raft over an arm of the
sea in the dead of night, leaving the women and children behind, and
escaped away to the westward, kindling the flames of war among the
tribes of Massachusetts and the Nipmuck country and threatening
the colony of Connecticut.

In this way Philip became a theme of universal apprehension. The
mystery in which he was enveloped exaggerated his real terrors. He
was an evil that walked in darkness, whose coming none could foresee
and against which none knew when to be on the alert. The whole
country abounded with rumors and alarms. Philip seemed almost
possessed of ubiquity, for in whatever part of the widely-extended frontier an irruption from the forest took place, Philip was said to be its
leader. Many superstitious notions also were circulated concerning
him. He was said to deal in necromancy, and to be attended by an old

Indian witch or prophetess, whom he consulted and who assisted him by her charms and incantations. This, indeed, was frequently the case with Indian chiefs, either through their own credulity or to act upon that of their followers; and the influence of the prophet and the dreamer over Indian superstition has been fully evidenced in recent instances of savage warfare.

At the time that Philip effected his escape from Pocasset his fortunes were in a desperate condition. His forces had been thinned by repeated fights and he had lost almost the whole of his resources. In this time of adversity he found a faithful friend in Canonchet. chief Sachem of all the Narragansetts. He was the son and heir of Miantonimo, the great sachem who, as already mentioned, after an honorable acquittal of the charge of conspiracy, had been privately put to death at the perfidious instigations of the settlers. "He was the heir," says the old chronicler, "of all his father's pride and insolence, as well as of his malice towards the English;" he certainly was the heir of his insults and injuries and the legitimate avenger of his murder. Though he had forborne to take an active part in this hopeless war, yet he received Philip and his broken forces with open arms and gave them the most generous countenance and support. This at once drew upon him the hostility of the English, and it was determined to strike a signal blow that should involve both the Sachems in one common ruin. A great force was therefore gathered together from Massachusetts, Plymouth, and Connecticut, and was sent into the Narragansett country in the depth of winter, when the swamps, being frozen and leafless, could be traversed with comparative facility and would no longer afford dark and impenetrable fastnesses to the Indians.

Apprehensive of attack, Canonchet had conveyed the greater part of his stores, together with the old, the infirm, the women and children of his tribe, to a strong fortress, where he and Philip had likewise drawn up the flower of their forces. This fortress, deemed by the Indians impregnable, was situated upon a rising mound or kind of island of five or six acres in the midst of a swamp; it was constructed with a degree of judgment and skill vastly superior to what is usually displayed in Indian fortification, and indicative of the martial genius of these two chieftains.

Guided by a renegado Indian, the English penetrated, through December snows, to this stronghold and came upon the garrison by surprise. The fight was fierce and tumultuous. The assailants were repulsed in their first attack, and several of their bravest officers were shot down in the act of storming the fortress, sword in hand. The assault was renewed with greater success. A lodgment was effected. The Indians were driven from one post to another. They disputed their ground inch by inch, fighting with the fury of despair. Most of their veterans were cut to pieces, and after a long and bloody battle, Philip and Canonchet, with a handful of surviving warriors, retreated from the fort and took refuge in the thickets of the surrounding forest.

The victors set fire to the wigwams and the fort; the whole was soon in a blaze; many of the old men, the women, and the children perished in the flames. This last outrage overcame even the stoicism of the savage. The neighboring woods resounded with the yells of rage and despair uttered by the fugitive warriors, as they beheld the destruction of their dwellings and heard the agonizing cries of their wives and offspring. "The burning of the wigwams," says a contemporary writer, "the shrieks and cries of the women and children, and the yelling of the warriors, exhibited a most horrible and affecting scene, so that it greatly moved some of the soldiers." The same writer cautiously adds, "They were in *much doubt* then, and afterwards seriously inquired, whether burning their enemies alive could be consistent with humanity, and the benevolent principles of the gospel."*

The fate of the brave and generous Canonchet is worthy of particular mention: the last scene of his life is one of the noblest instances on record of Indian magnimity.

Broken down in his power and resources by this signal defeat, yet faithful to his ally and to the hapless cause which he had espoused, he rejected all overtures of peace offered on condition of betraying Philip and his followers, and declared that "he would fight it out to the last man, rather than become a servant to the English." His home being destroyed, his country harassed and laid waste by the incursions of the conquerors, he was obliged to wander away to the banks of the Connecticut, where he formed a rallying-point to the whole body of western Indians and laid waste several of the English settlements.

Early in the spring he departed on a hazardous expedition, with only thirty chosen men, to penetrate to Seaconck, in the vicinity of Mount Hope, and to procure seed corn to plant for the sustenance of his troops. This little band of adventurers had passed safely through the Pequod country, and were in the centre of the Narragansett, rest-

---

*MS. of the Rev. W. Ruggles.

ing at some wigwams near Pautucket River, when an alarm was given of an approaching enemy. Having but seven men by him at the time, Canonchet despatched two of them to the top of a neighboring hill to bring intelligence of the foe.

Panic-struck by the appearance of a troop of English and Indians rapidly advancing, they fled in breathless terror past their chieftain, without stopping to inform him of the danger. Canonchet sent another scout, who did the same. He then sent two more, one of whom, hurrying back in confusion and affright, told him that the whole British army was at hand. Canonchet saw there was no choice but immediate flight. He attempted to escape round the hill, but was perceived and hotly pursued by the hostile Indians and a few of the fleetest of the English. Finding the swiftest pursuer close upon his heels, he threw off, first his blanket, then his silver-laced coat and belt of peag, by which his enemies knew him to be Canonchet and redoubled the eagerness of pursuit.

At length, in dashing through the river, his foot slipped upon a stone, and he fell so deep as to wet his gun. This accident so struck him with despair that, as he afterwards confessed, "his heart and his bowels turned within him, and he became like a rotten stick, void of strength."

To such a degree was he unnerved that, being seized by a Pequod Indian within a short distance of the river, he made no resistance, though a man of great vigor of body and boldness of heart. But on being made prisoner the whole pride of his spirit arose within him, and from that moment we find, in the anecdotes given by his enemies, nothing but repeated flashes of elevated and prince-like heroism. Being questioned by one of the English who first came up with him, and who had not attained his twenty second year, the proud-hearted warrior, looking with lofty contempt upon his youthful countenance, replied, "You are a child—you cannot understand matters of war; let your brother or your chief come: him will I answer."

Though repeated offers were made to him of his life on condition of submitting with his nation to the English, yet he rejected them with disdain, and refused to send any proposals of the kind to the great body of his subjects, saying that he knew none of them would comply. Being reproached with his breach of faith towards the whites, his boast that he would not deliver up a Wampanoag nor the paring of a Wampanoag's nail, and his threat that he would burn the English alive in their houses, he disdained to justify himself, haughtily answering that others were as forward for the war as himself, and "he desired to hear no more thereof."

So noble and unshaken a spirit, so true a fidelity to his cause and his friend, might have touched the feelings of the generous and the brave; but Canonchet was an Indian, a being towards whom war had no courtesy, humanity no law, religion no compassion: he was condemned to die. The last words of his that are recorded are worthy the greatness of his soul. When sentence of death was passed upon him, be observed "that he liked it well, for he should die before his heart was soft or he had spoken anything unworthy of himself." His enemies gave him the death of a soldier, for he was shot at Stoning ham by three young Sachems of his own rank.

The defeat at the Narraganset fortress and the death of Canonchet were fatal blows to the fortunes of King Philip. He made an ineffectual attempt to raise a head of war by stirring up the Mohawks to take arms; but, though possessed of the native talents of a statesman, his arts were counteracted by the superior arts of his enlightened enemies, and the terror of their warlike skill began to subdue the resolution of the neighboring tribes. The unfortunate chieftain saw himself daily stripped of power, and his ranks rapidly thinning around him. Some were suborned by the whites; others fell victims to hunger and fatigue and to the frequent attacks by which they were harassed. His stores were all captured; his chosen friends were swept away from before his eyes; his uncle was shot down by his side; his sister was carried into captivity; and in one of his narrow escapes he was compelled to leave his beloved wife and only son to the mercy of the enemy. "His ruin," says the historian, "being thus gradually carried on, his misery was not prevented, but augmented thereby; being himself made acquainted with the sense and experimental feeling of the captivity of his children, loss of friends, slaughter of his subjects, bereavement of all family relations, and being stripped of all outward comforts before his own life should be taken away."

To fill up the measure of his misfortunes, his own followers began to plot against his life, that by sacrificing him they might purchase dishonorable safety. Through treachery a number of his faithful adherents, the subjects of Wetamoe, an Indian princess of Pocasset, a near kinswoman and confederate of Philip, were betrayed into the hands of the enemy. Wetamoe was among them at the time, and attempted to make her escape by crossing a neighboring river: either exhausted by swimming or starved with cold and hunger, she was found dead and naked near the water-side. But persecution ceased not at the grave. Even death, the refuge of the wretched, where the wicked commonly cease from troubling, was no protection to this outcast female, whose great crime was affectionate fidelity to her kinsman and her friend. Her corpse was the object of unmanly and dastardly vengeance: the head was severed from the body and set upon a pole, and was thus exposed at Taunton to the view of her captive subjects. They immediately recognized the features of their unfortunate queen, and were so affected at this barbarous spectacle that we are told they broke forth into the "most horrid and diabolical lamentations."

However Philip had borne up against the complicated miseries and misfortunes that surrounded him, the treachery of his followers seemed to wring his heart and reduce him to despondency. It is said that "he never rejoiced afterwards, nor had success in any of his designs." The spring of hope was broken—the ardor of enterprise was extinguished; he looked around, and all was danger and darkness; there was no eye to pity nor any arm that could bring deliverance. With a scanty band of followers, who still remained true to his desperate fortunes, the unhappy Philip wandered back to the vicinity of Mount Hope, the ancient dwelling of his fathers. Here he lurked about like a spectre among the scenes of former power and prosperity, now bereft of home, of family, and of friend. There needs no better picture of his destitute and piteous situation than that furnished by the homely pen of the chronicler, who is unwarily enlisting the feelings of the reader in favor of the hapless warrior whom he reviles. "Philip," he says, "like a savage wild beast, having been hunted by the English forces through the woods above a hundred miles backward and forward, at last was driven to his own den upon Mount Hope, where he retired, with a few of his best friends, into a swamp, which proved but a prison to keep him fast till the messengers of death came by divine permission to execute vengeance upon him."

Even in this last refuge of desperation and despair a sullen grandeur gathers round his memory. We picture him to ourselves seated among his care-worn followers, brooding in silence over his blasted fortunes, and acquiring a savage sublimity from the wildness and dreariness of his lurking-place. Defeated, but not dismayed—crushed to the earth, but not humiliated—he seemed to grow more haughty beneath disaster, and to experience a fierce satisfaction in draining the last dregs of bitterness. Little minds are tamed and subdued by misfortune, but great minds rise above it. The very idea of submission awakened the fury of Philip, and he smote to death one of his followers who proposed an expedient of peace. The brother of the victim made his escape, and in revenge betrayed the retreat of his chieftain, A body of white men and Indians were immediately despatched to the swamp where Philip lay crouched, glaring with fury and despair. Before he was aware of their approach they had begun to surround him. In a little while he saw five of his trustiest followers laid dead at his feet; all resistance was vain; he rushed forth from his covert, and made a head-long attempt to escape, but was shot through the heart by a renegado Indian of his own nation.

Such is the scanty story of the brave but unfortunate King Philip, persecuted while living, slandered and dishonored when dead. If, however, we consider even the prejudiced anecdotes furnished us by his enemies, we may perceive in them traces of amiable and loftly character sufficient to awaken sympathy for his fate and respect for his memory. We find that amidst all the harassing cares and ferocious passions of constant warfare he was alive to the softer feelings of connubial love and paternal tenderness and to the generous sentiment of friendship. The captivity of his "beloved wife and only son" are mentioned with exultation as causing him poignant misery: the death of any near friend is triumphantly recorded as a new blow on his sensibilities; but the treachery and desertion of many of his followers, in whose affections he had confided, is said to have desolated his heart and to have bereaved him of all further comfort. He was a patriot attached to his native soil—a prince true to his subjects and indignant of their wrongs—a soldier daring in battle, firm in adversity, patient of fatigue, of hunger, of every variety of bodily suffering, and ready to perish in the cause he had espoused. Proud of heart and with an untamable love of natural liberty, he preferred to enjoy it among the beasts of the forests or in the dismal and famished recesses of swamps and morasses, rather than bow his haughty spirit to submission and live dependent and despised in the ease and luxury of the settlements. With heroic qualities and bold achievements that would have graced a civilized warrior, and have rendered him the theme of the poet and the historian, he lived a wanderer and a fugitive in his native land, and went down, like a lonely bark foundering amid darkness and tempest, without a pitying eye to weep his fall or a friendly hand to record his struggle.

The Pride of the Village

May no wolfe howle; no screech owle stir
A wing about thy sepulchre!
No boysterous winds or stormes come hither,
To starve or wither
Thy soft sweet earth! but, like a spring,
Love kept it ever flourishing.

—Herrick

In the course of an excursion through one of the remote counties of England, I had struck into one of those cross-roads that lead through the more secluded parts of the country, and stopped one afternoon at a village the situation of which was beautifully rural and retired. There was an air of primitive simplicity about its inhabitants not to be found in the villages which lie on the great coach-roads. I determined to pass the night there, and, having taken an early dinner, strolled out to enjoy the neighboring scenery.

My ramble, as is usually the case with travellers, soon led me to the church, which stood at a little distance from the village. Indeed, it was an object of some curiosity, its old tower being completely overrun with ivy so that only here and there a jutting buttress, an angle of gray wall, or a fantastically carved ornament peered through the verdant covering. It was a lovely evening. The early part of the day had been dark and showery, but in the afternoon it had cleared up, and, though sullen clouds still hung overhead, yet there was a broad tract of golden sky in the west, from which the setting sun gleamed through the dripping leaves and lit up all Nature into a melancholy smile. It seemed like the parting hour of a good Christian smiling on the sins and sorrows of the world, and giving, in the serenity of his decline, an assurance that he will rise again in glory.

I had seated myself on a half-sunken tombstone, and was musing, as one is apt to do at this sober-thoughted hour, on past scenes and early friends—on those who were distant and those who were dead—and indulging in that kind of melancholy fancying which has in it something sweeter even than pleasure. Every now and then the stroke of a bell from the neighboring tower fell on my ear; its tones were in unison with the scene, and, instead of jarring, chimed in with my feelings; and it was some time before I recollected that it must be tolling the knell of some new tenant of the tomb.

Presently I saw a funeral train moving across the village green; it wound slowly along a lane, was lost, and reappeared through the breaks of the hedges, until it passed the place where I was sitting. The pall was supported by young girls dressed in white, and another, about the age of seventeen, walked before, bearing a chaplet of white flowers—a token that the deceased was a young and unmarried female. The corpse was followed by the parents. They were a venerable couple of the better order of peasantry. The father seemed to repress his feelings, but his fixed eye, contracted brow, and deeply-furrowed face showed the struggle that was passing within. His wife hung on his arm, and wept aloud with the convulsive bursts of a mother's sorrow.

I followed the funeral into the church. The bier was placed in the centre aisle, and the chaplet of white flowers, with a pair of white gloves, was hung over the seat which the deceased had occupied.

Every one knows the soul-subduing pathos of the funeral service, for who is so fortunate as never to have followed some one he has loved to the tomb? But when performed over the remains of innocence and beauty, thus laid low in the bloom of existence, what can be more affecting? At that simple but most solemn consignment of the body to the grave—"Earth to earth, ashes to ashes, dust to dust!"—the tears of the youthful companions of the deceased flowed unrestrained. The father still seemed to struggle with his feelings, and to comfort himself with the assurance that the dead are blessed which die in the Lord; but the mother only thought of her child as a flower of the field cut down and withered in the midst of its sweetness; she was like Rachel, "mourning over her children, and would not be comforted."

On returning to the inn I learnt the whole story of the deceased. It was a simple one, and such as has often been told. She had been the beauty and pride of the village. Her father had once been an opulent farmer, but was reduced in circumstances. This was an only child, and brought up entirely at home in the simplicity of rural life. She had been the pupil of the village pastor, the favorite lamb of his little flock. The good man watched over her education with paternal care; it was limited and suitable to the sphere in which she was to move, for he only sought to make her an ornament to her station in life, not to raise her above it. The tenderness and indulgence of her parents and the exemption from all ordinary occupations had fostered a natural

grace and delicacy of character that accorded with the fragile loveliness of her form. She appeared like some tender plant of the garden
blooming accidentally amid the hardier natives of the fields.

The superiority of her charms was felt and acknowledged by her
companions, but without envy, for it was surpassed by the unassum-
ing gentleness and winning kindness of her manners. It might be truly
said of her:

> This is the prettiest low-born lass, that ever
> Ran on the green-sward: nothing she does or seems
> But smacks of something greater than herself;
> Too noble for this place.

The village was one of those sequestered spots which still retain
some vestiges of old English customs. It had its rural festivals and
holiday pastimes, and still kept up some faint observance of the once
popular rites of May. These, indeed, had been promoted by its present
pastor, who was a lover of old customs and one of those simple Chris-
tians that think their mission fulfilled by promoting joy on earth and
good-will among mankind. Under his auspices the May-pole stood
from year to year in the centre of the village green; on Mayday it was
decorated with garlands and streamers, and a queen or lady of the
May was appointed, as in former times, to preside at the sports and
distribute the prizes and rewards. The picturesque situation of the
village and the fancifulness of its rustic fetes would often attract the
notice of casual visitors. Among these, on one May-day, was a young
officer whose regiment had been recently quartered in the neighborhood. He was charmed with the native taste that pervaded this village
pageant, but, above all, with the dawning loveliness of the queen of
May. It was the village favorite who was crowned with flowers, and
blushing and smiling in all the beautiful confusion of girlish diffi-
dence and delight. The artlessness of rural habits enabled him readily
to make her acquaintance; be gradually won his way into her intimacy, and paid his court to her in that unthinking way in which young
officers are too apt to trifle with rustic simplicity.

There was nothing in his advances to startle or alarm. He never
even talked of love, but there are modes of making it more eloquent
than language, and which convey it subtilely and irresistibly to the
heart. The beam of the eye, the tone of voice, the thousand tendernesses
which emanate from every word and look and action—these form the

true eloquence of love, and can always be felt and understood, but never described. Can we wonder that they should readily win a heart young, guileless, and susceptible? As to her, she loved almost unconsciously; she scarcely inquired what was the growing passion that was absorbing every thought and feeling, or what were to be its consequences. She, indeed, looked not to the future. When present, his looks and words occupied her whole attention; when absent, she thought but of what had passed at their recent interview. She would wander with him through the green lanes and rural scenes of the vicinity. He taught her to see new beauties in Nature; he talked in the language of polite and cultivated life, and breathed into her ear the witcheries of romance and poetry.

Perhaps there could not have been a passion between the sexes more pure than this innocent girl's. The gallant figure of her youthful admirer and the splendor of his military attire might at first have charmed her eye, but it was not these that had captivated her heart. Her attachment had something in it of idolatry. She looked up to him as to a being of a superior order. She felt in his society the enthusiasm of a mind naturally delicate and poetical, and now first awakened to a keen perception of the beautiful and grand. Of the sordid distinctions of rank and fortune she thought nothing; it was the difference of intellect, of demeanor, of manners, from those of the rustic society to which she had been accustomed, that elevated him in her opinion. She would listen to him with charmed ear and downcast look of mute delight, and her cheek would mantle with enthusiasm; or if ever she ventured a shy glance of timid admiration, it was as quickly withdrawn, and she would sigh and blush at the idea of her comparative unworthiness.

Her lover was equally impassioned, but his passion was mingled with feelings of a coarser nature. He had begun the connection in levity, for he had often heard his brother-officers boast of their village conquests, and thought some triumph of the kind necessary to his reputation as a man of spirit. But he was too full of youthful fervor. His heart had not yet been rendered sufficiently cold and selfish by a wandering and a dissipated life: it caught fire from the very flame it sought to kindle, and before he was aware of the nature of his situation he became really in love.

What was he to do? There were the old obstacles which so incessantly occur in these heedless attachments. His rank in life, the prejudices of titled connections, his dependence upon a proud and unyielding

father, all forbade him to think of matrimony; but when he looked
down upon this innocent being, so tender and confiding, there was a
purity in her manners, a blamelessness in her life, and a beseeching
modesty in her looks that awed down every licentious feeling. In vain
did he try to fortify himself by a thousand heartless examples of men
of fashion, and to chill the glow of generous sentiment with that cold
derisive levity with which he had heard them talk of female virtue:
whenever he came into her presence she was still surrounded by that
mysterious but impassive charm of virgin purity in whose hallowed
sphere no guilty thought can live.

The sudden arrival of orders for the regiment to repair to the Con-
tinent completed the confusion of his mind. He remained for a short
time in a state of the most painful irresolution; he hesitated to com-
municate the tidings until the day for marching was at hand, when he
gave her the intelligence in the course of an evening ramble.

The idea of parting had never before occurred to her. It broke in at
once upon her dream of felicity; she looked upon it as a sudden and
insurmountable evil, and wept with the guileless simplicity of a child.
He drew her to his bosom and kissed the tears from her soft cheek;
nor did he meet with a repulse, for there are moments of mingled
sorrow and tenderness which hallow the caresses of affection. He was
naturally impetuous, and the sight of beauty apparently yielding in his
arms, the confidence of his power over her, and the dread of losing
her forever all conspired to overwhelm his better feelings: he ventured
to propose that she should leave her home and be the companion of
his fortunes.

He was quite a novice in seduction, and blushed and faltered at his
own baseness; but so innocent of mind was his intended victim that
she was at first at a loss to comprehend his meaning, and why she
should leave her native village and the humble roof of her parents.
When at last the nature of his proposal flashed upon her pure mind,
the effect was withering. She did not weep; she did not break forth
into reproach; she said not a word, but she shrunk back aghast as from
a viper, gave him a look of anguish that pierced to his very soul, and,
clasping her hands in agony, fled, as if for refuge, to her father's cottage.

The officer retired confounded, humiliated, and repentant. It is
uncertain what might have been the result of the conflict of his feelings, had not his thoughts been diverted by the bustle of departure.
New scenes, new pleasures, and new companions soon dissipated his

self-reproach and stifled his tenderness; yet, amidst the stir of camps, the revelries of garrisons, the array of armies, and even the din of battles, his thoughts would sometimes steal back to the scenes of rural quiet and village simplicity—the white cottage, the footpath along the silver brook and up the hawthorn hedge, and the little village maid loitering along it, leaning on his arm and listening to him with eyes beaming with unconscious affection.

The shock which the poor girl had received in the destruction of all her ideal world had indeed been cruel. Faintings and hysterics had at first shaken her tender frame, and were succeeded by a settled and pining melancholy. She had beheld from her window the march of the departing troops. She had seen her faithless lover borne off, as if in triumph, amidst the sound of drum and trumpet and the pomp of arms. She strained a last aching gaze after him as the morning sun glittered about his figure and his plume waved in the breeze; he passed away like a bright vision from her sight, and left her all in darkness.

It would be trite to dwell on the particulars of her after story. It was, like other tales of love, melancholy. She avoided society and wandered out alone in the walks she had most frequented with her lover. She sought, like the stricken deer, to weep in silence and loneliness and brood over the barbed sorrow that rankled in her soul. Sometimes she would be seen late of an evening sitting in the porch of the village church, and the milk-maids, returning from the fields, would now and then overhear her singing some plaintive ditty in the hawthorn walk. She became fervent in her devotions at church, and as the old people saw her approach, so wasted away, yet with a hectic gloom and that hallowed air which melancholy diffuses round the form, they would make way for her as for something spiritual, and looking after her, would shake their heads in gloomy foreboding.

She felt a conviction that she was hastening to the tomb, but looked forward to it as a place of rest. The silver cord that had bound her to existence was loosed, and there seemed to be no more pleasure under the sun. If ever her gentle bosom had entertained resentment against her lover, it was extinguished. She was incapable of angry passions, and in a moment of saddened tenderness she penned him a farewell letter. It was couched in the simplest language, but touching from its very simplicity. She told him that she was dying, and did not conceal from him that his conduct was the cause. She even depicted the sufferings which she had experienced, but concluded with saying that she could not die in peace until she had sent him her forgiveness and her blessing.

By degrees her strength declined that she could no longer leave the cottage. She could only totter to the window, where, propped up in her chair, it was her enjoyment to sit all day and look out upon the landscape. Still she uttered no complaint nor imparted to any one the malady that was preying on her heart. She never even mentioned her lover's name, but would lay her head on her mother's bosom and weep in silence. Her poor parents hung in mute anxiety over this fading blossom of their hopes, still flattering themselves that it might again revive to freshness and that the bright unearthly bloom which sometimes flushed her cheek might be the promise of returning health.

In this way she was seated between them one Sunday afternoon; her hands were clasped in theirs, the lattice was thrown open, and the soft air that stole in brought with it the fragrance of the clustering honeysuckle which her own hands had trained round the window.

Her father had just been reading a chapter in the Bible: it spoke of the vanity of worldly things and of the joys of heaven: it seemed to have diffused comfort and serenity through her bosom. Her eye was fixed on the distant village church: the bell had tolled for the evening service; the last villager was lagging into the porch, and everything had sunk into that hallowed stillness peculiar to the day of rest. Her parents were gazing on her with yearning hearts. Sickness and sorrow, which pass so roughly over some faces, had given to hers the expression of a seraph's. A tear trembled in her soft blue eye. Was she thinking of her faithless lover? or were her thoughts wandering to that distant churchyard, into whose bosom she might soon be gathered?

Suddenly the clang of hoofs was heard: a horseman galloped to the cottage; he dismounted before the window; the poor girl gave a faint exclamation and sunk back in her chair: it was her repentant lover. He rushed into the house and flew to clasp her to his bosom; but her wasted form, her deathlike countenance—so wan, yet so lovely in its desolation—smote him to the soul, and he threw himself in agony at her feet. She was too faint to rise—she attempted to extend her trembling hand—her lips moved as if she spoke, but no word was articulated; she looked down upon him with a smile of unutterable tenderness, and closed her eyes forever.

Such are the particulars which I gathered of this village story. They are but scanty, and I am conscious have little novelty to recommend them. In the present rage also for strange incident and high-seasoned narrative they may appear trite and insignificant, but they interested me strongly at the time; and, taken in connection with the affecting ceremony which I had just witnessed, left a deeper impression on my mind than many circumstances of a more striking nature. I have passed through the place since, and visited the church again from a better motive than mere curiosity. It was a wintry evening: the trees were stripped of their foliage, the churchyard looked naked and mournful, and the wind rustled coldly through the dry grass. Evergreens, however, had been planted about the grave of the village favorite, and osiers were bent over it to keep the turf uninjured.

The church-door was open and I stepped in. There hung the chaplet of flowers and the gloves, as on the day of the funeral: the flowers were withered, it is true, but care seemed to have been taken that no dust should soil their whiteness. I have seen many monuments where art has exhausted its powers to awaken the sympathy of the spectator, but I have met with none that spoke more touchingly to my heart than this simple but delicate memento of departed innocence.

The Angler

This day Dame Nature seem'd in love,
The lusty sap began to move,
Fresh juice did stir th' embracing vines,
And birds had drawn their valentines.
The jealous trout that low did lie,
Rose at a well-dissembled flie.
There stood my friend, with patient skill,
Attending of his trembling quill.
　　　　　　　　　　　　　–Sir H. Wotton

It is said that many an unlucky urchin is induced to run away from his family and betake himself to a seafaring life from reading the history of Robinson Crusoe; and I suspect that, in like manner, many of those worthy gentlemen who are given to haunt the sides of pastoral streams with angle-rods in hand may trace the origin of their passion to the seductive pages of honest Izaak Walton. I recollect studying his *Compleat Angler* several years since in company with a knot of friends in America, and moreover that we were all completely bitten with the angling mania. It was early in the year, but as soon as the weather was auspicious, and that the spring began to melt into the verge of summer, we took rod in hand and sallied into the country, as stark mad as was ever Don Quixote from reading books of chivalry.

One of our party had equalled the Don in the fulness of his equipments, being attired cap-a-pie for the enterprise. He wore a broad-skirted fustian coat, perplexed with half a hundred pockets; a pair of stout shoes and leathern gaiters; a basket slung on one side for fish; a patent rod, a landing net, and a score of other inconveniences only to be found in the true angler's armory. Thus harnessed for the field, he was as great a matter of stare and wonderment among the country folk, who had never seen a regular angler, as was the steel-clad hero of La Mancha among the goatherds of the Sierra Morena.

Our first essay was along a mountain brook among the Highlands of the Hudson—a most unfortunate place for the execution of those piscatory tactics which had been invented along the velvet margins of quiet English rivulets. It was one of those wild streams that lavish, among our romantic solitudes, unheeded beauties enough to fill the sketch-book of a hunter of the picturesque. Sometimes it would leap down rocky shelves, making small cascades, over which the trees threw their broad balancing sprays and long nameless weeds hung in fringes from the impending banks, dripping with diamond drops. Sometimes it would brawl and fret along a ravine in the matted shade of a forest, filling it with murmurs, and after this termagant career would steal forth into open day with the most placid, demure face imaginable, as I have seen some pestilent shrew of a housewife, after filling her home with uproar and ill-humor, come dimpling out of doors, swimming and curtseying and smiling upon all the world.

How smoothly would this vagrant brook glide at such times through some bosom of green meadowland among the mountains, where the quiet was only interrupted by the occasional tinkling of a bell from the lazy cattle among the clover or the sound of a woodcutter's axe from the neighboring forest!

For my part, I was always a bungler at all kinds of sport that required either patience or adroitness, and had not angled above half an hour before I had completely "satisfied the sentiment," and convinced myself of the truth of Izaak Walton's opinion, that angling is something like poetry—a man must be born to it. I hooked myself instead of the fish, tangled my line in every tree, lost my bait, broke my rod, until I gave up the attempt in despair, and passed the day under the trees reading old Izaak, satisfied that it was his fascinating vein of honest simplicity and rural feeling that had bewitched me, and not the passion for angling. My companions, however, were more persevering in their delusion. I have them at this moment before eyes, stealing along the border of the brook where it lay open to the day or was merely fringed by shrubs and bushes. I see the bittern rising with hollow scream as they break in upon his rarely-invaded haunt; the kingfisher watching them suspiciously from his dry tree that overhangs the deep black millpond in the gorge of the hills; the tortoise letting himself slip sideways from off the stone or log on which he is sunning himself; and the panic-struck frog plumping in headlong as they approach, and spreading an alarm throughout the watery world around.

I recollect also that, after toiling and watching and creeping about for the greater part of a day, with scarcely any success in spite of all our admirable apparatus, a lubberly country urchin came down from the hills with a rod made from a branch of a tree, a few yards of twine, and, as Heaven shall help me! I believe a crooked pin for a hook, baited with a vile earthworm, and in half an hour caught more fish than we had nibbles throughout the day!

But, above all, I recollect the "good, honest, wholesome, hungry" repast which we made under a beech tree just by a spring of pure sweet water that stole out of the side of a hill, and how, when it was over, one of the party read old Izaak Walton's scene with the milkmaid, while I lay on the grass and built castles in a bright pile of clouds until I fell asleep. All this may appear like mere egotism, yet I cannot refrain from uttering these recollections, which are passing like a strain of music over my mind and have been called up by an agreeable scene which I witnessed not long since.

In the morning's stroll along the banks of the Alun, a beautiful little stream which flows down from the Welsh hills and throws itself into the Dee, my attention was attracted to a group seated on the margin. On approaching I found it to consist of a veteran angler and two rustic disciples. The former was an old fellow with a wooden leg, with clothes very much but very carefully patched, betokening poverty honestly come by and decently maintained. His face bore the marks of former storms, but present fair weather, its furrows had been worn into an habitual smile, his iron-gray locks hung about his ears, and he had altogether the good-humored air of a constitutional philosopher who was disposed to take the world as it went. One of his companions was a ragged wight with the skulking look of an arrant poacher, and I'll warrant could find his way to any gentleman's fish-pond in the neighborhood in the darkest night. The other was a tall, awkward country lad, with a lounging gait, and apparently somewhat of a rustic beau. The old man was busy in examining the maw of a trout which he had just killed, to discover by its contents what insects were seasonable for bait, and was lecturing on the subject to his companions, who appeared to listen with infinite deference. I have a kind feeling towards all "brothers of the angle" ever since I read Izaak Walton. They are men, he affirms, of a "mild, sweet, and peaceable spirit;" and my esteem for them has been increased since I met with an old *Tretyse of Fishing with the Angle*, in which are set forth many of the maxims of their inoffensive fraternity. "Take good hede," sayeth this honest little tretyse, "that in going about your disportes ye open no man's gates but that ye shet them again. Also ye shall not use this forsayd crafti disport for no covetousness to the encreasing and sparing of your money only, but principally for your solace, and to cause the helth of your body and specyally of your soule."*

I thought that I could perceive in the veteran angler before me an exemplification of what I had read; and there was a cheerful content-edness in his looks that quite drew me towards him. I could not but remark the gallant manner in which he stumped from one part of the brook to another, waving his rod in the air to keep the line from dragging on the ground or catching among the bushes, and the adroit-ness with which he would throw his fly to any particular place, some-times skimming it lightly along a little rapid, sometimes casting it into one of those dark holes made by a twisted root or overhanging bank in which the large trout are apt to lurk. In the meanwhile he was giving instructions to his two disciples, showing them the manner in which they should handle their rods, fix their flies, and play them along the surface of the stream. The scene brought to my mind the instructions of the sage Piscator to his scholar. The country around was of that pastoral kind which Walton is fond of describing. It was a part of the great plain of Cheshire, close by the beautiful vale of Gessford, and just where the inferior Welsh hills begin to swell up from among fresh-smelling meadows. The day too, like that recorded in his work, was mild and sunshiny, with now and then a soft-dropping shower that sowed the whole earth with diamonds.

I soon fell into conversation with the old angler, and was so much entertained that, under pretext of receiving instructions in his art, I kept company with him almost the whole day, wandering along the banks of the stream and listening to his talk. He was very communica-tive, having all the easy garrulity of cheerful old age, and I fancy was a little flattered by having an opportunity of displaying his piscatory lore, for who does not like now and then to play the sage?

He had been much of a rambler in his day, and had passed some years of his youth in America, particularly in Savannah, where he had entered into trade and had been ruined by the indiscretion of a part-

---

*From this same treatise it would appear that angling is a more industrious and devout employment than it is generally considered: "For when ye pur-pose to go on your disportes in fishynge ye will not desyre greatlye many persons with you, which might let you of your game. And that ye may serve God devoutly in saying effectually your customable prayers. And thus doying, ye shall eschew and also avoyde many vices, as ydelness, which is principall cause to induce man to many other vices, as it is right well known."

ner. He had afterwards experienced many ups and downs in life until he got into the navy, where his leg was carried away by a cannon-ball at the battle of Camperdown. This was the only stroke of real good-fortune he had ever experienced, for it got him a pension, which, together with some small paternal property, brought him in a revenue of nearly forty pounds. On this he retired to his native village, where he lived quietly and independently, and devoted the remainder of his life to the "noble art of angling."

I found that he had read Izaak Walton attentively, and he seemed to have imbibed all his simple frankness and prevalent good-humor. Though he had been sorely buffeted about the world, he was satisfied that the world, in itself, was good and beautiful. Though he had been as roughly used in different countries as a poor sheep that is fleeced by every hedge and thicket, yet he spoke of every nation with candor and kindness, appearing to look only on the good side of things; and, above all, he was almost the only man I had ever met with who had been an unfortunate adventurer in America and had honesty and magnanimity enough to take the fault to his own door, and not to curse the country. The lad that was receiving his instructions, I learnt, was the son and heir-apparent of a fat old widow who kept the village inn, and of course a youth of some expectation, and much courted by the idle gentleman-like personages of the place. In taking him under his care, therefore, the old man had probably an eye to a privileged corner in the tap-room and an occasional cup of cheerful ale free of expense.

There is certainly something in angling—if we could forget, which anglers are apt to do, the cruelties and tortures inflicted on worms and insects—that tends to produce a gentleness of spirit and a pure serenity of mind. As the English are methodical even in their recreations, and are the most scientific of sportsmen, it has been reduced among them to perfect rule and system. Indeed, it is an amusement peculiarly adapted to the mild and highly-cultivated scenery of England, where every roughness has been softened away from the landscape. It is delightful to saunter along those limpid streams which wander, like veins of silver, through the bosom of this beautiful country, leading one through a diversity of small home scenery—sometimes winding through ornamented grounds; sometimes brimming along through rich pasturage, where the fresh green is mingled with sweet-smelling flowers; sometimes venturing in sight of villages and hamlets, and then running capriciously away into shady retirements. The sweetness and serenity of Nature and the quiet watchfulness of the sport gradually bring on pleasant fits of musing, which are now and then agreeably interrupted by the song of a bird, the distant whistle of the peasant, or perhaps the vagary of some fish leaping out of the still water and skimming transiently about its glassy surface. "When I would beget content," says Izaak Walton, "and increase confidence in the power and wisdom and providence of Almighty God, I will walk the meadows by some gliding stream, and there contemplate the lilies that take no care, and those very many other little living creatures that are not only created, but fed (man knows not how) by the goodness of the God of Nature, and therefore trust in Him."

I cannot forbear to give another quotation from one of those ancient champions of angling which breathes the same innocent and happy spirit:

> Let me live harmlessly, and near the brink
>   Of Trent or Avon have a dwelling-place:
> Where I may see my quill, or cork, down sink
>   With eager bite—of Pike, or Bleak, or Dace;
> And on the world and my Creator think:
>   Whilst some men strive ill-gotten goods t' embrace:
> And others spend their time in base excess
>   Of wine, or worse, in war or wantonness.
>
> Let them that will, these pastimes still pursue,
>   And on such pleasing fancies feed their fill;
> So I the fields and meadows green may view,
>   And daily by fresh rivers walk at will,
> Among the daisies and the violets blue,
>   Red hyacinth and yellow daffodil.*

On parting with the old angler I inquired after his place of abode, and, happening to be in the neighborhood of the village a few evenings afterwards, I had the curiosity to seek him out. I found him living in a small cottage containing only one room, but a perfect curiosity in its method and arrangement. It was on the skirts of the village, on a green bank a little back from the road, with a small garden in front stocked with kitchen herbs and adorned with a few flowers. The whole front of the cottage was overrun with a honeysuckle. On

---

*J. Davors.

the top was a ship for a weathercock. The interior was fitted up in a truly nautical style, his ideas of comfort and convenience having been acquired on the berth-deck of a man-of-war. A hammock was slung from the ceiling which in the daytime was lashed up so as to take but little room. From the centre of the chamber hung a model of a ship, of his own workmanship. Two or three chairs, a table, and a large sea-chest formed the principal movables. About the wall were stuck up naval ballads, such as "Admiral Hosier's Ghost," "All in the Downs," and "Tom Bowling," intermingled with pictures of sea-fights, among which the battle of Camperdown held a distinguished place. The mantelpiece was decorated with sea-shells, over which hung a quadrant, flanked by two wood-cuts of most bitter-looking naval commanders. His implements for angling were carefully disposed on nails and hooks about the room. On a shelf was arranged his library, containing a work on angling, much worn, a Bible covered with canvas, an odd volume or two of voyages, a nautical almanac, and a book of songs.

His family consisted of a large black cat with one eye, and a parrot which he had caught and tamed and educated himself in the course of one of his voyages, and which uttered a variety of sea-phrases with the hoarse brattling tone of a veteran boatswain. The establishment reminded me of that of the renowned Robinson Crusoe; it was kept in neat order, everything being "stowed away" with the regularity of a ship of war; and he informed me that he "scoured the deck every morning and swept it between meals."

I found him seated on a bench before the door, smoking his pipe in the soft evening sunshine. His cat was purring soberly on the threshold, and his parrot describing some strange evolutions in an iron ring that swung in the centre of his cage. He had been angling all day, and gave me a history of his sport with as much minuteness as a general would talk over a campaign, being particularly animated in relating the manner in which he had taken a large trout, which had completely tasked all his skill and wariness, and which he had sent as a trophy to mine hostess of the inn.

How comforting it is to see a cheerful and contented old age, and to behold a poor fellow like this, after being tempest-tost through life, safely moored in a snug and quiet harbor in the evening of his days! His happiness, however, sprung from within himself and was independent of external circumstances, for he had that inexhaustible good-nature which is the most precious gift of Heaven, spreading itself like oil over the troubled sea of thought, and keeping the mind smooth and equable in the roughest weather.

On inquiring further about him, I learnt that he was a universal favorite in the village and the oracle of the tap-room, where he delighted the rustics with his songs, and, like Sindbad, astonished them with his stories of strange lands and shipwrecks and sea-fights. He was much noticed too by gentlemen sportsmen of the neighborhood, had taught several of them the art of angling, and was a privileged visitor to their kitchens. The whole tenor of his life was quiet and inoffensive, being principally passed about the neighboring streams when the weather and season were favorable; and at other times he employed himself at home, preparing his fishing-tackle for the next campaign or manufacturing rods, nets, and flies for his patrons and pupils among the gentry.

He was a regular attendant at church on Sundays, though he generally fell asleep during the sermon. He had made it his particular request that when he died he should be buried in a green spot which he could see from his seat in church, and which he had marked out ever since he was a boy, and had thought of when far from home on the raging sea in danger of being food for the fishes: it was the spot where his father and mother had been buried.

I have done, for I fear that my reader is growing weary, but I could not refrain from drawing the picture of this worthy "brother of the angle," who has made me more than ever in love with the theory, though I fear I shall never be adroit in the practice, of his art; and I will conclude this rambling sketch in the words of honest Izaak Walton, by craving the blessing of St. Peter's Master upon my reader, "and upon all that are true lovers of virtue, and dare trust in His providence, and be quiet, and go a-angling."

Wolfert Webber, or Golden Dreams

In the year of grace one thousand seven hundred and . . .blank —for I do not remember the precise date; however, it was somewhere in the early part of the last century—there lived in the ancient city of the Manhattoes a worthy burgher, Wolfert Webber by name. He was descended from old Cobus Webber of the Brill in Holland, one of the original settlers, famous for introducing the cultivation of cabbages, and who came over to the province during the protectorship of Oloffe Van Kortlandt, otherwise called "the Dreamer."

The field in which Cobus Webber first planted himself and his cabbages had remained ever since in the family, who continued in the same line of husbandry with that praiseworthy perseverance for which our Dutch burghers are noted. The whole family genius, during several generations, was devoted to the study and development of this one noble vegetable, and to this concentration of intellect may doubtless be ascribed the prodigious renown to which the Webber cabbages attained.

The Webber dynasty continued in uninterrupted succession, and never did a line give more unquestionable proofs of legitimacy. The eldest son succeeded to the looks as well as the territory of his sire, and had the portraits of this line of tranquil potentates been taken, they would have presented a row of heads marvelously resembling, in shape and magnitude, the vegetables over which they reigned.

The seat of government continued unchanged in the family mansion—a Dutch-built house, with a front, or rather gable end, of yellow brick, tapering to a point, with the customary iron weathercock at the top. Everything about the building bore the air of long-settled ease and security. Flights of martins peopled the little coops nailed against its walls, and swallows built their nests under the eaves, and everyone knows that these house-loving birds bring good luck to the dwelling where they take up their abode. In a bright summer morning in early summer, it was delectable to hear their cheerful notes as they sported about in the pure, sweet air, chirping forth, as it were, the greatness and prosperity of the Webbers.

Thus quietly and comfortably did this excellent family vegetate under the shade of a mighty buttonwood tree, which by little and little grew so great as entirely to overshadow their palace. The city gradually spread its suburbs round their domain. Houses sprang up to interrupt their prospects. The rural lanes in the vicinity began to grow into the bustle and pWolopulousness of streets; in short, with all the habits of rustic life they began to find themselves the inhabitants of a city. Still, however, they maintained their hereditary character and hereditary possessions, with all the tenacity of petty German princes in the midst of the empire. Wolfert was the last of the line, and succeeded to the patriarchal bench at the door, under the family tree, and swayed the scepter of his fathers—a kind of rural potentate in the midst of the metropolis.

To share the cares and sweets of sovereignty he had taken unto himself a helpmate, one of that excellent kind called "stirring women"; that is to say, she was one of those notable little housewives who are always busy where there is nothing to do. Her activity, however, took one particular direction—her whole life seemed devoted to intense knitting; whether at home or abroad, walking or sitting, her needles were continually in motion, and it is even affirmed that by her unwearied industry she very nearly supplied her household with stockings throughout the year. This worthy couple were blessed with one daughter who was brought up with great tenderness and care; uncommon pains had been taken with her education, so that she could stitch in every variety of way, make all kinds of pickles and preserves, and mark her own name on a sampler. The influence of her taste was seen also in the family garden, where the ornamental began to mingle with the useful; whole rows of fiery marigolds and splendid hollyhocks bordered the cabbage beds, and gigantic sunflowers lolled their broad, jolly faces over the fences, seeming to ogle most affectionately the passers-by.

Thus reigned and vegetated Wolfert Webber over his paternal acres, peacefully and contentedly. Not but that, like all other sovereigns, he had his occasional cares and vexations. The growth of his native city sometimes caused him annoyance. His little territory gradually became hemmed in by streets and houses, which intercepted air and sunshine. He was now and then subjected to the eruptions of the border population that infest the streets of a metropolis, who would make midnight forays into his dominions, and carry off captive whole platoons of his noblest subjects. Vagrant swine would make a descent, too, now and then, when the gate was left open, and lay all waste before them; and mischievous urchins would decapitate the illustrious sunflowers, the glory of the garden, as they lolled their heads so fondly over the walls. Still all these were petty grievances, which might now and then ruffle the surface of his mind, as a summer breeze will ruffle the surface of a mill pond, but they could not disturb the deep-seated quiet of his soul. He would but seize a trusty staff that stood behind the door, issue suddenly out, and anoint the back of the aggressor, whether pig or urchin, and then return within doors, marvelously refreshed and tranquilized.

The chief cause of anxiety to honest Wolfert, however, was the growing prosperity of the city. The expenses of living doubled and trebled, but he could not double and treble the magnitude of his cabbages, and the number of competitors prevented the increase of price; thus, therefore, while everyone around him grew richer, Wolfert grew poorer, and he could not, for the life of him, perceive how the evil was to be remedied.

This growing care, which increased from day to day, had its gradual effect upon our worthy burgher, insomuch that it at length implanted two or three wrinkles in his brow, things unknown before in the family of the Webbers, and it seemed to pinch up the corners of his cocked hat into an expression of anxiety totally opposite to the tranquil, broad-brimmed, low-crowned beavers of his illustrious progenitors.

Perhaps even this would not have materially disturbed the serenity of his mind had he had only himself and his wife to care for; but there was his daughter gradually growing to maturity, and all the world knows that when daughters begin to ripen, no fruit nor flower requires so much looking after. I have no talent at describing female charms, else fain would I depict the progress of this little Dutch beauty: how her blue eyes grew deeper and deeper, and her cherry lips redder and redder, and how she ripened and ripened, and rounded and rounded, in the opening breath of sixteen summers, until, in her seventeenth spring, she seemed ready to burst out of her bodice, like a half-blown rosebud.

Ah, well-a-day! Could I but show her as she was then, tricked out on a Sunday morning in the hereditary finery of the old Dutch clothespress, of which her mother had confided to her the key! The wedding dress of her grandmother, modernized for use, with sundry ornaments, handed down as heirlooms in the family. Her pale brown hair smoothed with buttermilk in flat, waving lines on each side of her fair forehead. The chain of yellow, virgin gold that encircled her neck; the little cross that just rested at the entrance of a soft valley of happiness, as if it would sanctify the place. The . . . but pooh! it is not for an old man like me to be prosing about female beauty; suffice it to say, Amy had attained her seventeenth year. Long since had her sampler exhibited hearts in couples desperately transfixed with arrows, and true lovers' knots worked in deep blue silk, and it was evident she began to languish for some more interesting occupation than the rearing of sunflowers or pickling of cucumbers.

At this critical period of female existence, when the heart within a damsel's bosom, like its emblem, the miniature which hangs without, is apt to be engrossed by a single image, a new visitor began to make his appearance under the roof of Wolfert Webber. This was Dirk Waldron, the only son of a poor widow, but who could boast of more fathers than any lad in the province, for his mother had had four husbands, and this only child, so that, though born in her last wedlock, he might fairly claim to be the tardy fruit of a long course of cultivation. This son of four fathers united the merits and the vigor of all his sires. If he had not had a great family before him he seemed likely to have a great one after him, for you had only to look at the fresh, buxom youth to see that he was formed to be the founder of a mighty race.

This youngster gradually became an intimate visitor of the family. He talked little, but he sat long. He filled the father's pipe when it was empty, gathered up the mother's knitting needle, or ball of worsted, when it fell to the ground, stroked the sleek coat of the tortoise-shell cat, and replenished the teapot for the daughter from the bright copper kettle that sang before the fire. All these quiet little offices may seem of trifling import, but when true love is translated into Low Dutch it is in this way that it eloquently expresses itself. They were not lost upon the Webber family. The winning youngster found marvelous favor in the eyes of the mother; the tortoise-shell cat, albeit the most staid and demure of her kind, gave indubitable signs of approbation of his visits; the teakettle seemed to sing out a cheering note of welcome at his approach; and if the sly glances of the daughter might be rightly read, as she sat bridling and dimpling, and sewing by her mother's side, she was not a whit behind Dame Webber, or grimalkin, or the teakettle, in good will.

Wolfert alone saw nothing of what was going on. Profoundly wrapped up in meditation on the growth of the city and his cabbages, he sat looking in the fire, and puffing his pipe in silence. One night, however, as the gentle Amy, according to custom, lighted her lover to the outer door, and he, according to custom, took his parting salute, the smack resounded so vigorously through the long, silent entry as to startle even the dull ear of Wolfert. He was slowly roused to a new source of anxiety. It had never entered into his head that this mere child, who, as it seemed, but the other day had been climbing about his knees and playing with dolls and baby houses, could all at once be thinking of lovers and matrimony. He rubbed his eyes, examined into the fact, and really found that while he had been dreaming of other matters, she had actually grown to be a woman, and, what was worse, had fallen in love. Here arose new cares for Wolfert. He was a kind father, but he was a prudent man. The young man was a lively, stirring lad, but then he had neither money nor land. Wolfert's ideas all ran in one channel, and he saw no alternative in case of a marriage but to portion off the young couple with a corner of his cabbage garden, the whole of which was barely sufficient for the support of his family.

Like a prudent father, therefore, he determined to nip this passion in the bud, and forbade the youngster the house, though sorely did it go against his fatherly heart, and many a silent tear did it cause in the bright eye of his daughter. She showed herself, however, a pattern of filial piety and obedience. She never pouted and sulked; she never flew in the face of parental authority; she never flew into a passion, nor fell into hysterics, as many romantic, novel-read young ladies would do. Not she, indeed. She was none such heroical, rebellious trumpery, I'll warrant ye. On the contrary, she acquiesced like an obedient daughter, shut the street door in her lover's face, and if ever she did grant him an interview, it was either out of the kitchen window or over the garden fence.

Wolfert was deeply cogitating these matters in his mind, and his brow wrinkled with unusual care, as he wended his way one Saturday afternoon to a rural inn, about two miles from the city. It was a favorite resort of the Dutch part of the community, from being always held by a Dutch line of landlords, and retaining an air and relish of the good old times. It was a Dutch-built house that had probably been a country seat of some opulent burgher in the early time of the settlement. It stood near a point of land called Corlear's Hook, which stretches out into the Sound, and against which the tide, at its flux and reflux, sets with extraordinary rapidity. The venerable and somewhat crazy mansion was distinguished from afar by a grove of elms and sycamores that seemed to wave a hospitable invitation, while a few weeping willows, with their dank, drooping foliage, resembling falling waters, gave an idea of coolness that rendered it an attractive spot during the heats of summer.

Here, therefore, as I said, resorted many of the old inhabitants of the Manhattoes, where, while some played at shuffleboard and quoits, and ninepins, others smoked a deliberate pipe, and talked over public affairs.

It was on a blustering autumnal afternoon that Wolfert made his visit to the inn. The grove of elms and willows was stripped of its leaves, which whirled in rustling eddies about the fields. The ninepin alley was deserted, for the premature chilliness of the day had driven the company within doors. As it was Saturday afternoon the habitual club was in session, composed principally of regular Dutch burghers, though mingled occasionally with persons of various character and country, as is natural in a place of such motley population.

Beside the fireplace, in a huge, leather-bottomed armchair, sat the dictator of this little world, the venerable Rem, or, as it was pronounced, "Ramm" Rapelye. He was a man of Walloon race, and illustrious for the antiquity of his line, his great-grandmother having been the first white child born in the province. But he was still more illustrious for his wealth and dignity. He had long filled the noble office of alderman, and was a man to whom the governor himself took off his hat. He had maintained possession of the leather-bottomed chair from time immemorial, and had gradually waxed in bulk as he sat in his seat of government, until in the course of years he filled its whole magnitude. His word was decisive with his subjects, for he was so rich a man that he was never expected to support any opinion by argument. The landlord waited on him with peculiar officiousness—not that he paid better than his neighbors, but then the coin of a rich man seems always to be so much more acceptable. The landlord had ever a pleasant word and a joke to insinuate in the ear of the august Ramm. It is true Ramm never laughed, and, indeed, ever maintained a mastiff-like gravity and even surliness of aspect; yet he now and then rewarded mine host with a token of approbation, which, though nothing more nor less than a kind of grunt, still delighted the landlord more than a broad laugh from a poorer man.

"This will be a rough night for the money diggers," said mine host, as a gust of wind bowled round the house and rattled at the windows.

"What! are they at their works again? " said an English half-pay captain, with one eye, who was a very frequent attendant at the inn.

"Aye are they," said the landlord, "and well may they be. They've had luck of late. They say a great pot of money has been dug up in the fields just behind Stuyvesant's orchard. Folks think it must have been buried there in old times by Peter Stuyvesant, the Dutch governor."

"Fudge!" said the one-eyed man of war, as he added a small portion of water to a bottom of brandy.

"Well, you may believe it or not, as you please," said mine host, somewhat nettled, "but everybody knows that the old governor buried a great deal of his money at the time of the Dutch troubles, when the English redcoats seized on the province. They say, too, the old gentleman walks, aye, and in the very same dress that he wears in the picture that hangs up in the family house."

"Fudge!" said the half-pay officer.

"Fudge, if you please! But didn't Corney Van Zandt see him at midnight, stalking about in the meadow with his wooden leg, and a drawn sword in his hand, that flashed like fire? And what can he be walking for but because people have been troubling the place where he buried his money in old times?"

Here the landlord was interrupted by several guttural sounds from Ramm Rapelye, betokening that he was laboring with the unusual production of an idea. As he was too great a man to be slighted by a prudent publican, mine host respectfully paused until he should deliver himself. The corpulent frame of this mighty burgher now gave all the symptoms of a volcanic mountain on the point of an eruption. First there was a certain heaving of the abdomen, not unlike an earthquake; then was emitted a cloud of tobacco smoke from that crater, his mouth; then there was a kind of rattle in the throat, as if the idea were working its way up through a region of phlegm; then there were several disjointed members of a sentence thrown out, ending in a cough; at length his voice forced its way into a slow, but absolute tone of a man who feels the weight of his purse, if not of his ideas, every portion of his speech being marked by a testy puff of tobacco smoke.

"Who talks of old Peter Stuyvesant's walking? (puff). Have people no respect for persons? (puff–puff). Peter Stuyvesant knew better what to do with his money than to bury it (puff). I know the Stuyvesant family (puff), every one of them (puff); not a more respectable family in the province (puff)–old standards (puff)–warm householders (puff)–

none of your upstarts (puff–puff–puff). Don't talk to me of Peter Stuyvesant's walking (puff–puff–puff– puff)."

Here the redoubtable Ramm contracted his brow, clasped up his mouth till it wrinkled at each corner, and redoubled his smoking with such vehemence that the cloudy volumes soon wreathed round his head, as the smoke envelops the awful summit of Mount Ætna. A general silence followed the sudden rebuke of this very rich man. The subject, however, was too interesting to be readily abandoned. The conversation soon broke forth again from the lips of Peechy Prauw Van Hook, the chronicler of the club, one of those prosing, narrative old men who seem to be troubled with an incontinence of words as they grow old.

Peechy could, at any time, tell as many stories in an evening as his hearers could digest in a month. He now resumed the conversation by affirming that, to his knowledge, money had, at different times, been dug up in various parts of the island.

The lucky persons who had discovered them had always dreamed of them three times beforehand, and, what was worthy of remark, those treasures had never been found but by some descendant of the good old Dutch families, which clearly proved that they had been buried by Dutchmen in the olden time.

"Fiddlestick with your Dutchmen! " cried the half-pay officer. "The Dutch had nothing to do with them. They were all buried by Kidd the pirate, and his crew."

Here a keynote was touched that roused the whole company. The name of Captain Kidd was like a talisman in those times, and was associated with a thousand marvelous stories.

The half-pay officer took the lead, and in his narrations fathered upon Kidd all the plunderings and exploits of Morgan, Blackbeard, and the whole list of bloody buccaneers.

The officer was a man of great weight among the peaceable members of the club, by reason of his warlike character and gunpowder tales. All his golden stories of Kidd, however, and of the booty he had buried, were obstinately rivaled by the tales of Peechy Prauw, who, rather than suffer his Dutch progenitors to be eclipsed by a foreign freebooter, enriched every field and shore in the neighborhood with the hidden wealth of Peter Stuyvesant and his contemporaries.

Not a word of this conversation was lost upon Wolfert Webber. He returned pensively home, full of magnificent ideas. The soil of his native island seemed to be turned into gold dust, and every field to teem with treasure. His head almost reeled at the thought how often he must have heedlessly rambled over places where countless sums lay, scarcely covered by the turf beneath his feet. His mind was in an uproar with this whirl of new ideas. As he came in sight of the venerable mansion of his forefathers, and the little realm where the Webbers had so long and so contentedly flourished, his gorge rose at the narrowness of his destiny. "Unlucky Wolfert!" exclaimed he; "others can go to bed and dream themselves into whole mines of wealth; they have but to seize a spade in the morning, and turn up doubloons like potatoes; but thou must dream of hardships, and rise to poverty, must dig thy field from year's end to year's end, and yet raise nothing but cabbages!"

Wolfert Webber went to bed with a heavy heart, and it was long before the golden visions that disturbed his brain permitted him to sink into repose. The same visions, however, extended into his sleeping thoughts, and assumed a more definite form. He dreamed that he had discovered an immense treasure in the center of his garden. At every stroke of the spade he laid bare a golden ingot; diamond crosses sparkled out of the dust; bags of money turned up their bellies, corpulent with pieces-of-eight or venerable doubloons; and chests wedged close with moidores, ducats, and pistareens, yawned before his ravished eyes, and vomited forth their glittering contents.

Wolfert awoke a poorer man than ever. He had no heart to go about his daily concerns, which appeared so paltry and profitless, but sat all day long in the chimney corner, picturing to himself ingots and heaps of gold in the fire. The next night his dream was repeated. He was again in his garden digging, and laying open stores of hidden wealth. There was something very singular in this repetition. He passed another day of reverie, and though it was cleaning day, and the house, as usual in Dutch households, completely topsy-turvy, yet he sat unmoved amidst the general uproar.

The third night he went to bed with a palpitating heart. He put on his red nightcap wrong side outward, for good luck. It was deep midnight before his anxious mind could settle itself into sleep. Again the golden dream was repeated, and again he saw his garden teeming with ingots and money bags.

Wolfert rose the next morning in complete bewilderment. A dream, three times repeated, was never known to lie, and if so, his fortune was made.

In his agitation he put on his waistcoat with the hind part before, and this was a corroboration of good luck. He no longer doubted that a huge store of money lay buried somewhere in his cabbage field, coyly waiting to be sought for, and he repined at having so long been scratching about the surface of the soil instead of digging to the center.

He took his seat at the breakfast table, full of these speculations, asked his daughter to put a lump of gold into his tea, and on handing his wife a plate of slapjacks, begged her to help herself to a doubloon.

His grand care now was how to secure this immense treasure without its being known. Instead of his working regularly in his grounds in the daytime, he now stole from his bed at night, and with spade and pickax went to work to rip up and dig about his paternal acres, from one end to the other. In a little time the whole garden, which had presented such a goodly and regular appearance, with its phalanx of cabbages, like a vegetable army in battle array, was reduced to a scene of devastation, while the relentless Wolfert, with nightcap on head and lantern and spade in hand, stalked through the slaughtered ranks, the destroying angel of his own vegetable world.

Every morning bore testimony to the ravages of the preceding night in cabbages of all ages and conditions, from the tender sprout to the full-grown head, piteously rooted from their quiet beds like worthless weeds, and left to wither in the sunshine. In vain Wolfert's wife remonstrated; in vain his darling daughter wept over the destruction of some favorite marigold. "Thou shalt have gold of another-guess sort," he would cry, chucking her under the chin; "thou shalt have a string of crooked ducats for thy wedding necklace, my child." His family began really to fear that the poor man's wits were diseased. He muttered in his sleep at night about mines of wealth, about pearls and diamonds, and bars of gold. In the daytime he was moody and abstracted, and walked about as if in a trance. Dame Webber held frequent councils with all the old women of the neighborhood; scarce an hour in the day but a knot of them might be seen wagging their white caps together round her door, while the poor woman made some piteous recital. The daughter, too, was fain to seek for more frequent consolation from the stolen interviews of her favored swain, Dirk Waldron. The delectable little Dutch songs with which she used to dulcify the house grew less and less frequent, and she would forget her sewing, and look wistfully in her father's face as he sat pondering by the fireside. Wolfert caught her eye one day fixed on him thus anxiously, and for a moment was roused from his golden reveries. "Cheer up, my girl," said he exultingly; "why dost thou droop? Thou shalt hold up thy head one day with the Brinckerhoffs, and the Schermer-horns, the Van Hornes, and the Van Dams. By St. Nicholas, but the patroon himself shall be glad to get thee for his son!"

Amy shook her head at his vainglorious boast, and was more than ever in doubt of the soundness of the good man's intellect. In the meantime Wolfert went on digging and digging; but the field was ex-tensive, and as his dream had indicated no precise spot, he had to dig at random. The winter set in before one tenth of the scene of promise had been explored.

The ground became frozen hard, and the nights too cold for the labors of the spade.

No sooner, however, did the returning warmth of spring loosen the soil, and the small frogs begin to pipe in the meadows, but Wolfert resumed his labors with renovated zeal. Still, however, the hours of industry were reversed.

Instead of working cheerily all day, planting and setting out his vegetables, he remained thoughtfully idle, until the shades of night summoned him to his secret labors. In this way he continued to dig from night to night, and week to week, and month to month, but not a stiver did he find. On the contrary, the more he dug the poorer he grew. The rich soil of his garden was dug away, and the sand and gravel from beneath was thrown to the surface, until the whole field presented an aspect of sandy barrenness.

In the meantime, the seasons gradually rolled on. The little frogs which had piped in the meadows in early spring croaked as bullfrogs during the summer heats, and then sank into silence. The peach tree budded, blossomed, and bore its fruit. The swallows and martins came, twittered about the roof, built their nests, reared their young, held their congress along the eaves, and then winged their flight in search of another spring. The caterpillar spun its winding sheet, dangled in it from the great buttonwood tree before the house, turned into a moth, fluttered with the last sunshine of summer, and disappeared; and finally the leaves of the buttonwood tree turned yellow, then brown, then rustled one by one to the ground, and whirling about in little eddies of wind and dust, whispered that winter was at hand.

Wolfert gradually woke from his dream of wealth as the year de-clined. He had reared no crop for the supply of his household during the sterility of winter. The season was long and severe, and for the first time the family was really straitened in its comforts. By degrees a revul-sion of thought took place in Wolfert's mind, common to those whose golden dreams have been disturbed by pinching realities. The idea gradually stole upon him that he should come to want. He already considered himself one of the most unfortunate men in the province, having lost such an incalculable amount of undiscovered treasure, and now, when thousands of pounds had eluded his search, to be perplexed for shillings and pence was cruel in the extreme.

Haggard care gathered about his brow; he went about with a money-seeking air, his eyes bent downward into the dust, and carrying his hands in his pockets, as men are apt to do when they have nothing else to put into them. He could not even pass the city almshouse without giving it a rueful glance, as if destined to be his future abode.

The strangeness of his conduct and of his looks occasioned much speculation and remark. For a long time he was suspected of being crazy, and then everybody pitied him; and at length it began to be suspected that he was poor, and then everybody avoided him. The rich old burghers of his acquaintance met him outside the door when he called, entertained him hospitably on the threshold, pressed him warmly by the hand at parting, shook their heads as he walked away, with the kindhearted expression of "poor Wolfert," and turned a corner nimbly if by chance they saw him approaching as they walked the streets. Even the barber and the cobbler of the neighborhood, and a tattered tailor in an alley hard by, three of the poorest and merriest rogues in the world, eyed him with that abundant sympathy which usually attends a lack of means, and there is not a doubt but their pockets would have been at his command, only that they happened to be empty.

Thus everybody deserted the Webber mansion, as if poverty were contagious, like the plague—everybody but honest Dirk Waldron, who still kept up his stolen visits to the daughter, and indeed seemed to wax more affectionate as the fortunes of his mistress were on the wane.

Many months had elapsed since Wolfert had frequented his old resort, the rural inn. He was taking a long, lonely walk one Saturday afternoon, musing over his wants and disappointments, when his feet took instinctively their wonted direction, and on awaking out of a reverie, he found himself before the door of the inn. For some moments he hesitated whether to enter, but his heart yearned for companionship, and where can a ruined man find better companionship than at a tavern, where there is neither sober example nor sober advice to put him out of countenance?

Wolfert found several of the old frequenters of the inn at their usual posts and seated in their usual places; but one was missing, the great Ramm Rapelye, who for many years had filled the leather-bottomed chair of state. His place was supplied by a stranger, who seemed, however, completely at home in the chair and the tavern. He was rather under size, but deep-chested, square, and muscular. His broad shoulders, double joints, and bow knees gave tokens of prodigious strength. His face was dark and weather-beaten; a deep scar, as if from the slash of a cutlass, had almost divided his nose, and made a gash in his upper lip, through which his teeth shone like a bulldog's. A mop of iron-gray hair gave a grisly finish to this hard-favored visage. His dress was of an amphibious character. He wore an old hat edged with tarnished lace, and cocked in martial style on one side of his head; a rusty blue military coat with brass buttons; and a wide pair of short petticoat trousers—or rather breeches, for they were gathered up at the knees. He ordered everybody about him with an authoritative air, talking in a brattling voice that sounded like the crackling of thorns under a pot, damned the landlord and servants with perfect impunity, and was waited upon with greater obsequiousness than had ever been shown to the mighty Ramm himself.

Wolfert's curiosity was awakened to know who and what was this stranger who had thus usurped absolute sway in this ancient domain. Peechy Prauw took him aside into a remote corner of the hall, and there, in an under voice and with great caution, imparted to him all that he knew on the subject. The inn had been aroused several months before, on a dark, stormy night, by repeated long shouts that seemed like the howlings of a wolf. They came from the water side, and at length were distinguished to be hailing the house in the seafaring manner, "House ahoy!" The landlord turned out with his head waiter, tapster, hostler, and errand boy—that is to say, with his old Negro Cuff. On approaching the place whence the voice proceeded, they found this amphibious-looking personage at the water's edge, quite alone, and seated on a great oaken sea chest. How he came there—whether he had been set on shore from some boat, or had floated to land on his chest—nobody could tell, for he did not seem disposed to answer questions, and there was something in his looks and manners that put a stop to all questioning. Suffice it to say, he took possession of a corner room of the inn, to which his chest was removed with great difficulty. Here he had remained ever since, keeping about the inn and its vicinity. Sometimes, it is true, he disappeared for one, two, or three days at a time, going and returning without giving any notice or account of his movements. He always appeared to have plenty of money, though often of very strange, outlandish coinage, and he regularly paid his bill every evening before turning in. He had fitted up his room to his own fancy, having slung a hammock from the ceiling instead of a bed, and decorated the walls with rusty pistols and cutlasses of foreign workmanship. A greater part of his time was passed in this room, seated by the window, which commanded a wide view of the Sound, a short, old-fashioned pipe in his mouth, a glass of rum toddy at his elbow, and a pocket telescope in his hand, with which he reconnoitered every boat that moved upon the water. Large square-rigged vessels seemed to excite but little attention; but the moment he descried anything with a shoulder-of-mutton sail, or that a barge or yawl or jolly-boat hove in sight, up went the telescope, and he examined it with the most scrupulous attention.

All this might have passed without much notice, for in those times the province was so much the resort of adventurers of all characters and climes that any oddity in dress or behavior attracted but small attention. In a little while, however, this strange sea monster, thus strangely cast upon dry land, began to encroach upon the long established customs and customers of the place, and to interfere in a dictatorial manner in the affairs of the ninepin alley and the barroom, until in the end he usurped an absolute command over the whole inn. It was all in vain to attempt to withstand his authority. He was not exactly quarrelsome, but boisterous and peremptory, like one accustomed to tyrannize on a quarter-deck; and there was a dare-devil air about everything he said and did that inspired wariness in all bystanders. Even the half-pay officer, so long the hero of the club, was soon silenced by him, and the quiet burghers stared with wonder at seeing their inflammable man of war so readily and quietly extinguished.

And then the tales that he would tell were enough to make a peaceable man's hair stand on end. There was not a sea fight, nor marauding nor freebooting adventure that had happened within the last twenty years, but he seemed perfectly versed in it. He delighted to talk of the exploits of the buccaneers in the West Indies and on the Spanish Main. How his eyes would glisten as he described the waylaying of treasure ships; the desperate fights, yardarm and yardarm, broadside and broadside; the boarding and capturing huge Spanish galleons! With what chuckling relish would he describe the descent upon some rich Spanish colony, the rifling of a church, the sacking of a convent!

You would have thought you heard some gormandizer dilating upon the roasting of a savory goose at Michaelmas, as he described the roasting of some Spanish don to make him discover his treasure—a detail given with a minuteness that made every rich old burgher present turn uncomfortably in his chair.

All this would be told with infinite glee, as if he considered it an excellent joke, and then he would give such a tyrannical leer in the face of his next neighbor that the poor man would be fain to laugh out of sheer faint-heartedness. If anyone, however, pretended to contradict him in any of his stories, he was on fire in an instant. His very cocked hat assumed a momentary fierceness, and seemed to resent the contradiction. "How the devil should you know as well as I? I tell you it was as I say;" and he would at the same time let slip a broadside of thundering oaths and tremendous sea phrases, such as had never been heard before within these peaceful walls.

Indeed, the worthy burghers began to surmise that he knew more of those stories than mere hearsay. Day after day their conjectures concerning him grew more and more wild and fearful. The strangeness of his arrival, the strangeness of his manners, the mystery that surrounded him—all made him something incomprehensible in their eyes. He was a kind of monster of the deep to them; he was a merman, he was a behemoth, he was a leviathan—in short, they knew not what he was.

The domineering spirit of this boisterous sea urchin at length grew quite intolerable. He was no respecter of persons; he contradicted the richest burghers without hesitation; he took possession of the sacred elbow chair, which time out of mind had been the seat of sovereignty of the illustrious Ramm Rapelye. Nay, he even went so far, in one of his rough, jocular moods, as to slap that mighty burgher on the back, drink his toddy, and wink in his face—a thing scarcely to be believed. From this time Ramm Rapelye appeared no more at the inn. His example was followed by several of the most eminent customers, who were too rich to tolerate being bullied out of their opinions or being obliged to laugh at another man's jokes. The landlord was almost in despair; but he knew not how to get rid of this sea monster and his sea chest, who seemed both to have grown like fixtures, or excrescences on his establishment.

Such was the account whispered cautiously in Wolfert's ear by the narrator, Peechy Prauw, as he held him by the button in a corner of the hall, casting a wary glance now and then toward the door of the barroom, lest he should be overheard by the terrible hero of his tale.

Wolfert took his seat in a remote part of the room in silence, impressed with profound awe of this unknown, so versed in freebooting history. It was to him a wonderful instance of the revolutions of mighty empires, to find the venerable Ramm Rapelye thus ousted from the throne, and a rugged tarpaulin dictating from his elbow chair, hectoring the patriarchs, and filling this tranquil little realm with brawl and bravado.

The stranger was, on this evening, in a more than usually communicative mood, and was narrating a number of astounding stories of plunderings and burnings on the high seas. He dwelt upon them with peculiar relish, heightening the frightful particulars in proportion to their effect on his peaceful auditors. He gave a swaggering detail of the capture of a Spanish merchantman. She was lying becalmed during a long summer's day, just off from the island which was one of the lurking places of the pirates. They had reconnoitered her with their spyglasses from the shore, and ascertained her character and force. At night a picked crew of daring fellows set off for her in a whaleboat. They approached with muffled oars, as she lay rocking idly with the undulations of the sea, and her sails flapping against the masts. They were close under the stern before the guard on deck was aware of their approach. The alarm was given; the pirates threw hand grenades on deck, and sprang up the main chains, sword in hand.

The crew flew to arms, but in great confusion; some were shot down, others took refuge in the tops, others were driven overboard and drowned, while others fought hand to hand from the main deck to the quarter-deck, disputing gallantly every inch of ground. There were three Spanish gentlemen on board, with their ladies, who made the most desperate resistance. They defended the companion way, cut down several of their assailants, and fought like very devils, for they were maddened by the shrieks of the ladies from the cabin.

One of the dons was old, and soon dispatched. The other two kept their ground vigorously, even though the captain of the pirates was among their assailants. Just then there was a shout of victory from the main deck. "The ship is ours!" cried the pirates.

One of the dons immediately dropped his sword and surrendered; the other, who was a hot-headed youngster, and just married, gave the captain a slash in the face that laid all open. The captain just made out to articulate the words, "No quarter."

"And what did they do with their prisoners? " said Peechy Prauw eagerly.

"Threw them all overboard," was the answer. A dead pause followed the reply. Peechy Prauw sank quietly back, like a man who had unwarily stolen upon the lair of a sleeping lion. The honest burghers cast fearful glances at the deep scar slashed across the visage of the stranger, and moved their chairs a little farther off. The seaman, however, smoked on without moving a muscle, as though he either did not perceive, or did not regard, the unfavorable effect he had produced upon his hearers.

The half-pay officer was the first to break the silence, for he was continually tempted to make ineffectual head against this tyrant of the seas, and to regain his lost consequence in the eyes of his ancient companions. He now tried to match the gunpowder tales of the stranger by others equally tremendous. Kidd, as usual, was his hero, concerning whom he seemed to have picked up many of the floating traditions of the province. The seaman had always evinced a settled pique against the one-eyed warrior. On this occasion he listened with peculiar impatience. He sat with one arm akimbo, the other elbow on the table, the hand holding on to the small pipe he was pettishly puffing, his legs crossed, drumming with one foot on the ground, and casting every now and then the side glance of a basilisk at the prosing captain. At length the latter spoke of Kidd's having ascended the Hudson with some of his crew, to land his plunder in secrecy.

"Kidd up the Hudson!" burst forth the seaman, with a tremendous oath; "Kidd never was up the Hudson!"

"I tell you he was," said the other. "Aye, and they say he buried a quantity of treasure on the little flat that runs out into the river, called the Devil's Dans Kammer."

"The Devil's Dans Kammer in your teeth!" cried the seaman. "I tell you Kidd never was up the Hudson. What a plague do you know of Kidd and his haunts?"

"What do I know?" echoed the half-pay officer. "Why, I was in London at the time of his trial; aye, and I had the pleasure of seeing him hanged at Execution Dock."

"Then, sir, let me tell you that you saw as pretty a fellow hanged as ever trod shoe leather. Aye!" putting his face nearer to that of the officer, "and there was many a landlubber looked on that might much better have swung in his stead."

The half-pay officer was silenced; but the indignation thus pent up in his bosom glowed with intense vehemence in his single eye, which kindled like a coal.

Peechy Prauw, who never could remain silent, observed that the gentleman certainly was in the right. Kidd never did bury money up the Hudson, nor indeed in any of those parts, though many affirmed such to be the fact. It was Bradish and others of the buccaneers who had buried money, some said in Turtle Bay, others on Long Island, others in the neighborhood of Hell Gate. "Indeed," added he, "I recollect an adventure of Sam, the Negro fisherman, many years ago, which some think had something to do with the buccaneers. As we are all friends here, and as it will go no further, I'll tell it to you.

"Upon a dark night many years ago, as Black Sam was returning from fishing in Hell Gate—"

Here the story was nipped in the bud by a sudden movement from the unknown, who, laying his iron fist on the table, knuckles downward, with a quiet force that indented the very boards, and looking grimly over his shoulder, with the grin of an angry bear—

"Hearkee, neighbor," said he, with significant nodding of the head, "you'd better let the buccaneers and their money alone; they're not for old men and old women to meddle with. They fought hard for their money—they gave body and soul for it; and wherever it lies buried, depend upon it he must have a tug with the devil who gets it!

This sudden explosion was succeeded by a blank silence throughout the room. Peechy Prauw shrunk within himself, and even the one-eyed officer turned pale. Wolfert, who from a dark corner of the room had listened with intense eagerness to all this talk about buried treasure, looked with mingled awe and reverence at this bold buccaneer, for such he really suspected him to be. There was a chinking of gold and a sparkling of jewels in all his stories about the Spanish Main that gave a value to every period, and Wolfert would have given anything for the rummaging of the ponderous sea chest, which his imagination crammed full of golden chalices, crucifixes, and jolly round bags of doubloons.

The dead stillness that had fallen upon the company was at length interrupted by the stranger, who pulled out a prodigious watch of curious and ancient workmanship, and which in Wolfert's eyes had a decidedly Spanish look. On touching a spring, it struck ten o'clock, upon which the sailor called for his reckoning, and having paid it out of a handful of outlandish coin, he drank off the remainder of his beverage, and without taking leave of anyone, rolled out of the room, muttering to himself as he stamped upstairs to his chamber.

It was some time before the company could recover from the silence into which they had been thrown. The very footsteps of the stranger, which were heard now and then as he traversed his chamber, inspired awe.

Still the conversation in which they had been engaged was too interesting not to be resumed. A heavy thunder gust had gathered up unnoticed while they were lost in talk, and the torrents of rain that fell forbade all thoughts of setting off for home until the storm should subside. They drew nearer together, therefore, and entreated the worthy Peechy Prauw to continue the tale which had been so discourteously interrupted. He readily complied, whispering, however, in a tone scarcely above his breath, and drowned occasionally by the rolling of the thunder; and he would pause every now and then and listen, with evident awe, as he heard the heavy footsteps of the stranger pacing overhead. The following is the purport of his story:

Adventure of the Black Fisherman

Everybody knows Black Sam, the old Negro fisherman, or, as he is commonly called, "Mud Sam," who has fished about the Sound for the last half century. It is now many years since Sam, who was then as active a young Negro as any in the province, and worked on the farm of Killian Suydam on Long Island, having finished his day's work at an early hour, was fishing, one still summer evening, just about the neighborhood of Hell Gate.

He was in a light skiff, and being well acquainted with the currents and eddies, had shifted his station, according to the shifting of the tide, from the Hen and Chickens to the Hog's Back, from the Hog's Back to the Pot, and from the Pot to the Frying Pan; but in the eagerness of his sport he did not see that the tide was rapidly ebbing, until the roaring of the whirlpools and eddies warned him of his danger, and he had some difficulty in shooting his skiff from among the rocks and breakers, and getting to the point of Blackwell's Island. Here he cast anchor for some time, waiting the turn of the tide to enable him to return homeward. As the night set in, it grew blustering and gusty. Dark clouds came bundling up in the west, and now and then a growl of thunder or a flash of lightning told that a summer storm was at hand. Sam pulled over, therefore, under the lee of Manhattan Island, and, coasting along, came to a snug nook, just under a steep, beetling rock, where he fastened his skiff to the root of a tree that shot out from a cleft, and spread its broad branches like a canopy over the water. The gust came scouring along, the wind threw up the river in white surges, the rain rattled among the leaves, the thunder bellowed worse than that which is now bellowing, the lightning seemed to lick up the surges of the stream; but Sam, snugly sheltered under rock and tree, lay crouching in his skiff, rocking upon the billows until he fell asleep.

When he woke all was quiet. The gust had passed away, and only now and then a faint gleam of lightning in the east showed which way it had gone. The night was dark and moonless, and from the state of the tide Sam concluded it was near midnight. He was on the point of making loose his skiff to return homeward when he saw a light gleaming along the water from a distance, which seemed rapidly approaching. As it drew near he perceived it came from a lantern in the bow of a boat gliding along under shadow of the land. It pulled up in a small cove close to where he was. A man jumped on shore, and searching about with the lantern, exclaimed, "This is the place—here's the iron ring." The boat was then made fast, and the man, returning on board, assisted his comrades in conveying something heavy on shore. As the light gleamed among them, Sam saw that they were five stout, desperate-looking fellows, in red woolen caps, with a leader in a three-cornered hat, and that some of them were armed with dirks, or long knives, and pistols. They talked low to one another, and occasionally in some outlandish tongue which he could not understand.

On landing they made their way among the bushes, taking turns to relieve each other in lugging their burden up the rocky bank. Sam's curiosity was now fully aroused, so leaving his skiff he clambered silently up a ridge that overlooked their path. They had stopped to rest for a moment, and the leader was looking about among the bushes with his lantern." Have you brought the spades?" said one. "They are here," replied another, who had them on his shoulder. "We must dig deep, where there will be no risk of discovery," said a third.

A cold chill ran through Sam's veins. He fancied he saw before him a gang of murderers, about to bury their victim. His knees smote together. In his agitation he shook the branch of a tree with which he was supporting himself as he looked over the edge of the cliff.

"What's that?" cried one of the gang. "Some one stirs among the bushes!"

The lantern was held up in the direction of the noise. One of the red-caps cocked a pistol, and pointed it toward the very place where Sam was standing. He stood motionless, breathless, expecting the next moment to be his last. Fortunately his dingy complexion was in his favor, and made no glare among the leaves.

"'Tis no one," said the man with the lantern." What a plague! you would not fire off your pistol and alarm the country!"

The pistol was uncocked, the burden was resumed, and the party slowly toiled along the bank. Sam watched them as they went, the light sending back fitful gleams through the dripping bushes, and it was not till they were fairly out of sight that he ventured to draw breath freely. He now thought of getting back to his boat, and making his escape out of the reach of such dangerous neighbors; but curiosity was all-powerful. He hesitated, and lingered, and listened. By and by he heard the strokes of spades. "They are digging the grave!" said he to himself, and the cold sweat started upon his forehead. Every stroke of a spade, as it sounded through the silent groves, went to his heart. It was evident there was as little noise made as possible; everything had an air of terrible mystery and secrecy. Sam had a great relish for the horrible; a tale of murder was a treat for him, and he was a constant attendant at executions. He could not resist an impulse, in spite of every danger, to steal nearer to the scene of mystery, and overlook the midnight fellows at their work. He crawled along cautiously, therefore, inch by inch, stepping with the utmost care among the dry leaves, lest their rustling should betray him. He came at length to where a steep rock intervened between him and the gang, for he saw the light of their lantern shining up against the branches of the trees on the other side. Sam slowly and silently clambered up the surface of the rock, and raising his head above its naked edge, beheld the villains immediately below him, and so near that though he dreaded discovery he dared not withdraw lest the least movement should be heard. In this way he remained, with his round black face peering above the edge of the rock, like the sun just emerging above the edge of the horizon, or the round-cheeked moon on the dial of a clock.

The red-caps had nearly finished their work, the grave was filled up, and they were carefully replacing the turf. This done they scattered dry leaves over the place. "And now," said the leader, "I defy the devil himself to find it out."

"The murderers!" exclaimed Sam involuntarily.

The whole gang started, and looking up beheld the round black head of Sam just above them, his white eyes strained half out of their orbits, his white teeth chattering, and his whole visage shining with cold perspiration.

"We're discovered!" cried one. "Down with him!" cried another.

Sam heard the cocking of a pistol, but did not pause for the report. He scrambled over rock and stone, through brush and brier, rolled down banks like a hedgehog, scrambled up others like a catamount. In every direction he heard some one or other of the gang hemming him in. At length he reached the rocky ridge along the river; one of the red-caps was hard behind him. A steep rock like a wall rose directly in his way; it seemed to cut off all retreat, when fortunately he espied the strong, cord-like branch of a grapevine reaching half way down it. He sprang at it with the force of a desperate man, seized it with both hands, and, being young and agile, succeeded in swinging himself to the summit of the cliff. Here he stood in full relief against the sky, when the red-cap cocked his pistol and fired. The ball whistled by Sam's head. With the lucky thought of a man in an emergency, he uttered a yell, fell to the ground, and detached at the same time a fragment of the rock, which tumbled with a loud splash into the river.

"I've done his business," said the red-cap to one or two of his comrades as they arrived panting. "He'll tell no tales, except to the fishes in the river."

His pursuers now turned to meet their companions. Sam, sliding silently down the surface of the rock, let himself quietly into his skiff, cast loose the fastening, and abandoned himself to the rapid current, which in that place runs like a mill stream, and soon swept him off from the neighborhood. It was not, however, until he had drifted a great distance that he ventured to ply his oars, when he made his skiff dart like an arrow through the strait of Hell Gate, never heeding the danger of Pot, Frying Pan, nor Hog's Back itself, nor did he feel himself thoroughly secure until safely nestled in bed in the cockloft of the ancient farmhouse of the Suydams.

Here the worthy Peechy Prauw paused to take breath, and to take a sip of the gossip tankard that stood at his elbow. His auditors remained with open mouths and outstretched necks, gaping like a nest of swallows for an additional mouthful.

"And is that all?" exclaimed the half-pay officer.

"That's all that belongs to the story," said Peechy Prauw.

"And did Sam never find out what was buried by the red-caps?" said Wolfert eagerly, whose mind was haunted by nothing but ingots and doubloons.

"Not that I know of," said Peechy; "he had no time to spare from his work, and, to tell the truth, he did not like to run the risk of another race among the rocks. Besides, how should he recollect the spot where the grave had been dug? Everything would look so different by daylight. And then, where was the use of looking for a dead body when there was no chance of hanging the murderers?"

"Aye, but are you sure it was a dead body they buried?" said Wolfert.

"To be sure," cried Peechy Prauw exultingly. "Does it not haunt in the neighborhood to this very day?"

"Haunts!" exclaimed several of the party, opening their eyes still wider, and edging their chairs still closer.

"Aye, haunts," repeated Peechy; "have none of you heard of Father Red-cap, who haunts the old burned farmhouse in the woods, on the border of the Sound, near Hell Gate?"

"Oh, to be sure, I've heard tell of something of the kind, but then I took it for some old wives' fable."

"Old wives' fable or not," said Peechy Prauw, "that farmhouse stands hard by the very spot. It's been unoccupied time out of mind, and stands in a lonely part of the coast, but those who fish in the neighborhood have often heard strange noises there, and lights have been seen about the wood at night, and an old fellow in a red cap has been seen at the windows more than once, which people take to be the ghost of the body buried there. Once upon a time three soldiers took shelter in the building for the night, and rummaged it from top to bottom, when they found old Father Red-cap astride of a cider barrel in the cellar, with a jug in one hand and a goblet in the other. He offered them a drink out of his goblet, but just as one of the soldiers was putting it to his mouth—whew!—a flash of fire blazed through the cellar, blinded every mother's son of them for several minutes, and when they recovered their eyesight, jug, goblet, and Red-cap had vanished, and nothing but the empty cider barrel remained."

Here the half-pay officer, who was growing very muzzy and sleepy, and nodding over his liquor, with half-extinguished eye, suddenly gleamed up like an expiring rush-light.

"That's all fudge!" said he, as Peechy finished his last story.

"Well, I don't vouch for the truth of it myself," said Peechy Prauw, "though all the world knows that there's something strange about that house and grounds; but as to the story of Mud Sam, I believe it just as well as if it had happened to myself."

The deep interest taken in this conversation by the company had made them unconscious of the uproar abroad among the elements, when suddenly they were electrified by a tremendous clap of thunder. A lumbering crash followed instantaneously, shaking the building to its very foundation. All started from their seats, imagining it the shock of an earthquake, or that old Father Red-cap was coming among them in all his terrors. They listened for a moment, but only heard the rain pelting against the windows and the wind howling among the trees. The explosion was soon explained by the apparition of an old Negro's bald head thrust in at the door, his white goggle eyes contrasting with his jetty poll, which was wet with rain, and shone like a bottle. In a jargon but half intelligible he announced that the kitchen chimney had been struck with lightning.

A sullen pause of the storm, which now rose and sank in gusts, produced a momentary stillness. In this interval the report of a musket was heard, and a long shout, almost like a yell, resounded from the shores. Everyone crowded to the window; another musket shot was heard, and another long shout, mingled wildly with a rising blast of wind. It seemed as if the cry came up from the bosom of the waters, for though incessant flashes of lightning spread a light about the shore, no one was to be seen.

Suddenly the window of the room overhead was opened, and a loud halloo uttered by the mysterious stranger. Several hailings passed from one party to the other, but in a language which none of the company in the barroom could understand, and presently they heard the window closed, and a great noise overhead, as if all the furniture were pulled and hauled about the room. The Negro servant was summoned, and shortly afterwards was seen assisting the veteran to lug the ponderous sea chest downstairs.

The landlord was in amazement. "What, you are not going on the water in such a storm?"

"Storm!" said the other scornfully, "do you call such a sputter of weather a storm?"

"You'll get drenched to the skin; you'll catch your death!" said Peechy Prauw affectionately.

"Thunder and lightning!" exclaimed the veteran; "don't preach about weather to a man that has cruised in whirlwinds and torna-does."

The obsequious Peechy was again struck dumb. The voice from the water was heard once more in a tone of impatience; the bystanders stared with redoubled awe at this man of storms, who seemed to have come up out of the deep, and to be summoned back to it again. As, with the assistance of the Negro, he slowly bore his ponderous sea chest toward the shore, they eyed it with a superstitious feeling, half doubting whether he were not really about to embark upon it and launch forth upon the wild waves. They followed him at a distance with a lantern.

"Dowse the light!" roared the hoarse voice from the water. "No one wants light here!"

"Thunder and lightning!" exclaimed the veteran, turning short upon them; "back to the house with you!"

Wolfert and his companions shrank back in dismay. Still their curiosity would not allow them entirely to withdraw. A long sheet of lightning now flickered across the waves, and discovered a boat, filled with men, just under a rocky point, rising and sinking with the heaving surges, and swashing the waters at every heave. It was with difficulty held to the rocks by a boat hook, for the current rushed furiously round the point. The veteran hoisted one end of the lumbering sea chest on the gunwale of the boat, and seized the handle at the other end to lift it in, when the motion propelled the boat from the shore, the chest slipped off from the gunwale, and, sinking into the waves, pulled the veteran headlong after it. A loud shriek was uttered by all on shore, and a volley of execrations by those on board, but boat and man were hurried away by the rushing swiftness of the tide. A pitchy darkness succeeded.

Wolfert Webber, indeed, fancied that he distinguished a cry for help, and that he beheld the drowning man beckoning for assistance; but when the lightning again gleamed along the water all was void; neither man nor boat was to be seen—nothing but the dashing and weltering of the waves as they hurried past.

The company returned to the tavern to await the subsiding of the storm. They resumed their seats and gazed on each other with dismay. The whole transaction had not occupied five minutes, and not a dozen words had been spoken. When they looked at the oaken chair they could scarcely realize the fact that the strange being who had so lately tenanted it, full of life and Herculean vigor, should already be a corpse.

There was the very glass he had just drunk from; there lay the ashes from the pipe which he had smoked, as it were, with his last breath. As the worthy burghers pondered on these things, they felt a terrible conviction of the uncertainty of existence, and each felt as if the ground on which he stood was rendered less stable by his awful example.

As, however, the most of the company were possessed of that valuable philosophy which enables a man to bear up with fortitude against the misfortunes of his neighbors, they soon managed to console themselves for the tragic end of the veteran. The landlord was particularly happy that the poor dear man had paid his reckoning before he went, and made a kind of farewell speech on the occasion.

"He came," said he, "in a storm, and he went in a storm; he came in the night, and he went in the night; he came nobody knows whence, and he has gone nobody knows where. For aught I know he has gone to sea once more on his chest, and may land to bother some people on the other side of the world; though it's a thousand pities," added he, "if he has gone to Davy Jones's locker, that he had not left his own locker behind him."

"His locker! St. Nicholas preserve us! " cried Peechy Prauw. "I'd not have had that sea chest in the house for any money; I'll warrant he'd come racketing after it at nights, and making a haunted house of the inn. And as to his going to sea in his chest, I recollect what happened to Skipper Onderdonk's ship on his voyage from Amsterdam.

"The boatswain died during a storm, so they wrapped him up in a sheet, and put him in his own sea chest, and threw him overboard; but they neglected, in their hurry-skurry, to say prayers over him, and the storm raged and roared louder than ever, and they saw the dead man seated in his chest, with his shroud for a sail, coming hard after the ship, and the sea breaking before him in great sprays like fire; and there they kept scudding day after day and night after night, expecting every moment to go to wreck; and every night they saw the dead boatswain in his sea chest trying to get up with them, and they heard his whistle above the blasts of wind, and he seemed to send great seas, mountain high, after them that would have swamped the ship if they had not put up the deadlights. And so it went on till they lost sight of him in the fogs off Newfoundland, and supposed he had veered ship and stood for Dead Man's Isle. So much for burying a man at sea without saying prayers over him."

The thunder gust which had hitherto detained the company was now at an end. The cuckoo clock in the hall told midnight; everyone

pressed to depart, for seldom was such a late hour of the night tres-
passed on by these quiet burghers. As they sallied forth they found the
heavens once more serene. The storm which had lately obscured them
had rolled away, and lay piled up in fleecy masses on the horizon,
lighted up by the bright crescent of the moon, which looked like a
little silver lamp hung up in a palace of clouds.

The dismal occurrence of the night, and the dismal narrations they
had made, had left a superstitious feeling in every mind. They cast a
fearful glance at the spot where the buccaneer had disappeared, almost expecting to see him sailing on his chest in the cool moonshine.
The trembling rays glittered along the waters, but all was placid, and
the current dimpled over the spot where he had gone down. The party
huddled together in a little crowd as they repaired homeward, particularly when they passed a lonely field where a man had been murdered,
and even the sexton, who had to complete his journey alone, though
accustomed, one would think, to ghosts and goblins, went a long way
round rather than pass by his own churchyard.

Wolfert Webber had now carried home a fresh stock of stories and
notions to ruminate upon. These accounts of pots of money and Spanish treasures, buried here and there and everywhere about the rocks
and bays of these wild shores, made him almost dizzy. "Blessed St.
Nicholas!" ejaculated he, half aloud, "is it not possible to come upon
one of these golden hoards, and to make oneself rich in a twinkling?
How hard that I must go on, delving and delving, day in and day out,
merely to make a morsel of bread, when one lucky stroke of a spade
might enable me to ride in my carriage for the rest of my life!"

As he turned over in his thoughts all that had been told of the
singular adventure of the Negro fisherman, his imagination gave a
totally different complexion to the tale. He saw in the gang of red-caps
nothing but a crew of pirates burying their spoils, and his cupidity was
once more awakened by the possibility of at length getting on the
traces of some of this lurking wealth. Indeed, his infected fancy tinged
everything with gold. He felt like the greedy inhabitant of Baghdad
when his eyes had been greased with the magic ointment of the der-
vish, that gave him to see all the treasures of the earth. Caskets of
buried jewels, chests of ingots, and barrels of outlandish coins seemed
to court him from their concealments, and supplicate him to relieve
them from their untimely graves.

On making private inquiries about the grounds said to be haunted
by Feather Red-cap, he was more and more confirmed in his surmise.

He learned that the place had several times been visited by experienced money diggers who had heard Black Sam's story, though none of them had met with success. On the contrary, they had always been dogged with ill luck of some kind or other, in consequence, as Wolfert concluded, of not going to work at the proper time and with the proper ceremonials. The last attempt had been made by Cobus Quackenbos, who dug for a whole night, and met with incredible difficulty, for as fast as he threw one shovelful of earth out of the hole, two were thrown in by invisible hands. He succeeded so far, however, as to uncover an iron chest, when there was a terrible roaring, ramping, and raging of uncouth figures about the hole, and at length a shower of blows, dealt by invisible cudgels, fairly belabored him off of the forbidden ground. This Cobus Quackenbos had declared on his deathbed, so that there could not be any doubt of it. He was a man that had devoted many years of his life to money digging, and it was thought would have ultimately succeeded had he not died recently of a brain fever in the almshouse.

Wolfert Webber was now in a worry of trepidation and impatience, fearful lest some rival adventurer should get a scent of the buried gold. He determined privately to seek out the black fisherman, and get him to serve as guide to the place where he had witnessed the mysterious scene of interment. Sam was easily found, for he was one of those old habitual beings that live about a neighborhood until they wear themselves a place in the public mind, and become, in a manner, public characters. There was not an unlucky urchin about town that did not know Sam the fisherman, and think that he had a right to play his tricks upon the old Negro. Sam had led an amphibious life for more than half a century, about the shores of the bay and the fishing grounds of the Sound. He passed the greater part of his time on and in the water, particularly about Hell Gate, and might have been taken, in bad weather, for one of the hobgoblins that used to haunt that strait. There would he be seen, at all times and in all weathers, sometimes in his skiff, anchored among the eddies, or prowling like a shark about some wreck, where the fish are supposed to be most abundant; sometimes seated on a rock from hour to hour, looking, in the mist and drizzle, like a solitary heron watching for its prey. He was well acquainted with every hole and corner of the Sound, from the Wallabout to Hell Gate, and from Hell Gate unto the Devil's Stepping-Stones; and it was even affirmed that he knew all the fish in the river by their Christian names.

Wolfert found him at his cabin, which was not much larger than a tolerable dog house. It was rudely constructed of fragments of wrecks and driftwood, and built on the rocky shore at the foot of the old fort, just about what at present forms the point of the Battery. A "very ancient and fishlike smell" pervaded the place. Oars, paddles, and fishing rods were leaning against the wall of the fort, a net was spread on the sand to dry, a skiff was drawn up on the beach, and at the door of his cabin was Mud Sam himself, indulging in the true Negro luxury of sleeping in the sunshine.

Many years had passed away since the time of Sam's youthful adventure, and the snows of many a winter had grizzled the knotty wool upon his head. He perfectly recollected the circumstances, however, for he had often been called upon to relate them, though in his version of the story he differed in many points from Peechy Prauw, as is not infrequently the case with authentic historians. As to the subsequent researches of money diggers, Sam knew nothing about them; they were matters quite out of his line; neither did the cautious Wolfert care to disturb his thoughts on that point. His only wish was to secure the old fisherman as a pilot to the spot, and this was readily effected. The long time that had intervened since his nocturnal adventure had effaced all Sam's awe of the place, and the promise of a trifling reward roused him at once from his sleep and his sunshine.

The tide was adverse to making the expedition by water, and Wolfert was too impatient to get to the land of promise to wait for its turning; they set off, therefore, by land. A walk of four or five miles brought them to the edge of a wood, which at that time covered the greater part of the eastern side of the island. It was just beyond the pleasant region of Bloomen-dael. Here they struck into a long lane, straggling among trees and bushes very much overgrown with weeds and mullein stalks, as if but seldom used, and so completely overshadowed as to enjoy but a kind of twilight. Wild vines entangled the trees and flaunted in their faces; brambles and briers caught their clothes as they passed; the garter snake glided across their path; the spotted toad hopped and waddled before them; and the restless catbird mewed at them from every thicket. Had Wolfert Webber been deeply read in romantic legend he might have fancied himself entering upon forbidden, enchanted ground, or that these were some of the guardians set to keep watch upon buried treasure. As it was, the loneliness of the place, and the wild stories connected with it, had their effect upon his mind.

On reaching the lower end of the lane they found themselves near the shore of the Sound, in a kind of amphitheater surrounded by forest trees. The area had once been a grass plot, but was now shagged with briers and rank weeds. At one end, and just on the river bank, was a ruined building, little better than a heap of rubbish, with a stack of chimneys rising like a solitary tower out of the center. The current of the Sound rushed along just below it, with wildly grown trees drooping their branches into its waves. Wolfert had not a doubt that this was the haunted house of Father Red-cap, and called to mind the story of Peechy Prauw. The evening was approaching, and the light, falling dubiously among the woody places, gave a melancholy tone to the scene well calculated to foster any lurking feeling of awe or superstition. The nighthawk, wheeling about in the highest regions of the air, emitted his peevish, boding cry. The woodpecker gave a lonely tap now and then on some hollow tree, and the firebird streamed by them with his deep red plumage.

They now came to an enclosure that had once been a garden. It extended along the foot of a rocky ridge, but was little better than a wilderness of weeds, with here and there a matted rosebush, or a peach or plum tree, grown wild and ragged, and covered with moss. At the lower end of the garden they passed a kind of vault in the side of a bank, facing the water. It had the look of a root house. The door, though decayed, was still strong, and appeared to have been recently patched up. Wolfert pushed it open. It gave a harsh grating upon its hinges, and striking against something like a box, a rattling sound ensued, and a skull rolled on the floor. Wolfert drew back shuddering, but was reassured on being informed by the Negro that this was a family vault, belonging to one of the old Dutch families that owned this estate, an assertion corroborated by the sight of coffins of various sizes piled within. Sam had been familiar with all these scenes when a boy, and now knew that he could not be far from the place of which they were in quest.

They now made their way to the water's edge, scrambling along ledges of rocks that overhung the waves, and obliged often to hold by shrubs and grapevines to avoid slipping into the deep and hurried stream. At length they came to a small cove, or rather indent of the shore. It was protected by steep rocks, and overshadowed by a thick copse of oaks and chestnuts, so as to be sheltered and almost concealed. The beach shelved gradually within the cove, but, the current swept deep and black and rapid along its jutting points. The Negro paused, raised his remnant of a hat, and scratched his grizzled poll for a moment, as he regarded this nook; then suddenly clapping his hands, he stepped exultingly forward, and pointed to a large iron ring, stapled firmly in the rock, just where a broad shelf of stone furnished a commodious landing place.

It was the very spot where the red-caps had landed. Years had changed the more perishable features of the scene; but rock and iron yield slowly to the influence of time. On looking more closely Wolfert remarked three crosses cut in the rock just above the ring, which had no doubt some mysterious signification. Old Sam now readily recognized the overhanging rock under which his skiff had been sheltered during the thunder gust. To follow up the course which the midnight gang had taken, however, was a harder task. His mind had been so much taken up on that eventful occasion by the persons of the drama as to pay but little attention to the scenes, and these places looked so different by night and day. After wandering about for some time, however, they came to an opening among the trees which Sam thought resembled the place. There was a ledge of rock of moderate height, like a wall, on one side, which he thought might be the very ridge whence he had overlooked the diggers. Wolfert examined it narrowly, and at length discovered three crosses similar to those on the above ring, cut deeply into the face of the rock, but nearly obliterated by moss that had grown over them. His heart leaped with joy, for he doubted not they were the private marks of the buccaneers. All now that remained was to ascertain the precise spot where the treasure lay buried, for otherwise he might dig at random in the neighborhood of the crosses, without coming upon the spoils, and he had already had enough of such profitless labor. Here, however, the old Negro was perfectly at a loss, and indeed perplexed him by a variety of opinions, for his recollections were all confused.

Sometimes he declared it must have been at the foot of a mulberry tree hard by; then beside a great white stone; then under a small green knoll, a short distance from the ledge of rocks, until at length Wolfert became as bewildered as himself.

The shadows of evening were now spreading themselves over the woods, and rock and tree began to mingle together. It was evidently too late to attempt anything further at present, and, indeed, Wolfert had come unprovided with implements to prosecute his researches. Satisfied, therefore, with having ascertained the place, he took note of all its landmarks, that he might recognize it again, and set out on his return homeward, resolved to prosecute this golden enterprise without delay.

The leading anxiety which had hitherto absorbed every feeling being now in some measure appeased, fancy began to wander, and to conjure up a thousand shapes and chimeras as he returned through this haunted region. Pirates hanging in chains seemed to swing from every tree, and he almost expected to see some Spanish don, with his throat cut from ear to ear, rising slowly out of the ground, and shaking the ghost of a money bag.

Their way back lay through the desolate garden, and Wolfert's nerves had arrived at so sensitive a state that the flitting of a bird, the rustling of a leaf, or the falling of a nut was enough to startle him. As they entered the confines of the garden, they caught sight of a figure at a distance advancing slowly up one of the walks, and bending under the weight of a burden. They paused and regarded him attentively. He wore what appeared to be a woolen cap, and, still more alarming, of a most sanguinary red. The figure moved slowly on, ascended the bank, and stopped at the very door of the sepulchral vault. Just before entering it he looked around. What was the affright of Wolfert when he recognized the grisly visage of the drowned buccaneer! He uttered an ejaculation of horror. The figure slowly raised his iron fist and shook it with a terrible menace. Wolfert did not pause to see any more, but hurried off as fast as his legs could carry him, nor was Sam slow in following at his heels, having all his ancient terrors revived. Away, then, did they scramble through bush and brake, horribly frightened at every bramble that tugged at their skirts, nor did they pause to breathe until they had blundered their way through this perilous wood, and fairly reached the highroad to the city.

Several days elapsed before Wolfert could summon courage enough to prosecute the enterprise, so much had he been dismayed by the apparition, whether living or dead, of the grisly buccaneer. In the meantime, what a conflict of mind did he suffer! He neglected all his concerns, was moody and restless all day, lost his appetite, wandered in his thoughts and words, and committed a thousand blunders. His rest was broken, and when he fell asleep the nightmare, in shape of a huge money bag, sat squatted upon his breast. He babbled about incalculable sums, fancied himself engaged in money-digging, threw the bedclothes right and left, in the idea that he was shoveling away the dirt, groped under the bed in quest of the treasure, and lugged forth, as he supposed, an inestimable pot of gold.

Dame Webber and her daughter were in despair at what they conceived a returning touch of insanity. There are two family oracles, one or other of which Dutch housewives consult in all cases of great doubt and perplexity—the dominie and the doctor. In the present instance they repaired to the doctor. There was at that time a little dark, moldy man of medicine, famous among the old wives of the Manhattoes for his skill, not only in the healing art, but in all matters of strange and mysterious nature. His name was Dr. Knipperhausen, but he was more commonly known by the appellation of the "High German Doctor." To him did the poor women repair for counsel and assistance touching the mental vagaries of Wolfert Webber.

They found the doctor seated in his little study, clad in his dark camlet robe of knowledge, with his black velvet cap, after the manner of Boerhaave, Van Helmont, and other medical sages, a pair of green spectacles set in black horn upon his clubbed nose, and poring over a German folio that reflected back the darkness of his physiognomy. The doctor listened to their statement of the symptoms of Wolfert's malady with profound attention, but when they came to mention his raving about buried money the little man pricked up his ears. Alas, poor women! they little knew the aid they had called in.

Dr. Knipperhausen had been half his life engaged in seeking the short cuts to fortune, in quest of which so many a long lifetime is wasted. He had passed some years of his youth among the Harz mountains of Germany, and had derived much valuable instruction from the miners touching the mode of seeking treasure buried in the earth. He had prosecuted his studies, also, under a traveling sage who united the mysteries of medicine with magic and legerdemain. His mind, therefore, had become stored with all kinds of mystic lore; he had dabbled a little in astrology, alchemy, divination; knew how to detect stolen money, and to tell where springs of water lay hidden; in a word, by the dark nature of his knowledge he had acquired the name of the "High German Doctor," which is pretty nearly equivalent to that of necromancer. The doctor had often heard rumors of treasure being buried in various parts of the island, and had long been anxious to get on the traces of it. No sooner were Wolfert's waking and sleeping vagaries confided to him than he beheld in them the confirmed symptoms of a case of money digging, and lost no time in probing it to the bottom. Wolfert had long been sorely oppressed in mind by the golden secret, and as a family physician is a kind of father confessor, he was glad of any opportunity of unburdening himself. So far from curing, the doctor caught the malady from his patient. The circumstances unfolded to him awakened all his cupidity; he had not a doubt of money being buried somewhere in the neighborhood of the mysterious crosses, and offered to join Wolfert in the search. He informed him that much secrecy and caution must be observed in enterprises of the kind; that money is only to be dug for at night, with certain forms and ceremonies and burning of drugs, the repeating of mystic words, and, above all, that the seekers must first be provided with a divining rod, which had the wonderful property of pointing to the very spot on the surface of the earth under which treasure lay hidden. As the doctor had given much of his mind to these matters he charged himself with all the necessary preparations, and, as the quarter of the moon was propitious, he undertook to have the divining rod ready by a certain night.

Wolfert's heart leaped with joy at having met with so learned and able a coadjutor. Everything went on secretly but swimmingly. The doctor had many consultations with his patient, and the good women of the household lauded the comforting effect of his visits. In the meantime the wonderful divining rod, that great key to nature's secrets, was duly prepared. The doctor had thumbed over all his books of knowledge for the occasion, and the black fisherman was engaged to take them in his skiff to the scene of enterprise, to work with spade and pickax in unearthing the treasure, and to freight his bark with the weighty spoils they were certain of finding.

At length the appointed night arrived for this perilous undertaking. Before Wolfert left his home he counseled his wife and daughter to go to bed, and feel no alarm if he should not return during the night. Like reasonable women, on being told not to feel alarm they fell immediately into a panic. They saw at once by his manner that something unusual was in agitation; all their fears about the unsettled state of his mind were revived with tenfold force; they hung about him, entreating him not to expose himself to the night air, but all in vain. When once Wolfert was mounted on his hobby, it was no easy manner to get him out of the saddle. It was a clear, starlight night when he issued out of the portal of the Webber palace. He wore a large flapped hat, tied under the chin with a handkerchief of his daughter's, to secure him from the night damp, while Dame Webber threw her long red cloak about his shoulders, and fastened it round his neck.

The doctor had been no less carefully armed and accoutered by his housekeeper, the vigilant Frau Ilsy, and sallied forth in his camlet robe by way of surcoat, his black velvet cap under his cocked hat, a thick clasped book under his arm, a basket of drugs and dried herbs in one hand, and in the other the miraculous rod of divination.

The great church clock struck ten as Wolfert and the doctor passed by the churchyard, and the watchman bawled in hoarse voice a long and doleful "All's well!" A deep sleep had already fallen upon this primitive little burgh; nothing disturbed this awful silence excepting now and then the bark of some profligate, night-walking dog, or the serenade of some romantic cat. It is true Wolfert fancied more than once that he heard the sound of a stealthy footfall at a distance behind them; but it might have been merely the echo of their own steps along the quiet streets. He thought also at one time that he saw a tall figure skulking after them, stopping when they stopped and moving on as they proceeded; but the dim and uncertain lamplight threw such vague gleams and shadows that this might all have been mere fancy.

They found the old fisherman waiting for them, smoking his pipe in the stern of the skiff, which was moored just in front of his little cabin. A pickax and spade were lying in the bottom of the boat, with a dark lantern, and a stone bottle of good Dutch courage, in which honest Sam no doubt put even more faith than Dr. Knipperhausen in his drugs.

Thus, then, did these three worthies embark in their cockleshell of a skiff upon this nocturnal expedition, with a wisdom and valor equaled only by the three wise men of Gotham, who adventured to sea in a bowl. The tide was rising and running rapidly up the Sound. The current bore them along, almost without the aid of an oar. The profile of the town lay all in shadow. Here and there a light feebly glimmered from some sick chamber, or from the cabin window of some vessel at anchor in the stream. Not a cloud obscured the deep, starry firmament, the lights of which wavered on the surface of the placid river, and a shooting meteor, streaking its pale course in the very direction they were taking, was interpreted by the doctor into a most propitious omen.

In a little while they glided by the point of Corlear's Hook, with the rural inn which had been the scene of such night adventures. The family had retired to rest, and the house was dark and still. Wolfert felt a chill pass over him as they passed the point where the buccaneer had disappeared. He pointed it out to Dr. Knipperhausen. While regarding it they thought they saw a boat actually lurking at the very place; but the shore cast such a shadow over the border of the water that they could discern nothing distinctly. They had not proceeded far when they heard the low sounds of distant oars, as if cautiously pulled. Sam plied his oars with redoubled vigor, and knowing all the eddies and currents of the stream, soon left their followers, if such they were, far astern.

In a little while they stretched across Turtle Bay and Kip's Bay, then shrouded themselves in the deep shadows of the Manhattan shore, and glided swiftly along, secure from observation. At length the Negro shot his skiff into a little cove, darkly embowered by trees, and made it fast to the well-known iron ring. They now landed, and lighting the lantern gathered their various implements and proceeded slowly through the bushes. Every sound startled them, even that of their own footsteps among the dry leaves, and the hooting of a screech owl, from the shattered chimney of the neighboring ruin, made their blood run cold.

In spite of all Wolfert's caution in taking note of the landmarks, it was some time before they could find the open place among the trees, where the treasure was supposed to be buried. At length they came to the ledge of rock, and on examining its surface by the aid of the lantern, Wolfert recognized the three mystic crosses. Their hearts beat quick, for the momentous trial was at hand that was to determine their hopes.

The lantern was now held by Wolfert Webber, while the doctor produced the divining rod. It was a forked twig, one end of which was grasped firmly in each hand, while the center, forming the stem, pointed perpendicularly upward. The doctor moved his wand about, within a certain distance of the earth, from place to place, but for some time without any effect, while Wolfert kept the light of the lantern turned full upon it, and watched it with the most breathless interest. At length the rod began slowly to turn. The doctor grasped it with greater earnestness, his hands trembling with the agitation of his mind. The wand continued to turn gradually, until at length the stem had reversed its position, and pointed perpendicularly downward, and remained pointing to one spot as fixedly as the needle to the pole.

"This is the spot!" said the doctor, in an almost inaudible tone. Wolfert's heart was in his throat.

"Shall I dig?" said the Negro, grasping the spade.

"Pots tausend, no!" replied the little doctor hastily. He now ordered his companions to keep close by him, and to maintain the most inflexible silence; that certain precautions must be taken and ceremonies used to prevent the evil spirits which kept about buried treasure from doing them any harm. He then drew a circle about the place, enough to include the whole party. He next gathered dry twigs and leaves and made a fire, upon which he threw certain drugs and dried herbs which he had brought in his basket. A thick smoke rose, diffusing a potent odor savoring marvelously of brimstone and asafetida, which, however grateful it might be to the olfactory nerves of spirits, nearly strangled poor Wolfert, and produced a fit of coughing and wheezing that made the whole grove resound. Dr. Knipperhausen then unclasped the volume which he had brought under his arm, which was printed in red and black characters in German text. While Wolfert held the lantern, the doctor, by the aid of his spectacles, read off several forms of conjuration in Latin and German. He then ordered Sam to seize the pickax and proceed to work. The close-bound soil gave obstinate signs of not having been disturbed for many a year. After having picked his way through the surface, Sam came to a bed of sand and gravel, which he threw briskly to right and left with the spade."

Hark!" said Wolfert, who fancied he heard a trampling among the dry leaves and a rustling through the bushes. Sam paused for a moment, and they listened. No footstep was near. The bat flitted by them in silence; a bird, roused from its roost by the light which glared up among the trees, flew circling about the flame. In the profound stillness of the woodland they could distinguish the current rippling along the rocky shore, and the distant murmuring and roaring of Hell Gate.

The Negro continued his labors, and had already dug a considerable hole. The doctor stood on the edge, reading formulae every now and then from his black-letter volume, or throwing more drugs and herbs upon the fire, while Wolfert bent anxiously over the pit, watching every stroke of the spade. Anyone witnessing the scene thus lighted up by fire, lantern, and the reflection of Wolfert's red mantle, might have mistaken the little doctor for some foul magician, busied in his incantations, and the grizzly- headed Negro for some swart goblin obedient to his commands. At length the spade of the fisherman struck upon something that sounded hollow. The sound vibrated to Wolfert's heart. He struck his spade again.

"'Tis a chest," said Sam.

"Full of gold, I'll warrant it!" cried Wolfert, clasping his hands with rapture.

Scarcely had he uttered the words when a sound from above caught his ear. He cast up his eyes, and lo! by the expiring light of the fire he beheld, just over the disk of the rock, what appeared to be the grim visage of the drowned buccaneer, grinning hideously down upon him.

Wolfert gave a loud cry and let fall the lantern. His panic communicated itself to his companions. The Negro leaped out of the hole, the doctor dropped his book and basket, and began to pray in German. All was horror and confusion. The fire was scattered about, the lantern extinguished. In their hurry-scurry they ran against and confounded one another. They fancied a legion of hobgoblins let loose upon them, and that they saw, by the fitful gleams of the scattered embers, strange figures, in red caps, gibbering and ramping around them. The doctor ran one way, the Negro another, and Wolfert made for the water side. As he plunged struggling onward through brush and brake, he heard the tread of some one in pursuit. He scrambled frantically forward. The footsteps gained upon him. He felt himself grasped by his cloak, when suddenly his pursuer was attacked in turn; a fierce fight and struggle ensued, a pistol was discharged that lit up rock and bush for a second, and showed two figures grappling together; all was then darker than ever. The contest continued, the combatants clinched each other, and panted and groaned, and rolled among the rocks. There was snarling and growling as of a cur, mingled with curses, in which Wolfert fancied he could recognize the voice of the buccaneer. He would fain have fled, but he was on the brink of a precipice, and could go no farther.

Again the parties were on their feet, again there was a tugging and struggling, as if strength alone could decide the combat, until one was precipitated from the brow of the cliff, and sent headlong into the deep stream that whirled below. Wolfert heard the plunge, and a kind of strangling, bubbling murmur, but the darkness of the night hid everything from him, and the swiftness of the current swept everything instantly out of hearing. One of the combatants was disposed of, but whether friend or foe Wolfert could not tell, nor whether they might not both be foes. He heard the survivor approach, and his terror revived. He saw, where the profile of the rocks rose against the horizon, a human form advancing. He could not be mistaken; it must be the buccaneer. Whither should he fly?—a precipice was on one side, a murderer on the other. The enemy approached—he was close at hand. Wolfert attempted to let himself down the face of the cliff. His cloak caught in a thorn that grew on the edge. He was jerked from off his feet, and held dangling in the air, half choked by the string with which his careful wife had fastened the garment around his neck. Wolfert thought his last moment was arrived; already had he committed his soul to St. Nicholas, when the string broke, and he tumbled down the bank, bumping from rock to rock and bush to bush, and leaving the red cloak fluttering like a bloody banner in the air.

It was a long while before Wolfert came to himself. When he opened his eyes, the ruddy streaks of morning were already shooting up the sky. He found himself grievously battered, and lying in the bottom of a boat. He attempted to sit up, but was too sore and stiff to move. A voice requested him in a friendly accents to lie still. He turned his eyes toward the speaker; it was Dirk Waldron. He had dogged the party, at the earnest request of Dame Webber and her daughter, who, with the laudable curiosity of their sex, had pried into the secret consultations of Wolfert and the doctor. Dirk had been completely distanced in following the light skiff of the fisherman, and had just come in time to rescue the poor money digger from his pursuer.

Thus ended this perilous enterprise. The doctor and Black Sam severally found their way back to the Manhattoes, each having some dreadful tale of peril to relate. As to poor Wolfert, instead of returning in triumph, laden with bags of gold, he was borne home on a shutter, followed by a rabble-rout of curious urchins. His wife and daughter saw the dismal pageant from a distance, and alarmed the neighborhood with their cries; they thought the poor man had suddenly settled the great debt of nature in one of his wayward moods. Finding him, however, still living, they had him speedily to bed, and a jury of old matrons of the neighborhood assembled to determine how he should be doctored.

The whole town was in a buzz with the story of the money-diggers. Many repaired to the scene of the previous night's adventures; but though they found the very place of the digging, they discovered nothing that compensated them for their trouble. Some say they found the fragments of an oaken chest, and an iron pot lid, which savored strongly of hidden money, and that in the old family vault there were traces of bales and boxes; but this is all very dubious.

In fact, the secret of all this story has never to this day been discovered. Whether any treasure were ever actually buried at that place; whether, if so, it were carried off at night by those who had buried it; or whether it still remains there under the guardianship of gnomes and spirits until it shall be properly sought for, is all matter of conjecture.

For my part, I incline to the latter opinion, and make no doubt that great sums lie buried, both there and in other parts of this island and its neighborhood, ever since the times of the buccaneers and the Dutch colonists; and I would earnestly recommend the search after them to such of my fellow citizens as are not engaged in any other speculations.

There were many conjectures formed, also, as to who and what was the strange man of the seas, who had domineered over the little fraternity at Corlear's Hook for a time, disappeared so strangely, and reappeared so fearfully. Some supposed him a smuggler stationed at that place to assist his comrades in landing their goods among the rocky coves of the island. Others, that he was one of the ancient comrades of Kidd or Bradish, returned to convey away treasures formerly hidden in the vicinity.

The only circumstance that throws anything like a vague light on this mysterious matter is a report which prevailed of a strange, foreign-built shallop, with much the look of a picaroon, having been seen hovering about the Sound for several days without landing or reporting herself, though boats were seen going to and from her at night; and that she was seen standing out of the mouth of the harbor, in the gray of the dawn, after the catastrophe of the money-diggers.

I must not omit to mention another report, also, which I confess is rather apocryphal, of the buccaneer who is supposed to have been drowned, being seen before daybreak, with a lantern in his hand, seated astride of his great sea chest, and sailing through Hell Gate, which just then began to roar and bellow with redoubled fury.

While all the gossip world was thus filled with talk and rumor, poor Wolfert lay sick and sorrowfully in his bed, bruised in body and sorely beaten down in mind. His wife and daughter did all they could to bind up his wounds, both corporal and spiritual. The good old dame never stirred from his bedside, where she sat knitting from morning till night, while his daughter busied herself about him with the fondest care. Nor did they lack assistance from abroad. Whatever may be said of the desertion of friends in distress, they had no complaint of the kind to make. Not an old wife of the neighborhood but abandoned her work to crowd to the mansion of Wolfert Webber, to inquire after his health and the particulars of his story. Not one came, moreover, without her little pipkin of pennyroyal, sage, balm, or other herb tea, delighted at an opportunity of signalizing her kindness and her doctorship. What drenchings did not the poor Wolfert undergo, and all in vain! It was a moving sight to behold him wasting away day by day, growing thinner and thinner and ghastlier and ghastlier, and staring with rueful visage from under an old patchwork counterpane, upon the jury of matrons kindly assembled to sigh and groan and look unhappy around him.

Dirk Waldron was the only being that seemed to shed a ray of sunshine into this house of mourning. He came in with cheery look and manly spirit, and tried to reanimate the expiring heart of the poor money digger, but it was all in vain. Wolfert was completely done over. If anything was wanting to complete his despair, it was a notice, served upon him in the midst of his distress, that the corporation was about to run a new street through the very center of his cabbage garden. He now saw nothing before him but poverty and ruin; his last reliance, the garden of his forefathers, was to be laid waste, and what then was to become of his poor wife and child?

His eyes filled with tears as they followed the dutiful Amy out of the room one morning. Dirk Waldron was seated beside him; Wolfert grasped his hand, pointed after his daughter, and for the first time since his illness broke the silence he had maintained. "I am going!" said he, shaking his head feebly, "and when I am gone, my poor daughter—" "Leave her to me, father!" said Dirk manfully; "I'll take care of her!"

Wolfert looked up in the face of the cheery, strapping youngster, and saw there was none better able to take care of a woman. "Enough," said he, "she is yours! And now fetch me a lawyer—let me make my will and die."

The lawyer was brought—a dapper, bustling, round-headed little man, Roorback (or Rollebuck, as it was pronounced) by name. At the sight of him the women broke into loud lamentations, for they looked upon the signing of a will as the signing of a death warrant. Wolfert made a feeble motion for them to be silent. Poor Amy buried her face and her grief in the bed curtain. Dame Webber resumed her knitting to hide her distress, which betrayed itself, however, in a pellucid tear, which trickled silently down, and hung at the end of her peaked nose; while the cat, the only unconcerned member of the family, played with the good dame's ball of worsted as it rolled about the floor.

Wolfert lay on his back, his nightcap drawn over his forehead, his eyes closed, his whole visage the picture of death. He begged the lawyer to be brief, for he felt his end approaching, and that he had no time to lose. The lawyer nibbed his pen, spread out his paper, and prepared to write.

"I give and bequeath," said Wolfert faintly, "my small farm—"

"What! all?" exclaimed the lawyer.

Wolfert half opened his eyes and looked upon the lawyer.

"Yes, all," said he.

"What! all that great patch of land with cabbages and sunflowers, which the corporation is just going to run a main street through?"

"The same," said Wolfert, with a heavy sigh, and sinking back upon his pillow.

"I wish him joy that inherits it!" said the little lawyer, chuckling and rubbing his hands involuntarily.

"What do you mean?" said Wolfert, again opening his eyes.

"That he'll be one of the richest men in the place," cried little Rollebuck.

The expiring Wolfert seemed to step back from the threshold of existence; his eyes again lighted up; he raised himself in his bed, shoved back his red worsted nightcap, and stared broadly at the lawyer.

"You don't say so!" exclaimed he.

"Faith but I do!" rejoined the other. "Why, when that great field and that huge meadow come to be laid out in streets and cut up into snug building lots—why, whoever owns it need not pull off his hat to the patroon!"

"Say you so?" cried Wolfert, half thrusting one leg out of bed; "why, then, I think I'll not make my will yet."

To the surprise of everybody, the dying man actually recovered. The vital spark, which had glimmered faintly in the socket, received fresh fuel from the oil of gladness which the little lawyer poured into his soul. It once more burned up into a flame.

Give physic to the heart, ye who would revive the body of a spirit-broken man! In a few days Wolfert left his room; in a few days more his table was covered with deeds, plans of streets and building lots. Little Rollebuck was constantly with him, his right hand man and adviser, and instead of making his will assisted in the more agreeable task of making his fortune. In fact Wolfert Webber was one of those worthy Dutch burghers of the Manhattoes whose fortunes have been made, in a manner, in spite of themselves; who have tenaciously held on to their hereditary acres, raising turnips and cabbages about the skirts of the city, hardly able to make both ends meet, until the corporation has cruelly driven streets through their abodes, and they have suddenly awakened out of their lethargy, and, to their astonishment, found themselves rich men.

Before many months had elapsed a great, bustling street passed through the very center of the Webber garden, just where Wolfert had dreamed of finding a treasure. His golden dream was accomplished; he did, indeed, find an unlooked-for source of wealth, for, when his paternal lands were distributed into building lots and rented out to safe tenants, instead of producing a paltry crop of cabbages they returned him an abundant crop of rent, insomuch that on quarter day it was a goodly sight to see his tenants knocking at the door from morning till night, each with a little round-bellied bag of money, a golden produce of the soil.

The ancient mansion of his forefathers was still kept up, but, instead of being a little yellow-fronted Dutch house in a garden, it now stood boldly in the midst of a street, the grand home of the neighborhood; for Wolfert enlarged it with a wing on each side, and a cupola or tea room on top, where he might climb up and smoke his pipe in hot weather, and in the course of time the whole mansion was overrun by the chubby-faced progeny of Amy Webber and Dirk Waldron.

As Wolfert waxed old and rich and corpulent he also set up a great gingerbread-colored carriage, drawn by a pair of black Flanders mares with tails that swept the ground; and to commemorate the origin of his greatness he had for his crest a full-blown cabbage painted on the panels, with the pithy motto, *Alles Kopf,* that is to say, *All Head,* meaning thereby that he had risen by sheer head work.

To fill the measure of his greatness, in the fullness of time the renowned Ramm Rapelye slept with his fathers, and Wolfert Webber succeeded to the leather-bottomed armchair in the inn parlor at Corlear's Hook; where he long reigned, greatly honored and respected, insomuch that he was never known to tell a story without its being believed, nor to utter a joke without its being laughed at.

BORDERS® CLASSICS

Charles Dickens, *A Christmas Carol and Other Holiday Tales*
Charles Dickens, *Great Expectations*
Charles Dickens, *Oliver Twist*
Charles Dickens, *A Tale of Two Cities*
George Eliot, *Silas Marner*
Kenneth Grahame, *The Wind in the Willows and Other Writings*
Thomas Hardy, *Tess of the d'Urbervilles*
Rudyard Kipling, *The Jungle Books*
William Shakespeare, *The Sonnets and Other Love Poems*
William Shakespeare, *Three Romantic Tragedies*
Mary Shelley, *Frankenstein*
Robert Louis Stevenson, *Dr. Jekyll and Mr. Hyde and Other Strange Tales*
Robert Louis Stevenson, *Treasure Island*
Bram Stoker, *Dracula*
Jonathan Swift, *Gulliver's Travels*
H. G. Wells, *The Time Machine* and *The War of the Worlds*
Oscar Wilde, *The Picture of Dorian Gray*
Oscar Wilde, *Selected Plays*

WORLD LITERATURE

Sir Robert Burton, *Tales from the 1001 Nights*
Miguel de Cervantes, *Don Quixote*
Dante Alighieri, *The Divine Comedy*
Fyodor Dostoevsky, *Crime and Punishment*
Alexandre Dumas, *The Count of Monte Cristo*
Alexandre Dumas, *The Three Musketeers*
Gustave Flaubert, *Madame Bovary*
Homer, *The Iliad*
Homer, *The Odyssey*
Victor Hugo, *The Hunchback of Notre-Dame*
Victor Hugo, *Les Misérables*
Gaston Leroux, *The Phantom of the Opera*
Guy de Maupassant, *The Necklace and Other Stories*
Michel de Montaigne, *Selected Essays*
Ovid, *Metamorphoses*
Virgil, *The Aeneid*
Voltaire, *Candide and The Maid of Orléans*

ANTHOLOGIES

Four Centuries of Great Love Poems

The text of this book is set in 11 point Goudy Old Style,
designed by American printer and typographer
Frederic W. Goudy (1865–1947).
This serif font was chosen for its readability
and beautiful characteristics.

The archival-quality, natural paper is composed of recyclable products
made from wood grown in sustainable forests;
the manufacturing processes conform to the
environmental regulations of the country of origin.
Binder's boards are made from 100% post-consumer waste.

The finished volume demonstrates the convergence of Old World
craftsmanship and modern technology that exemplifies
books manufactured by Edwards Brothers, Inc.
Established in 1893, the family-owned business is a well-respected
leader in book manufacturing, recognized the world
over for quality and attention to detail.
In addition, Ann Arbor Media Group's editorial and design services
provide full-service book publication to business partners.